Moonborn

By

Terry Maggert

First published in USA in 2017 by
Terry Maggert
Portland
Tennessee

Copyright © Terry Maggert 2017

Formatted by LionheART Publishing House

Ten years, M.C. We're winning.

CHAPTER ONE:

CHAOS

Three angels arrowed out of the sun at top speed, their swords drawn to gleam in the dying light of the fifth day since the war began in the floating city of Sliver. Their armor was red on red, well-used, and marked them as experienced fighters rather than emissaries of a neighboring faction. They were not stopping by for a chat.

"Visitors?" Saiinov mused. He'd been expecting an incursion from another House, but his tone revealed that, if anything, he was surprised it had taken this long. Along with his wife, Vasa, he led House Windhook and its devastating coup against the tyrannical control of the Crescent Council. He was dark of hair and eyes and tanned from countless hours in the sky as a warrior who knew his business well. For someone confronted with murderous invaders, he was oddly placid. His wings were folded and still as he watched the approaching triad from the east.

"And from House Carillon, it would seem. An unwise decision on their part."

Habira laughed wickedly at his side. His daughter was a Skywatcher, too, her body honed to lethality from years of combat training with and without her father. Her curly dark hair was plaited and tucked under a metallic cap of scaled armor; the material glittered in the last rays of the sun as she followed the invaders with her gaze. She turned to the third member on the platform of House Windhook. Livvy Foster stood silently, her eyes narrowed as she drank in the details of what was transpiring. A recent addition from elsewhere, she was new to the idea of armed combat.

That did not mean she was unwilling.

Livvy's hand dropped to her longsword, a plain but vicious weapon that hung at her hip in a scabbard made from the hide of a beast far more dangerous than the approaching angels.

"Show me what to do," she said.

Her words were smooth, even clipped. She knew her role as a new member and relished the opportunity to learn under masters of political and martial warfare such as House Windhook. In her chest pounded the heart of Saiinov's youngest son, Keiron, who had given his life that he might save a girl from long ago and far away. Livvy's cheeks were flushed with health and excitement at the prospects of a lesson to be had; her smile caused an array of freckles to move about like merry stars that gave away her secret joy. For years, Livvy had smiled little and laughed less, but those days were over. For now, she was safe. She was whole.

She was a soldier if she could learn. At the altar of House Windhook, she would learn to fight as if she were breathing, with Saiinov and Habira as her instructors. Vasa was a different kind of teacher. As a Scholar, Vasa peered into the past--and the future--to pry glyphs of magical power away from a history that jealously guarded its secrets. The power of the past was not meant for angels, a fact which Vasa cheerfully ignored as she went about the business of reconstructing skills that brought her to the forefront of an uprising against the Crescent

Council.

The eldest daughter of Windhook, Prista, was a Scholar, as well. Brilliant and secretive, she had her own House well underway, spending the bulk of her time in unseen preparations to the west. By message, Saiinov and Vasa learned that she'd chosen the name for her residence, meaning that House Valuri had no elemental being living in its center. For the time being, all House business would be left to the eminently capable Prista, who would doubtless set the interior and exterior defenses exactly to her liking. By creating a tidy, safe environment, the chance of attracting a wandering Elemental was that much greater, and neither Vasa nor Saiinov had any concerns about their daughter being joined by one of the powerful beings who roamed among the clouds when they weren't ensconced in the heart of a house. They both made mental notes to look in on their daughter, for her dedication to work was nearly identical to that of Vasa. Outwardly, they favored each other, as well, with their honey hair and blue-grey eyes. Their only noticeable difference was height. Where Vasa was tall and lean, Prista was small and thin, with an eternally harried look on her beautiful features.

For the past several days, Livvy had been debriefed in a casual, if thorough, method by the entire family she was now a part of. The questions ranged from minor to grave; no detail was too small regarding her former life as a young woman who lived with half a heart and had only recently struggled for every breath. An excellent student, Livvy asked as many questions in return, for the world she lived in was violent, yet beautiful and filled with elements that were oddly familiar, like the faces of people she'd met once and dismissed. She asked for and received a costly diary of thick parchment so that she could write down questions as they came to her. Paper was a luxury item since the fibers were from plants were hunted, not picked, and could injure or kill the harvesters. That fact imbued her diary with value even before she'd written her first word in it, and she knew that, someday, it would unlock even more of the secrets around her. To record questions for future reference was both mature and thoughtful; these were traits that worked well in the life of a young woman who had reason enough to be cautious. She'd lived without a working heart for most of her life; being careful was a default setting she could not yet abandon.

Livvy ceased her musings and let her eyes focus on the three shapes as they grew closer. Two were male, and one was female; all looked capable and grim. "I'm the new guy here, sir." She grinned, a sign that her comfort around Saiinov was growing.

"Please, Saiinov will do." He returned her smile then flicked his sword out of its scabbard with a whisper of ringing steel. Turning into the house, he lifted his voice slightly. "Dear heart, if you would?"

There was no response. No human response, that is, but a blast of malevolent white light sizzled forth to split the triad of invaders, toasting their feathers and scattering them like frightened children who saw the shadow of a Windbeast. "I'm rather busy. Was that close enough?" Vasa's words were light with humor.

"Quite so, dear. They're regrouping, but I think they'll prefer to talk now rather than engage in something as brutish as an armed landing." He cupped his hands and bellowed into the wind, "Blades away if you please. We can discuss your intent like civilized people, over wine."

As one, the experienced triad backwinged to hover a short distance away. At an imperceptible nod from the

4

middle angel, all three sheathed their weapons, opting for discretion rather than senseless valor. In the face of Vasa's immense power, their decision was only reasonable.

"Permission to alight, Windhook?" The angel on the left spoke. She was middle-aged, with a thin, sour expression of barely-contained distaste. Her light hair was cut short to be worn under a helmet, revealing her as an experienced flyer at the very least. Based on her stance as she landed, it was entirely possible she was a seasoned combat veteran. The remaining two angels landed, their scowls matching hers, although they were taller and more heavily built. Both had black hair, visible scars, and the body posture of natural brawlers. A family relation was likely, given their matching gray eyes and long noses.

Saiinov nodded professionally to all three. "Welcome to House Windhook. We'll join my wife for wine and a discussion if that's amenable?" He was the picture of grace. He could afford to be. Vasa, no doubt, had another glyph of something unpleasant ready to ruin the day for House Carillon.

"Agreed," replied the leading angel, her tone clipped. Habira motioned everyone forward into the wide spaces of the central house, its area filled with breezes and the variant light of sundown. When everyone was seated around a depression in the shell-like material of the floor, Vasa entered, casually attaching an earring as if caught by unexpected company.

"House Carillon. What a delight." Vasa's tone left no doubt that their visit was anything but a delight. She followed her pointed greeting with a brilliant, predatory smile, then moved toward a high serving bar where Cressa stood, silently watching the new arrivals. Cressa was a Blightwing, having been convicted of killing a family member, so her wings were gray, fading to black. The world would know that the young woman with the dark, tilted eyes of an Easterner and a flyer's tan was a murderer. Her young face, long black hair, and mobile, small mouth looked like anything except that of a killer. She was plain, verging into pretty, tall, and held herself well. She was also fearless and honorable and possessing many other invisible qualities if one only looked at the color of her wings. As Livvy's lieutenant, Cressa occupied a new position in the house, but one that was nonetheless critical. For the moment, she wordlessly helped Vasa pour tall flutes of wine to observe some semblance of hospitality although anyone with sense could see that the visit was not going to go well.

"Thank you for the excellent wine," said the leading angel despite not having touched her glass. "It would appear that your family is, in fact, alive and well, despite reports to the contrary." She didn't seem happy to admit this inconvenience.

Saiinov gestured amiably around him. "We are, as is our house. More to the point, it is my utmost desire that this condition continues." Putting his glass down with a firm click on the smooth table, he regarded the visitors for a long moment before leaning back in a relaxed posture. "Perhaps we could begin with introductions?" He left the opening for the messengers, both from manners and curiosity.

A flash of relief passed over the grim woman's face. There was strain and not the simple variety involved in long-distance flight, which Saiinov silently doubted they had used as their means of reaching the distant outpost of House Windhook. The lines in her face were something else—they indicated worry, and a lot of it if he was any judge.

"My apologies for not announcing ourselves more

clearly. It's been a long night." She nodded to her left and right in quick succession, indicating the angels who sat, unmoving but thawing slightly as they sipped their wine and relaxed. "*Don* Treo and *Don* Verga. They're my lieutenants. I'm *Doña* Helia. I'm third in command of the House, but that status is in question."

"Why?" The word blurted from Livvy before she could hold her tongue, but she managed to control her impulse to apologize. It was a legitimate question brought on by her instincts, if not her collapse in manners.

Saiinov nodded slightly to indicate that her question, no matter how impertinent, should be answered.

Helia's face went through a range of emotions, settling on confused acceptance. She was an experienced fighter and leader, but there was an air of defeat behind her professional exterior. Saiinov could sense it easily, as could Vasa. Livvy felt it, but couldn't identify what the woman with tired eyes was hiding. After a brief pause, she spoke, her voice low and careful.

"I say our situation is fluid because we haven't seen Lord and Lady Carillon since the day of your, ahh, trial." Helia pointedly avoided using the term rebellion, but it was understood. Her face was a maze of tiny motions despite being still and smooth from experience. There was a storm underneath her expression of calm, revealing a commander who was sick with worry.

"You suspect something happened?" Vasa asked. She knew something of the people in question; they were aggressive but seasoned. They wouldn't abandon their house without just cause, and it was unthinkable that they would do so during a time of upheaval. It left House Carillon vulnerable and rudderless, two qualities that could lead to the end of the line for their family.

Helia only shook her head, but both of her companions

snorted with disgust. She stilled them with a gesture before returning her gaze back to Vasa. "I know it. My century of duty knows it. My bones know it. There's no reason for them to leave, and they've never done it before in the history of our house. We're in a delicate balance with the other families who span our length of sky. You know how things are." She grinned, a sour look that spoke volumes about her mental state. "My brother and his wife are at the outer edge of houses that span the skies between Windhook and the rogue armies. Our location isn't accidental."

"I can imagine. I'm not sure we would be comfortable in your place." Saiinov's response avoided the fact that Windhook was directly responsible for much of the added chaos that swept the skies around them. After some consideration, he asked, "Were there any direct threats against your house, other than the usual background chatter?"

"Spoken or real?" Helia's eyes cut toward her companions. Their scowls deepened.

"Let's try real." Saiinov sensed that she'd been withholding information, probably with good reason. The skies were dangerous enough without giving an advantage of any kind without provocation or necessity.

"In that case, I am almost certain that the lord and lady are dead, although I have no bodies or evidence, except for this. The jar, please?" Helia nodded to Treo, who reached into his carryall with a delicacy at odds with his size and shape. He seemed almost fearful as he lifted the hide flap and withdrew a sealed glass jar. It was twice as long as a hand and came to a stoppered end. There was a length of hide wrapped around the end to add extra security to the carved plug. Even through the pale blue glass, the creature inside gleamed with malevolence.

At Livvy's involuntary gasp, everyone turned to look at her with great interest. "You know this—creature?" Vasa's query was low and intense. She knew fear when she heard it.

Livvy moved without a sound to kneel next to the table where the jar stood, a robust clicking coming from inside it. As she grew closer, the creature paused and then hurled itself at the glass, tail first. It was a sickly yellow, shining like a poisonous fruit, and alive with danger in every fractious movement. After staring for a silent moment, Livvy turned her head slightly towards Helia. "Where did you find this?"

"Them. We found a dozen of them in the Lord and Lady's bed. Their sleeping chamber is on the aerie ledge at House Carillon, when weather permits. We found these things and no sign of my masters. There was some blood, but very little. Just an odd drop or two."

Livvy considered that before answering. She tapped a bold finger against the jar, sending the thing inside into wild spasms of violence. Clear fluid ran down the inner wall of the jar where it struck. Vasa shivered, while Saiinov looked unnerved. Cressa alone looked curious. "That would figure. These do not eat people; they eat angels. They sting. And that sting is venomous, even fatal under certain conditions. Many stings would do it, I think."

"What is it?" Helia asked, her voice rough with worry and fatigue.

"More importantly, where did it come from?" Saiinov interjected. He was thinking ahead to the larger implications of a murder that, at this point, had no obvious motive.

Livvy pulled her finger away from the jar, her expression deep with concern. "It's called a scorpion.

They live all over the place, but I think that one is from the Middle East." She looked at the jar with unease. "I think that one is called a Deathstalker. They're extremely dangerous, and they live in the desert."

"What is a desert?" Helia asked.

Livvy was surprised but then realized that angels would have no working knowledge of a desert or its inhabitants. The skies were dangerous but hardly filled with sand, which was a rare commodity harvested from fine nets that hung below airships traversing the endless skies. "It's an environment, a place, with animals and sand and heat. There isn't a lot of water, and it's incredibly difficult to survive there." She raised a hand to stall further questions as a look of disbelief crossed her features. "Look, I don't mean to seem uncaring, but aren't we missing the big picture here?" Livvy pointed at the scorpion, its legs scrabbling against the glass with mechanical, unnerving precision. "*That* doesn't exist here naturally, does it? Please tell me scorpions don't fly around because, if they do, I'm moving to Mars."

Saiinov chuckled despite the tension. "No need. We have some rather aggressive beasts but nothing that small." He examined the scorpion with a critical eye before adding, "Or that land bound. You'll come to learn that even the fish can fly here, Livvy."

"That's a small favor. But it doesn't answer my question, nor does it explain how a bunch of nasties from the desert got in the bed of two angels who live far"—

Vasa smoothly interrupted. "—away from their natural habitat?" She gave Livvy an obscure look before resuming her thoughts. "Perhaps we should be more concerned with the missing people, yes?"

Helia looked grateful at that. For all their love of war, angels preferred order within their houses. A missing leadership was the guaranteed fall of a house, especially at a time when the political landscape was so unsettled. Although the upheaval was courtesy of House Windhook, that didn't mean that Saiinov and Vasa wanted disorder and panic to spread.

"What can we do to assist?" Saiinov asked, simply.

Helia's face was a mask of control, but her wings rustled with nervous energy. "I don't know. We can't go much longer without someone asking questions, and when that happens--" She trailed off, the unspoken reality of their house looming large. House Carillon would be attacked, and soon, if the Lord and Lady were missing. It would happen even sooner if, as Saiinov suspected, someone had murdered them.

Vasa placed a hand on her husband's shoulder, squeezing lightly. "I propose an alliance, but it won't come without cost." Helia remained impassive, but there was an air of hunger about her at the possibility of deliverance. "Are there any other houses in your area who might be interested joining forces, if only to forestall a local war?"

Helia gave the question thought, then nodded. "Perhaps." She was too savvy to leap at an extended hand, no matter what the conditions.

Vasa looked at the two silent angels flanking Helia. They were capable fighters at worst and potent warriors at best. The kind of people who made better allies than enemies, even if the terms were less than perfect. "I apologize for bringing politics into this time of strife and loss. Let me assure you that we do not wish to make enemies of Carillon, nor any of your favored circle. House Windhook had only one enemy, that being the former Crescent Council. We will not shed the blood of anyone save their supporters. You have our word."

"Quite generous of you, Lady Vasa." Treo's comment was dry but pleasant, breaking some of the building tension that clouded the air. It also happened to be true, given that House Carillon faced a crisis in which they could easily cease existing in less than a day if things went wrong.

Throughout the exchange, Livvy remained silent but watchful. She was far from healed, and still uncertain as to her actual purpose, other than being an interested observer in a game that she didn't fully understand. The scorpion scuttled in its glass prison, frustrated and restless. Livvy cast a sympathetic look at the creature before focusing on the discussion at hand.

Helia responded after due thought, as the decision she made would likely determine whether she lived or died. Lone angels from fallen houses had notoriously short lifespans, and Helia was nothing if not practical. "What do you need from us?" She pointedly didn't ask for anything in return, choosing to throw the fate of House Carillon in with the growing power of Windhook.

Vasa's reply was instant. "Information. Specifically, who, why, and how this could have happened to your house. Anything at all that might help us protect you from further harm, and we ask nothing in return."

"Nothing?" Helia's reply was hopeful despite the reality before them.

Saiinov spoke, his voice soothing and calm. "Nothing. We seek no expansion of our territory beyond the air around this house, and would not inflict further pain on you and your people. Despite what you may think of us, we are not empire builders. We want freedom for all, and we were willing to risk our lives to gain it."

"You gave much more than that." Livvy's quiet statement brought everyone up short. She touched her chest with meaning, and the members of House Windhook understood. The trio of visitors didn't know what she meant but sensed the change in the air. Vasa's eyes were bright, while Cressa looked stricken. Only Saiinov maintained his composure, and even that cracked, making him turn away. After a hard few seconds, he regained his outward calm and smiled sadly at Livvy.

"It's true, but that's a personal issue for Windhook. Forgive us if we keep counsel of our recent losses." Vasa reclaimed her role as lady and arbiter, eliciting a nod from Helia.

"Then, excuse my boldness, but what can you do to help in exchange for our information, such as it is?" Helia's question was direct, her tone even. She was a capable being of some strength, and worthy of cultivation for future issues. Of that, Vasa and Saiinov were certain.

"Friends." Saiinov said without fanfare. "We have precious few right now, and we're going to need a stable sky, filled with houses who can tolerate each other rather than prey on the weak." He shook his head, looking tired in that instant. "I'm finished with watching people like the council use our sons and daughters like pawns. No more. Vasa thinks that we can have a working society without using force to cure every ill, and I agree. We want to make that happen, but we won't be able to do so without allies. So, we start with your house, and then, we move on. We form an alliance with Carillon, and then our houses reach out to build a network of clear skies and open hands."

Helia nodded at this, grasping the importance of a beginning. Peace had to start somewhere, and she had the means to embrace it immediately. She squared her shoulders and stood, extending a hand to Vasa, who was closest. "Agreed. It starts with us, then." She gave the scorpion a withering glare of disgust. "I know they're dead, but I have no idea how such a creature came to be in their bed. It's not natural."

Livvy picked up the jar, causing the scorpion to wriggle with menace. Its tail waved about like a questing weapon, and she peered close to the jar while speaking. Never taking her eyes from the creature, she said, "I know. It's where I came from."

CHAPTER TWO:

BRIGHA

$\mathcal{F}$or the first decades of her life, she hated being beautiful. Then, the realization that weakness surrounded her allowed Brigha to link her physical perfection with an intellect that was diamond-edged, ruthless, and vast. She was, in many ways, the most angelic being to ever fly the skies of her region, a cluster of houses and outposts known as the Seven Sisters. Brigha was the youngest of a house that produced brilliant minds and quarrelsome leaders, but her talents swiftly surpassed those of her older siblings, whom she disposed of by treachery or reassignment in the complicated trade agreements House Selinus used to dominate the local economy. Her shift from petty warlord to something new was due to the visitation. In the night, her mind began to unfurl a knotty plan filled with desires, violence, and sweeping vision. Like a Windbeast reaching full growth, she became something incredibly dangerous. The whispered plans clicked into place, and with each passing moment, Brigha began to grow well past the confines of a sky that was too small for her dreams.

Tall, olive skinned, and red-haired, she spent the majority of her days surveying the world in one of two expressions: the brilliant smile of a winning negotiator or the threatening scowl of a predator who was barely under control. Brigha's dark green eyes flashed between joy and rage, depending on her goals; she used emotion and appeal like weapons when and where it suited her. She was free of shame or morals or anything like a sense of decency. For those reasons, she sat atop a small conglomeration of Houses who both feared and respected her and the unknowable goals she sought to gain with each arcane move of her trade network. She like her men clever and ruthless, and, when she finished with them, they invariably vanished or moved on, for there was no room for anyone in Brigha's world other than herself.

At her hip, she carried a long, wicked blade of silvered steel embossed with the runes of a type unknown to all who had seen them up close and survived. The list of such fighters was small, for Brigha was known to kill first and ask questions later. House Selinus was a secretive, paranoid castle of whispers, lies, and the occasional scream, but it was undisputedly the crown of the region, and Brigha, the queen in control. Despite her youth, she governed with the suspicion and control of a much older angel, although this could not be considered an asset. Like the wind, Brigha's acquisitiveness and violence were simple facts, and nothing more.

She stood in the swirling winds of Selinus' aerie, a platform that curved around underneath the expanse of the house in a design that was graceful and practical. Two small windships bobbed at their moorings, sails furled and silent in the ever-present currents of a sky that was brilliant, blue, and cloudless. Her boots rapped smartly on the hollowed deck as she mounted the ramp into the inner chamber of the house; it was a sanctuary free from wind and sun, cool and calm in muted tones of gold and blue. Veins of silver shot through the walls of the shell-like home, their glints adding a merry element of light to the serenity of space that was broad, open, and free of clutter.

The furnishings were minimalist, elegant. Low couches and chairs huddled near the scrying pool, a circular divot in the floor filled with deep blue liquid that verged into black depending on the viewer's angle. Small creeper vines climbed around columns carved from the ribs of a Skybeast so large that it could have eaten a windship without noticing. The leaves and vines were lurid green, with flowers of soft white the color of a spring moon. They opened as Brigha passed, emitting a soothing vapor that made the area smell of living things and falling water. She stood, inhaling their velvety scent before easing to a couch after flicking her wings into the resting position. There was no sound save the burble of a fountain in the distance, and the subtle hum of winds that were denied by the walls of Selinus.

"I know you're there. You may as well come out." Brigha sounded mildly irked, but too comfortable to be truly upset. In such a setting, rage seemed out of place, unless she decided that it was necessary.

Hesitant footsteps announced her sister's presence; then, a shadow fell across the couch. "I was reading." The voice was small and timid, but clear. Marti was small, darker than Brigha, and quiet. She walked to the opposite seat and eased onto it with care as if she moved only after some degree of consideration. Her eyes were brown, like her hair, and her olive skin had the hint of a windburn despite her preference for quiet study. Marti was a thinker and kept company with books rather than other angels.

She was also incredibly dangerous because at the heart of the tidy, silent angel was a moral code that threatened everything Brigha hoped to achieve. Even when they'd been mere children, Marti worried over some small point of honor or truth. She'd been a humorless child who grew to fear her beautiful sister as one might keep a weapon hidden in its sheath until the day it's needed. Despite that, Marti worshiped her sister, for she was all the things that angels craved—brave, beautiful, and aggressive. For that reason alone, Marti felt shame each and every time Brigha insulted her habits, even though both were powerless to stop the deeply ingrained habits of their family's abusive nature. Since Brigha began influencing the houses in their local cluster, Marti had withdrawn ever deeper into her world of books and secrets, and there was only one thing that she craved more than the comfort of her library or house. In a secret place far from the surface, Marti nursed the need for recognition. Until that moment, she never imagined being anything other than a ghost who lived in the shadow of her vibrant, powerful sister. For an instant, there was blank fear on her face as she sat quietly across from the angel who regarded her as a liability and nothing more.

That was about to change.

"Reading," Brigha snorted. "Of course you were. What is it today? A moldy account of a mythical beast? Or a legend of angels soaring to the stars in metal Houses?" Her mocking knew no bounds, not when it came to the fanciful tales that Marti would relate on the rare occasions they spoke. Brigha was a realist—she had faith in the sword, and her cunning, and little else. True, the power of sorcery was something to be reckoned with, but even that was a known quantity, not an aging rumor pulled from legends and whispers.

Marti looked down at her hands. She cradled a small black shell covered in a single inscription that began at the bottom and ran around in tiny, neat lettering without a break. It was a language from the old world; even at a glance, Brigha could tell it was something she had no interest in deciphering. That's why she allowed Marti to waste away in the shadows of her chamber, poring over such trivialities while Brigha herself plunged through the light of days on a regular basis despite the pain and danger. She'd mastered the use of Timeslip to dive deep into the past, find useful things to further her cause, and rise like a thunderhead back to Selinus, where she could dispense her treachery as she saw fit.

But she was tiring. Under her greedy, perfect exterior, Brigha was worn thin and grew ever more fearful of making a mistake that would strand her in the distant past of a world that was now little more than a scorched ruin, if the stories were true. She needed rest, and help, and anything that might grant her dominion over the skies surrounding their house while the chaos of a civil war erupted.

"I saw one of the scorpions you brought back." Marti's words struck home like a spear, leaving her sister speechless for a long, windy moment.

"*What* did you just say?" Brigha's tone was colder than open sky.

Marti regarded her with eyes that had gone flat. The angel looking back at her magnificent sister wasn't scared. She was hungry. Marti wanted something, and she thought it was within reach. Something broke free in the girl, letting an undertone of desire come to the surface in a wave of jealousy and greed. "I said I know what you brought back. From your little trips. I've watched every time you go, and I didn't stop you because I was frightened of what might happen to me, but not anymore." She tapped the small shell in her hand with a loving pat. "Not since I found this."

Brigha said nothing. The intellect glittering in her

sister's eyes was a new facet that disturbed the air between them, like an oncoming storm. It left her uncertain, and she muffled her naturally arrogant response with a generous wave of one hand.

Marti tapped a nail against her tooth, thinking. It was a gesture so unlike her that Brigha merely stared, waiting to see what else might unfold from the depths of her sister's personality. "When I came with you to Selinus, I thought I was following someone who cared about me and our family. I know I was wrong." She waited to see if Brigha would protest, but there was none. It was true, and they both knew it. "Then you decided that building your house wasn't enough, and things started happening to our rivals."

"We live in a dangerous time."

"Yes, and there are dangerous people all around us. And you're one of them, Brigha. For the first time in my life, I'm scared of you." Marti's words hit her sister like a punch, but some of the tension in the room faded. It was better than the previous months, where Marti's days had been spent walking around in fear from watching Brigha become more ruthless, secretive, and alien. Their house was a place of secrets, not joy, and Marti had cracked. She needed to know why these things were happening, though up until now, she'd been afraid to ask.

No longer. Marti felt the stirrings of hunger that plagued her family, even though her natural state of kindness had kept such things at bay while Brigha chased the trappings of power, no matter what the cost.

"I only did it"- Brigha began, but stopped when she saw the disbelief on her younger sister's face.

"No, you didn't. Please don't insult me. You did this because you wanted to, and the Crescent Council is no more thanks to Windhook. You don't understand how they think, but you saw an opportunity, and started using the tools at hand to make your little empire if you could." Marti grinned, and it was cold. "You never cared about the past like I do because you were so busy being in the moment. But you should have cared. You can't believe the things that used to be real, and now we've forgotten all about them. The people spend their days hunting beasts in the clouds, and crafting storms, or angling for position in Sliver." Marti sighed, and it was the noise of an angel who was disgusted by her wings. "I don't know how to fight like you do, but I know you want our house to succeed now that the council is gone. I have an idea how you can do that, but you're going to need my help because it's a lot more dangerous than a jar filled with scorpions."

She had Brigha's full attention. "How?" It was one word, filled with greed.

Marti patted the shell, smiling. "I think that everything we are used to exist down there, in the other place and time before there were angels. I don't know why, entirely, but it's like a mirror or a window through time. That's why you can only go into the past for short trips before you have to come back. That's why you can only bring little things with you. There seems to be a balance or something." She looked into the distance, her eyes losing focus as she sifted through thoughts and conclusions before shrugging. "I'm not sure about any of it, but I think I've found a way to make a stable link to the past."

"You have?" Brigha sat forward, breathless. A doorway would give her unlimited access to everything that she'd only glimpsed. The possibilities were dizzying.

"Mm-hmm. Someone tried it once before, according to this shell, but they did it from the wrong side. I think it'll work if we try it here, but there's one tiny little problem." Marti smiled through her lie, and this time, it was genuine and wicked. She'd seen the writings of the connection between the sky and past. The Moondiver who'd gone before them had left detailed notes, and the possibilities were tantalizing. In truth, Marti wouldn't mind being a goddess, even if she didn't entirely understand why it made sense to build an empire between worlds.

Brigha's face closed up. She didn't have time for games, not when there was something close at hand that might give her a path to power. "What is it?" She ground out the question like a curse.

Marti raised a hand, placating the growing anger in her sister. "You'll have to convince some humans that you're a goddess."

The laughter rang through their house was like the pealing of bells. Brigha finally calmed herself enough to raise her hands in question. "*That* is something I've always wanted to do." Sobering, she scowled at the implications of dealing with humans and all of their quirks. In her brief visits, they'd proved to be stupid and greedy, but superstitious to a fault. She found them to be too much like angels, in a sense. They made her nervous. "I can do that. Rather, we can do that. I'll need your help."

"You have it." Marti had no intentions of playing goddess among the people of a distant past. She'd read enough of their stories to know what happened to kings and queens, let alone gods. They always ended up dead. Or worse.

Brigha stood, letting her wings fall outward in a gentle flare. She was a magnificent being, and she knew it. Playing a goddess would be second nature for her, and the fulfillment of every arrogant wish that lived in the depths of her heart. Turning to Marti, she raised a brow.

"How will you build a doorway to the lands of distant earth?" Greed rippled under her words, thick and obvious.

Placing the shell on the table between them, Marti held it an angle and began to read. "Let me tell you about the *Augur*."

CHAPTER THREE:

QUESTIONS

" How many more are dead, do you think?" Saiinov asked as the three angels from Carillon winged away, their shapes vanishing into a thickening cloud bank to the east. They hadn't left fully trusting each other, but it had been a good start. In troubled times, that was more than many families could hope for if Saiinov were any good at predicting the coming breakup of their system.

Vasa thought before replying. "More than two, but less than five. We would know if someone had removed leaders in any number. Whoever did this has a plan, but it's local. It doesn't feel"—

"Grandiose?" Livvy asked, a smile playing at her lips. She hadn't missed the irony in Windhook judging another power play as being large or small.

Saiinov and Vasa laughed as one, but it was Cressa who spoke up, her words brittle with nerves. "Aren't you worried? Angels are dying, and someone is using things from Livvy's world to do it."

"For our safety? I've been worried every day we lived under the shadow of the council, but now? Not really." Saiinov pointed toward the heart of Windhook, smiling broadly. "We have protections that other do not, but we're also on guard. No one will attack us here, at least not since we reduced the council."

24

"Nor will we be subject to attacks from organized forces. We selected the location of this house with care. The skies around us are relatively empty by design, not chance." Vasa looked over the expanse of blue, darkening as the day began to fade. Fingers of rose and orange crept upward from the horizon as shadows began to lengthen across the features of the house. Clouds were distant, the sky clear, and the moon a fat early wedge of brilliant white. Other than a single clump of wind herbs stretching out in serpentine curls, there was nothing to be seen around Windhook.

"What is that?" Livvy asked, pointing toward the drifting plants. Even at a distance, thorns glinted in the sunset as the wind herbs coiled slowly, turning to and fro like a sluggish worm. It unnerved Livvy, who was used to plants being still.

"Wind herbs? You've not seen them?" Vasa looked surprised. She hadn't given great thought to what Livvy's world had been. It was time to remedy that, beginning with the sight before them. When Livvy shook her head, Vasa brightened. Teaching was among her favorite occupations after research. "They're predatory and tough to kill. We harvest them for the buds, but it's a dangerous business that claims a life nearly every season. Still, the profits are considerable, so angels in financial need will don armor and fight the drifting forests to fill their coffers with wind herbs."

"Or use them for themselves." Cressa's disgust was evident in her words, but her expression contorted with something like pity.

"What do they do? The herbs?" Livvy's curiosity burned for her new world.

"The buds are chewed, but not swallowed. They stain the teeth but add vigor and focus. They're quite addictive, but some angels need them to fly. The herbs seem to have a medicinal effect, relieving the rare headaches that long distant flights can cause. Do you have anything like them where you—back there?" Saiinov faltered, but only momentarily as he struggled to define exactly where Livvy had come from.

"We do." Livvy flexed her wings slightly with a rueful smile. "They do, I mean. There was caffeine, which is in drinks called coffee, or tea, but I wasn't ever allowed to have it because it would make my heart race. Too risky." Talk of her new heart was still a raw topic, so she cut her eyes away, ashamed and conflicted by the simple wonder of drawing a deep breath. "But coffee plants never fought back, and they certainly don't attack people."

"Everything attacks you here. Even other angels." Vasa looked momentarily saddened by the danger around them, but she was working to see that the skies were safer, no matter what the cost. "You'll need to understand this now that you're one of us, and I can't think of a better way than immersing you in our culture. We'd like you to go to the Electra Outpost with Garrick. He's a good flyer and knows the skies well. He could also use your influence, Livvy, I won't lie."

"You can help him, just as he can help you." Saiinov's face was a neutral mask. He wasn't giving anything away except the truth. Garrick would need Livvy's kindness and potential to drag him back into the fold of the family. Windhook could not live without any of them, no matter how childish and sour their presence.

Livvy was no fool. She drew her lips to one side, clucking her tongue in a noise of thoughtful hesitation. She knew little of Garrick other than the tension that seemed to follow him when he entered the room. He was physically perfect and mentally prone to pettiness and sneering, two things that didn't wear well on him at all. To go anywhere with him meant that she was being used, but it also meant that Livvy could begin answering the deluge of questions piling up in her mind. As her confidence grew around Vasa and Saiinov, so did her curiosity, and while they were caring and attentive, there was an avalanche of interest building within her that must be satisfied. Livvy didn't even know what she didn't know, a state of ignorance completely unlike her previous seventeen years as a thoughtful, studious girl who wondered about the world every day. She squared herself to the room and looked at the lord and lady of Windhook with eyes that were steady and uncompromising. This would be where she made her first stand and damn the consequences.

"Why do I need to go to Electra?" Her question was simple and direct. She waited quietly while the leaders of Windhook chose their words with care.

It was Vasa who chose to answer, her tone plain and thoughtful. "Because we need things from their stores, and we need you to become more like us. Right now, you're somewhere between a lost soul and warrior's gift, but we don't know which and keeping you here in the walls of Windhook won't help change that. You need to fly, and talk, and listen, and feel the sting of rain in your face. Until you do all of those things, you're still at risk. And frankly, so are we."

Garrick landed in a flurry of shadow, but with little sound. He moved like a wraith, folding his wings behind a body that was tall and lean. He radiated the petulance of a spoiled child, and Livvy questioned her decision to go anywhere with him. Garrick had nearly colorless blue eyes and a face of cut planes that made him seem less human than any of the angels she'd met. His smile was smug; his teeth even and white. He was beautiful, and he knew it, so the only sensible thing for Livvy to do was treat him like he wore his soul on the outside where she could see the ugliest part of him.

She rounded on Garrick, pointing a menacing finger nearly even with his eyes. He withdrew slightly, then caught himself and opened his mouth to say something. Livvy was having none of it. "If you try to be coy or condescending, I'll cut my wings off and dive into that pool in the middle of this house. Whether or not I end up in my past isn't relevant, because I won't be here, and I won't help you. I'm not anyone's toy. I'm not your younger brother or sister and—I suggest you listen closely to this part, Garrick—I will treat you *exactly* how you treat me. I got the best part of the best brother, and if you so much as sneeze in my direction, you'll regret it."

Garrick's face flushed with anger before he regained control, but only because Saiinov shot him a look that could freeze water. "Angels don't sneeze." It was weak, but he had to reclaim some of the high ground from the upstart human with his brother's heart beating in her chest. He hadn't liked Keiron, but they were blood. The girl before him was a joke made by the gods of wind and air. He knew it, but he couldn't get rid of her because it would be the end of him.

Garrick was also, at his core, scared.

The council was gone. Angels and houses were falling, and in the middle of it sat his family, pulling strings in a web of long-range actions that left him wondering if they knew what they were doing. He feared and loved his parents, but destroying an empire was beyond his most runaway fantasies. Garrick's joke had fallen flat, dying away in the last evening breeze as the sun began to settle over the horizon, far from the prying eyes of angels

28

returning to their respective homes. He watched Livvy's mouth curl upward and decided she was pretty but dangerous. He didn't know what that meant, but for now, he would obey her wishes, at least until the skies began to settle down. Garrick had plans for his houses someday, and he wouldn't achieve it without his parents' help.

Livvy shrugged. "I don't care if they do or not. What I'm saying to you is that we better fly straight and your answers better be good. I have a lot to learn."

Garrick's teeth clenched together at being spoken to like that, but he pasted a smile on his face and delivered a mocking bow that was both respectful and insulting. The air was thick with uncertainty, a rare thing among Windhook, where decisions were made years in advance.

After a long, searching look at her son, Vasa clapped her hands together with an air of finality. "You leave in the morning, and you'll fly rather than take the windship."

"As you wish, Mother." Garrick nodded pleasantly to everyone and stepped away into the growing gloom of the outer hall. His forced amiability was a transparent necessity. He had thin skin, and appearances still mattered, especially given the discovery that he wasn't back into the graces of his parents. Had he been in their favor, they never would have let a usurper with a stolen heart and new wings speak to him like a spoiled child. The fact he was both spoiled and young had nothing to do with it, in his mind, but in a rare demonstration of will, he managed not to glare over his shoulder as he left.

In the silence, Livvy laughed brightly. "We're going to get along just fine." She smiled in the darkness, a blaze of white teeth and subtle challenge.

"I hope so for his sake," muttered Cressa. Above, a beast cooed as it slid past on a current, its destination as uncertain as everyone in Windhook was feeling just then. The night closed in, and Livvy felt the ache of longing for things that she was already having trouble remembering.

CHAPTER FOUR:

ANSWERS

*B*reakfast consisted of berries so sour that Livvy almost choked.

"They're an acquired taste," Saiinov said with a smile. He was in high spirits since all of his children would be filtering in and out as the day wore on. Habira, Prista, and the twins, Banu and Vesta were busy doing the quiet work that House Windhook needed to position itself as a regional power. There was a vacuum opening across the greater skies, and Windhook would be ready to fill it. When she pressed him for details, Livvy was met with a shrug.

"Am I a member of this family?" Her question brought Saiinov up short. Seated around the table, Vasa, Cressa, and Garrick watched the interplay between Livvy and the man who would now assume a role, not unlike that of her father. After a long moment, he simply nodded. "Then tell me what's going on." There was no negotiation, or pleading. She stated her needs, and sat back, hands folded in her lap like a judge waiting to hear the story of an accused criminal.

"She needs to know, even if the context isn't clear." Vasa sipped something from a tall glass and inclined her head toward Saiinov. The tiny signal was only possible after years of marriage; like many couples, they had visual code that spoke more clearly than any words ever could.

He wiped his mouth with care, stalling for time. When he spoke, it was with the voice of a teacher. "Contrary to my hopes, Sliver didn't fall through the clouds. It still exists, and it will remain a center of power, but reduced. We aim to gather allies and tools to make certain there *is* no rebirth of the Crescent Council. Our children are eminently able, and we all know our roles. Even you have a part to play, and I hope you're ready. I know we're asking a great deal of you so soon after your surgery." He looked askance at Vasa, who shrank for a moment, awash with the remembrance of Keiron.

Livvy's fingers traced her scar, but not from shame. She felt too good to let regret rob her of the vitality that hummed in her body. "You still haven't answered my question."

Saiinov chuckled, shaking his head at her tenacity. "You're right." His sigh was long and shallow. "You're more than a part of this family, Livvy. We gave something precious so that you might live, and now we're going to ask you to give it all back. And more." His eyes were hard.

"I figured this wasn't a sightseeing trip." She sounded resigned but in control. The girl who left earth was gone, but vestiges of her practicality lingered on.

"That's true. At least for the next three days or so. You're going to learn a great deal in a short span of time, and Garrick is going to help you." Saiinov's tone matched his expression, and Livvy saw the light of command in his eyes.

"She'll do more than that." Vasa looked outward, where a shadow indicated someone was wheeling into land on the aerie. "But that must wait. Livvy, I'll speak to you tonight. For now, I've left something for you in your room. You're going to need proper equipment for tomorrow."

"What am I learning?" Livvy burned with curiosity. Everything about her newfound life was a revelation that wavered between joy and fear.

Vasa's smile was bland. "We're going to teach you how to be an angel."

Hours later, Livvy sat at the edge of her bed, restless and distracted by the low hiss of the wind outside the walls. Sleep had been a troubled, broken thing, with each night marked with dreams of a crescent moon rising over the night sky. In the dreams, her head felt heavy, tilting back and forth as if it was no longer hers to command. She'd learned, in a short time, to fear sleep as well as a general suspicion of the rising moon. Both issues left her edgy and tired, a mix that made healing from the surgery and her transition to a new life harder than she'd ever imagined. Adding to her state of exhausted fear was her large, open, and lonely room, which was new and unwelcome, so unlike the life she had left behind. The bed was wide and low, the walls curved, and rippling fabrics hung to create a sense of privacy, but their constant motion was a distraction. Everything in the skies seemed to be alive, including the interior of Windhook. Other than the bed, the only furniture was a tall, shallow closet where she would hang her armor and clothes. Lights burned in the walls, but she knew that a wave of her hand would dim or snuff them entirely. The whole room was impersonal and cool despite the underlying sensation of life that suffused everything around her.

She felt the sob beginning deep underneath her, like an earthquake that could not be denied. The wind and the loneliness were too much at that moment. The first tears began to splash her cheeks with a savage indictment of her reality. She was far from home. She was among strangers who wanted things from her she didn't understand, and for the first time in her life, Livvy could breathe. It was a whirling contradiction of her pain and future that left her slumped on the side of the bed, drifting in possibilities, sure of nothing.

She missed her parents. She missed her room, and books, and the way that the top step creaked when she stood on it, announcing to her mom that she was coming downstairs to be kissed on the cheek, embraced. Wrapped in love each day, a lifetime of support and caring at the hands of people who knew every pain of her body and wished, just once, that they could have taken it all away. Every hurt, every surgery, all of the days and nights in agony, her mother and father would have given their blood to replace her during those moments when the pain would push her to the brink of darkness and beyond.

Yet, here she sat, one hand on her chest as the steady beat of a heart reminded her with every quiet thump that it was Keiron whom she ached for. Keiron, whom she'd known for a blink in her life--a boy who folded time itself to create a place of quiet calm where she could know him, and, in turn, love him.

And then, he finished his arc to the earth, completing a fall that would see her cut twice. Once by the surgeons, and once by the memory of his love, gone without a trace save the rhythms inside her chest. There was no denying the tears, not when she could feel him with every waking second, yet knew that they would never touch again. He was with the stars, a thing of light and beauty, but not hers. Not anyone's.

"You are safe here, Livvy." Vasa's words were low as she stepped through into the gloom of Livvy's cavernous room.

"Am I?" A wipe at her face. She felt shame for the tears but didn't know why.

Vasa paused, then moved to the bed and sat next to her, looking away through a massive window. The stars were silver points sprayed across a cloudless sky, far brighter than Livvy was used to. House Windhook sailed high above the bulk of the atmosphere, in air so thin that the skies were a show like no other. For Vasa, this was home. To Livvy, it was legend made real, a floating castle of seashell and mystery, carved in colored whorls and populated by angels who thought magic was simply another means of work. To some, it would be a dream.

Or a nightmare, depending on what the lady of Windhook planned on saying as she sat looking at the young woman who had so much to learn. Not for the first time, Livvy felt small in Vasa's presence. Her serene beauty was a physical thing, filling the space between them with something more than quiet perfection. It was nobility covering steel, and it made looking directly into Vasa's gray eyes more difficult than she imagined.

The lady waved, a simple gesture with her fingertips that encompassed everything around them. "This is my home, and you are safer here than anywhere else in the world. Tomorrow is another story. You'll learn to fly— really fly, and you're going to see to the dangers that we consider part of our everyday lives. Garrick is my son, and I love him despite his flaws, but that doesn't make him any less capable as a warrior and guide. He's brave and strong and decisive."

"He's also vain and petty."

Vasa inclined her head slightly. "True. And that's where you will teach him. The flight will take you more than a day, and you'll overnight to rest. Your body was made for

35

this, but you'll have to train yourself to such exertions. You are," and she slowed her speech, letting the words fall with understanding, "a work in progress thanks to your new heart. As you heal, you will learn that this world is far different from the one you left behind."

Livvy looked around at the room, a wan grin curling her lips. "I can see that."

"Not just the physical world, Livvy. We are a people of war, and everything in the skies is locked in a deadly competition to survive, including us. You'll need to live your life as an aggressor now. Do you think you can do that?" Vasa looked intently into Livvy's face, searching for something bold. She found it.

The new angel did a most human thing, letting out a gusty sigh of resignation. Decisions were made, and Livvy's eyes brightened, newly minted in the light of wonder. "I'll have to. I was never afraid, before, but now I'm mostly curious. I mean, how do I sleep with wings? What are all of the monsters flying through the clouds? It seems like the entire sky is filled with danger, and I don't have anything except a sword and a desire to see it all." Her smile was sheepish, but it was present despite the tracks of her tears. She wasn't sure how to regard Vasa. Not yet.

Vasa laughed at such brazen admission. "You'll have more than your share of adventure, child. I need you to temper your enthusiasm with good sense. We need you, and it's all too possible to die up here in the clouds. It's my preference that you learn such things through observation rather than actual danger."

"I'll be careful," Livvy said, her voice small. She was still young, and reprimands carried weight.

Vasa took her hand, looking down at the youthful fingers, free of scars and age. "I know you will. You've always been careful, haven't you?"

The answering grin was touched with regret as if being wistful was a default setting for the girl who had always needed a heart. "I had to, but for different reasons. I'm stronger now, and you have plans for me that I don't know—please don't lie, Vasa. You're the closest thing I'll have to a mother now, in time. She never lied to me, and I don't want you to break that confidence."

Vasa tugged at her lip in thought. "Fair enough." She let a small sigh gutter forth before nodding to herself. "You deserve the truth, and you'll get it. I'll warn you now that not everything will make sense. Some of it isn't clear even to me, and I've spent the better part of a century planning this."

"Planning what?"

Vasa's smile was brilliant even in the gloom. "Why, saving the world, of course. You didn't think we would invite you here for anything less?"

There was a moment of silence before Livvy found her voice once again as she let the enormity of her oncoming life wash over her. Turning inward, she listened to the strong, clear beat of a heart that was as new as her surroundings, and it gave her strength. "Okay. But let's be honest. I've never held a sword before three days ago, and I'm not even really sure how to fly without feeling like I'm going to faint. I don't know the art of war, or magic, or anything about this house or your world. Does that sound about right?"

"It does." Vasa inclined her head in agreement. A regal gesture, but with a smile. It made her even more appealing if that were possible.

"Then even I know that there's something else coming from over the horizon, and you may or may not want to tell me. I'm no general, but I know people who are versed in keeping their plans secret. This house reeks of secrets, and you're better off including me. Do you know why?"

"I think I do," Vasa said, noting the steel in Livvy's voice.

"I'm not afraid of pain, Vasa. I'll take that pretty sword and cut my wings off if I have to, and dive through the clouds in hopes of going home. Or, I'll take a dip in that pool you're so careful to steer me away from, even though I know the other end of it is in my parent's backyard. I can go home, or die trying, and I'm not scared of either. So it's best if you tell me what the hell I'm doing surrounded by angels and floating cities and everything else that makes up your life." She settled back on the seat, her mouth a flat line. Livvy had taken her position and wasn't going to budge, no matter how intimidating Vasa might be.

The air hummed with tension until Vasa scooted forward ever so slightly. It was a motion of compromise, and her eyes were deep with thought. After a long moment, she began to speak, but softly, as if she was building the sentences with great care. "I think that it might be possible to save your world."

"What?" Of all the things Vasa could have said, that was not among the things Livvy expected. "You can't reverse time, not on the scale you're proposing."

Vasa shook her head decisively. "No, not time. An event. A—a wave, a tide. Some cataclysm that ended the world you knew and drove people into the sky, into our floating habitats that speak back to us and defy the laws of the world. We weren't always here, Livvy, and I need to know why. If I understand that, then it may be possible to save *your* world as well as stabilize ours. Do you understand?"

Livvy looked down out of habit. "What's down there?"

"Death. Ghosts. There are storms, and mists, and beings that hunt the most fearsome Windbeasts who have ever flown. We don't know, but one thing is certain. When angels fly too low, they don't come back." Her voice was cool with acceptance and fear.

"Something happened to the entire planet? Like a war?" Livvy mulled the options. She could think of a dozen ways the planet ended, and none of them offered a reason for angels being made real.

"Something is one way of describing it. I know it was sorcery on a massive scale, but you could call it anything and still be just as close to the truth as I am. People left the surface, and, somehow, we were born. A warrior race of scholars whose wings could take us high above the terrors of the surface. There are early records of the first houses, fashioned from materials lost to us now. Windhook was once alive, but the beast who gave us this floating husk is long gone, or far away. At first, I assumed that sorcery kept us aloft, but it's far more complex than that."

"It's gasses in the walls, right?" Livvy looked at the opalescent expanse of ceiling. It was riddled with beautiful curls of light and dark, like a shell.

"I believe so, yes. But that doesn't explain how or why the beasts of the sky came to life, which brings me back to my original thought. There was an event of such devastation that life as you knew it ended, replaced by what you see around us. The world became a howling wasteland of fangs and storms, and we ascended to begin our endless squabbles over open patches of sky when we should have tried to grasp our history." Vasa's full lips twisted in disapproval. "If we don't unify and help each other, we're dead. All of us."

"Why? What will happen? You seem to live for a long

time, and you can obviously have children. Do so many of you fall in war that you'll, um, die out?"

"Let me show you something." Vasa reached into her robe and drew out an enormous feather. It had been white but was now singed to a molten gray, fading to black. The vanes were curled and wild with abuse. It smelled of death. "Here, take it."

Livvy held it like a venomous snake. "Is this from an angel?"

"At one time, yes. Right wing, I would guess, and the main feather that runs just along the spine. It is from a tall angel, most likely a man." Vasa took the feather back with care, running a thoughtful finger over the quill. It was cracked from heat. Or fire.

"You used the past tense. What happened?" Livvy knew it was something terrible. She also knew that the most important thing she could do right then was listen.

"Habira found this clinging to a grove of berries, like many plants they drift on the currents and emit little jets of air to drive them towards rain. She'd gone under a bank of storm clouds to escape any lightning, so she was far lower than we would normally fly, but still high enough to be safe from any unknown dangers." Vasa twirled the feather slowly, contemplating the ruin of something that had been beautiful.

Livvy's breath stopped as the pieces began to fit. "Something from the surface came up and grabbed an angel? In a place that should have been safe?"

"Exactly. And whatever it was, there was fire. That's how I know that our time here is limited. In all of our written history, there was always a wide swath of clear sky that we owned. There was danger, to be sure, but that was simply part of our life. Wind herbs and other predatory plants could be avoided—just steer around

40

them. Storms are natural, and while unpredictable, we understand their general parameters. We've even grown to master many of the wild animals that fly and hunt around us, because though they are fierce, we are smarter. But this?" She looked at the feather with something like fear, and it rested awkwardly on her beautiful features. "Everything about this feather tells me that our truce with the underworld has ended, and we must plan for something far worse than a disagreement with the Crescent Council." Vase clucked her tongue at the thought of explaining her fears to the council.

"Is that why you removed them? Because they would ruin your chances to fight? And win?"

"They would have assured our destruction. I'm sure of it. The council ruled for so long that they only saw threats from around them, not below. In all my years of digging, each and every shell has revealed something new to fear, and it's always been on the surface," Vasa said.

"Why do you write on shells?" Livvy asked.

"They're permanent and cheap, and it's tradition." Vasa smiled at her response. She'd been conditioned by the traditions of her people and asking why was a relatively new thing. She was thankful Livvy was there because that was exactly the kind of thing she needed to hear if they were going to survive as a house.

And as a people.

"You don't dig them up, do you? I haven't exactly seen anything like solid ground in three days." Livvy looked down at the floor of Windhook with meaning. Even the enormous house moved slightly underfoot, its bulk subject to the pressure of wind and weather.

"I say dig, but no, you're right. We find shells in caches, usually in the hidden places of houses that are in disrepair or abandoned. There are places where these drifting hulks collect before they're reclaimed or broken apart by storms. It isn't considered theft to go inside and take what you want; in the East, it's a fact of life. Where we are is a bit different, since few houses are ever unoccupied. We're a more lightly populated place, but the families tend to survive longer. Not so to the East, or in the areas of the rogue armies. There, life can be fluid, just like the alliances." Vasa pulled a small shell from her robe, holding it up for Livvy to see. "I found this in a ladies' bath. You can't read the script, but it's a series of complaints about her husband's mother. She seems to have moved into their home without warning, and brought a considerable fuss along with her."

Livvy chuckled, admiring the small, dark blue shell. "It's nice to know angels have trouble with their in-laws. Makes it more like home."

"Family squabbles are like the wind. Inescapable and likely to change at a whim. That's why I love my children, but don't judge them for their choices. I've given them everything I can to see them over the horizon, and gods willing, I'll be alive to see them live a stable existence in a place that knows far less war than my own time." Vasa's eyes were bright with desire. She had wings, and sorcery, and power, but she was a mother first. It settled Livvy's mind, for some reason. There was strength in the familiar, and a mother's love was nothing if not calming.

"About that. What do I expect from Garrick? I won't be his doormat, no matter what he thinks." Livvy's voice was grim with facts. She hadn't come this far to waste her heart on giving in to a spoiled brat with wings.

"Then don't. Garrick can teach you a great deal of your new world, but it's up to you. We'll rise together at dawn, which is not far away. You'd best make your wishes known at that time." Vasa frowned slightly, and somehow it only enhanced her beauty. "I find it difficult to change the rules once the fight begins."

"I thought I was going to learn and go to Electra Outpost. That doesn't sound like a fight", she said, dubious.

Vasa laughed, a low note that fell away in the rising wind. When she looked into Livvy's eyes, the girl she had once been shone through. "It's most certainly a fight, Livvy. And we're betting on you."

CHAPTER FIVE:

CLOUDBURST

"Pay attention just there," Brigha said with authority. After the initial shock had worn off, Brigha was fostering an uneasy peace with her sister, leading her to the moment where she pointed at a distant bank of roiling clouds. They were neither black nor gray, falling somewhere in between, with flashes of lightning deep within. The bolts sizzling through the air cast enormous shadows on the solid walls of a storm that was growing before their eyes, despite the fact the Brigha and Marti were several miles distant. They hovered above and away from the maelstrom, choosing to observe for the reason that only Brigha knew.

Marti was content to wait for an explanation. Their dynamic had changed, but there would be nothing like trust between them. Despite Brigha's flaws, Marti knew there was an excellent reason for them to watch the blooming storm.

"There. Can you see?" Brigha pointed again, this time with a sharp gesture at a slim crack of golden light that spilled up and through the vicious clouds raging around it. It was sunlight, pure and bright, and it meant that the storm had an eye. "This storm has been growing for months. It's stable enough that I think it will last for years. Angels are already marking trade routes with it, meaning that flyers more experienced than us are planning for it to be here a long time." Since angels had taken control of the skies, long-lasting storms were a part of life. Some storms lasted for years, and there were at least two in the south that had been raging for decades. The skies were dangerous in ways far beyond the predators and warring houses.

Marti was unmoved. "How can we get to the heart of the storm? The lightning alone could kill us, even with a protective spell." She'd read tales of angels burned to char by savage chain lightning that sent their blackened bodies plummeting to the surface. It wasn't a myth; it was a real possibility.

Brigha laughed, and it was a sneer turned into sound. Her face lost all hints of beauty as she savored her moment of superiority. "You're not the one capable of pawing through abandoned piles of message shells. I've been doing my research as well. You'd be surprised what people leave behind when they think their house is going to crash through the clouds to the unseen land."

"You? Research?" Brigha flinched as if stung by her sister's outright laughter. "Dear sister, there is a difference between theft and study," Marti said. The girl she had been would have choked on such an insult, but that was yesterday. She wasn't that girl.

Brigha grew still but mastered herself after a faint change in her wing speed. She had more important things to consider just then and tabled the insult for a later date when she could wield it like a weapon. "You'll learn, dear sister, that there is also a difference between your room and the open skies. Knowledge is worthless without the ability to apply it." She waved at the boiling mass of clouds, now hiding the light within. "There were methods of defeating lightning, but those require being grounded to the earth, a trick that is beyond us at this time. I found a sorcerous solution that costs us little or nothing, and it can be tuned to perfection."

"You? Sorcery?" Marti laughed in her face. Brigha viewed the power of magic as a necessary evil. The smile faded from Marti's face as she realized her sister had found a reason to tolerate the use of magic. Brigha was wicked, but not wasteful. "Why?"

The patronizing look from Brigha was almost too much. "I prefer my sword, but there are some things it won't cut. That storm is one such thing, and I aim to use it without fear of being killed. I have enough enemies without adding *that* to the list."

"You still haven't answered the question. What is your solution?" Marti chewed at the inside of her cheek, angry that her impetuous sister knew something she didn't. She liked Brigha more when she acted like a dangerous child; a smart, careful Brigha was a new thing and therefore unpredictable.

Brigha rolled her eyes but relented after squeezing every ounce of enjoyment from her sister's rising anger. "It's this." She held up an oblong shell with a single spiral curling from end to end. The inscribed line was filled with silver, glittering pure in the sunlight. "The spell is simple enough that a child could do it, which means it was well within my reach. Yes, I know what you think of my skills, and I'm not offended in the slightest, so spare me your sympathy."

"I was"—Marti began but closed her mouth with a click. Brigha was right, galling her even further.

"Yes, you were. But that matters not one bit because a silly little spell converts this ordinary shell into an elongated chain of silver beads."

Marti made a noise of appreciation. It was brilliant, and

it would work. "Thus drawing the lightning toward it."

"And away from us." Brigha tucked the shell away, smiling. "I have more than a dozen of them in reserve, but we'll need more if we plan on piercing that storm with any regularity."

"Why do we need to go to the surface?"

"We don't, or at least not *just* the surface. We need to go to the past, and we must have a stable pathway to do so. Everything depends on our ability to travel safely, and at will." Brigha sounded uncertain for the first time. Her plans hinged on something so unknown, there was only one way to make it work.

"When do we go?" Marti was resigned, but excited. As a scholar, the unknown was her harbor rather than something to be feared. They were going to a place and time out of her dreams, and she felt her body respond with a shudder of the first joy she'd known in years. "How will we know, ah, when we are? Does it matter?" The stars were a vibrant part of angelic science, but judging their travel would be a delicate matter, especially if they would be using the transit of guide stars. Time and the stars were related, but she was confident Brigha had planned for such a thing. It was in her nature.

Brigha withdrew two shells, handing one to her sister. The silver chasing was like a slender mirror spiraling away in an endless circle, all the way to the fine point of the pearlescent tip. She looked into the storm, her eyes crinkling at the blaze of lightning that danced across their field of vision, and then she smiled. Dipping one wing, she called, "No time like the present."

Toward the whirling chaos of the clouds, the sisters fell.

CHAPTER SIX:

ISLAND HOPPERS

The wind was cool but tolerable. Livvy thought her new body was insulated against the weather, somehow, but she didn't want to ask Vasa, who stood next to her watching the first blush of dawn creeping upward over the horizon. The silence had a weight that was not unwelcome. Both women savored the beginning of a day that held promise, letting the air rush past them in mute witness to their observations.

The day held lessons, too. Both Livvy and Garrick would learn a great deal if all went well. If things went badly, then one or both of them would not come home. Taking an inexperienced flyer across wide sections of unguarded sky was risky, but not without reward. If Livvy proved to be all that Windhook suspected, he would emerge from the journey a more seasoned angel, and one with a working knowledge of what it meant to live and play among dangerous things.

Saiinov's boots tapped softly as he approached across the wide veranda. "Beautiful morning, dear heart." He dropped a kiss on Vasa's upturned mouth, as both of them smiled in the growing dawn.

"'Tis. And fine skies, too." Vasa turned her expert gaze to the eastern skies, a wide expanse of clear air spotted only with the odd random wisp of cloud. As far as the horizon, there were no storms or patches of drifting plants to catch at wing and body. It was, in every way, optimal.

"I hope she's ready." Garrick's voice was saturated with his usual blend of boredom and arrogance. He'd intended to startle everyone but failed, leaving him to frown with childish anger. He wore light armor in the blue and silver of Windhook, and twin short swords nestled across his back via slender straps that avoided his wings. He moved like a vision of justice and radiated the personality of a wall of ice. Near colorless blue eyes regarded Livvy with contemptuous disdain, making her heart race with a burst of unbridled anger. She opened her mouth to blister the arrogant fool, but Vasa beat her to the punch, her silken voice cutting through the tense air.

"I know what you're thinking, son." She stepped forward to place a calming hand on the chest of a child who had been alternately wild, or insolent, or sullen, despite their best efforts to instill him with a sense of purpose. Garrick was beautiful but untethered, and Vasa saw this trip as a rite of passage for him as well as Livvy.

Garrick's mouth twisted with uncertainty as he fought to suppress the comfort his mother's presence brought him. He was dead set against playing shepherd to a girl from another place and time, let alone one who had taken the heart of his brother. The fact that he'd detested Keiron had no bearing on his anger whatsoever; if anything it gave him free reign to sulk even more. In his eyes, Windhook replaced a relative problem with something similar, and he couldn't understand why.

"Let me tell you what we need as a family so that there are no misunderstandings between us." Vasa took Garrick's face in her hands, drawing his gaze downward.

He was tall and lean; a male version of his mother, but with none of her kindness in his eyes. His blonde hair ruffled in the wind as he stood mutely awaiting her decree. There was mulish resentment in the muscles of his jaw, but he said nothing. "Like it or not, Livvy is a part of our world and our family. She serves a purpose you cannot imagine because you see only your needs. That has to end, but I don't expect you to change over the span of a flight. I'd rather you were concerned with why we're sending you and not the twins or Cressa. For that matter, we could take the airship and be at Electra station in a day. Have you considered this, son?"

It was clear he had not, but his pride kept him silent yet again.

Saiinov spoke up. "You're good in the sky, and when you aren't holding a grudge or delivering an insult, you have the potential to be a brilliant fighter. You know the beasts and currents of the clouds. Your sense of place and direction is flawless, and you're intelligent enough to understand danger before it's within striking distance. In short, if you can master your emotions, you're going to be someone I'll be proud of." He sighed, realizing the harshness of his words. When he continued, his voice was subdued to the point of muttering. "I'm proud of you now if only you would leave your anger behind us."

"And anger will bring you harm. As your mother, I can't allow that. As a leader in this house, I can't permit the hint of danger to strike you or Livvy from the sky, but she *must* learn what it means to live in our world. She needs to understand that there is more than just wings that make up one of our race." Vasa's eyes were adamant with a demand that her son listen. That, he understand.

"Our race?" Garrick sounded confused, a rarity for him. Even when uncertain, his natural arrogance hid such things, but not now. Not in the grip of his mother's gaze.

"Yes. She *needs* you, and we need her. Our future has never been more uncertain, son, and without teaching Livvy to thrive here, we've given too much for no good reason," Vasa said.

"You mean you gave Keiron for nothing." The sulky boy was returning with each word.

"I've explained this before, and you know the truth. He was never really ours, and your denial of that is like a curse upon my heart. I carried him and birthed him. I fed him from my body, and watched as you pushed him through the reaches of time and distance to save Livvy." Garrick turned as if scalded by her words. When she spoke again, there was a gentleness to her voice that hadn't been there before. "You need this, too, just as we need you. Look around, son of mine. We're at war. Do you think we can stand alone? Your father and I, perhaps the twins? Habira? Who would die first in that idiocy?" She shook her head slowly, watching him absorb the weight of her words.

"We would all die, and our world with us," Saiinov said flatly. "Do not mistake the open skies as being empty of threat. I've tried for years to make you understand that our world is vast, but that doesn't mean a hot war is not at hand. You needn't see the battles to grasp how tenuous our position, is, son. We are at war. *All* houses are at war, with each other, themselves, and the undiscovered future. This is about our survival, not your childish pride, and until you can see the broader context, your emotions are going to render you a liability to this family. I can't have that. None of us can, least of all you."

"If I may?" Livvy interjected, holding a hand up like a schoolchild. "No one asked me if I want to fly *anywhere* with him."

Vasa released Garrick and turned to Livvy, who stood

rigid with distrust. "No, we didn't, not in so many words. Last night you didn't object, and I thought you understood exactly what was going to happen today."

"No, I didn't. I understand bits and pieces of this--- of you, and this place, and these stupid wings, but not all of it. Why am I learning to fly to go to some glorified grocery store in the sky? If it's so dangerous, why aren't we all going? I know you said that I need education and training, but aren't you the leaders of this house? Why not you?" Livvy waved a hand in frustration as everyone merely listened. She felt the first heat of real anger rising in her cheeks, and resisted the urge to touch her chest. She wouldn't do that, not if she could help it.

"Because it isn't a—whatever a grocery store is, it isn't that, and we have other places to be." Saiinov seemed determined to leave it at that, but Livvy's cheeks flushed with anger, prompting Vasa to offer something more.

"You're going to get legitimate sorcerous things that I need. You'll select weapons as well, but those are secondary," Vasa began.

"I hope that my education isn't the primary reason because there have been some incredibly scary creatures in the clouds around us. I could learn about them here and fly in circles to get stronger, for that matter," Livvy interjected.

Vasa sighed in exasperation. She was coming to the conclusion that Livvy was smart, brave, and clever, but she was also a teenager. "The owner of the outpost you're going to deals in something more precious than weapons."

Livvy raised a brow, saying nothing. Saiinov chuckled, a rumble that made it clear he knew Livvy was a teenager.

"Information. He's a collector of it, and he sells it as well. We need information outside our zone, and we need it now. The more we understand about alliances that may be to our advantage, the greater our chance of surviving what is coming. You'll watch Garrick, who will deliver a message from me. What happens next will neither be your fault nor your triumph, but it will be invaluable. As to why we won't be going with you? There are many directions in the sky, Livvy. We'll be visiting other sources of rumor and secrets, in hopes of assembling the best possible picture we can." Vasa tilted her head in conclusion. If that weren't good enough for Livvy, then they would be at an impasse.

"I—I'll do the best I can, then. But I have conditions." Livvy's tone was respectful but firm.

"Which are?" Vasa replied, warily.

Livvy turned to Garrick. "Do you have any of those wind herbs?"

"Of course. I keep the pouch in my armor." His derisive snort matched his sneer.

"Can I see them? What they look like?" Livvy smiled, a bit shyly. Garrick handed over a small silken pouch, tied at the top with a small length of threaded hide. It was gray, stitched with red, and bulging with the light gray herbs when she opened it. She inhaled the scent, judging it to be somewhere between burning tires and mud, then smiled and threw the pouch over the veranda into the sky.

"Hey! What the—did you see what she did?" Sputtered Garrick.

"They give you an advantage on long range flights, right? Well, I'm not having you tell me I can't keep up when you've got the equivalent of an espresso machine tucked in your lip. Also, it's gross." Livvy flicked her hands with dismissal at Garrick's ongoing rage, even as everyone else laughed.

"I think she'll be fine. Remember what we said." Vasa

looked into the growing light of day, judging a cloud bank that had appeared in the distance. "Time to go, son. And as for you, listen to him. Watch the skies. Breathe from your belly and let your wings do the work." Vasa was strapping a belt and small pack to Livvy as she spoke, crossing thin leather straps across the smooth muscles of her back with practiced ease. When she attached a small pack to the straps, she explained its purpose after a sharp tug to verify that it was secure. "Food, and barter goods. A small knife for eating, and some other things you might need."

Livvy looked thoughtful. "How will we drink? In the sky, I mean."

"Ahh, good question. You'll use this." Vasa pulled a small, shimmering thing from the pack, which expanded into something that looked like the finest silk she'd ever seen. "Dewcatcher. You fly through a cloud and fill your net. Sadly, I haven't enchanted one to catch wine, but maybe someday." She smiled at Livvy; then, her face grew somber. "You'll also stop at the Blue Hole, but that's something you need to see to believe."

"The Blue Hole? Is that something in the sky?" Livvy thought that there was no limit to the wonders around her. She was learning that empty sky wasn't really empty.

Saiinov pointed with relish. It was clearly a place he favored. "One of the few bodies of water in our world, so to speak. The water is clean and sweet. You can rest there, as well as gather food stock. It's what you might call an oasis. One of the more peaceful—and beautiful—places in our realm."

"I can't wait." Livvy's enthusiasm was genuine; the Blue Hole sounded like a rarity in a world designed around danger.

Vasa gave her a warm smile before gesturing to Garrick.

"It's time." She kissed Livvy on the cheek, stepping back to let the newly minted angel spread her spectacular wings in small testing motions. Vasa muttered, "Be careful. You're mine, now. All of ours."

"It's true. And you have a friend who will need you to return with grace and experience." Saiinov hugged her lightly, then let Cressa approach.

"It's a big sky, and there's a lot to see. Come back safe," Cressa said, her eyes blinking rapidly to keep tears away.

They hugged as sisters might, then Livvy turned to Garrick. "I'm ready. Show me."

Garrick's face was neutral as he stepped to the edge and said, "Follow me." His wings flared in a magnificent spray of white; then, he leaped outward with a powerful down stroke.

For an eternal moment, Livvy watched him climb as time slowed all around her. The wind was a steady pressure in her face, whistling in musical tones as her blood began to roar with anticipation. Livvy took a breath, crouched, and jumped into the rising sun. With pure instinct, her wings flared into a stretched position as she felt her body contract and then—

Flying. A smile of wonder spread across her fine-drawn features as she took one, then two massive leaps forward with beats of her wings. The air lifted underneath her like an invisible hand, pushing her upward as the pressure above each wing dropped, and she began to climb. Tears streaked her face, and she wasn't sure if it was from the biting wind or the sheer joy of it all, but she knew at that moment that all of the pain in her entire life had been worth it. She was meant for this, and in seconds, her body took the last vestiges of her doubt and cast it aside with every elegant stroke of her wings.

"Not too far from me, now," Garrick said from nearby.

He didn't shout but directed his voice to her in a manner so that she could hear him without turning her head. She fought not to grimace at even that minor command, but it would take a lot more than Garrick to ruin the sensation of streaking through the sky with such a complete sense of freedom.

"Okay." She couldn't say anything else, although there was no pain in her chest or lungs from the effort of flying. Livvy marveled at the rightness of it all; she'd expected to have been out of breath at the very least, but her long wings were well up to the task of flying without causing her to feel the slightest twinge.

"Slow down and pace yourself, we're not racing." Garrick was just off her right wingtip, watching her with a neutral expression. "We're going sunward. Let me know when you begin to tire because I'll need some warning for us to find a proper aerie for midday rest."

"We're flying all morning?" Livvy asked, alarmed. She felt good now, but the idea of doing anything for more than a few minutes was still alien to a girl who'd lived her whole life fighting for each breath.

"You're thinking like one of *them*," Garrick said with a sneer. After a moment of nearly kind behavior, his arrogance returned to remind Livvy or her origins. "You'll get thirsty before me, so we'll steer toward the closest clouds to fill our nets."

"Thanks for ruining my first flight as an angel, jerk," Livvy muttered. When Garrick didn't answer, she stuck her tongue out at him and made a face before returning her concentration to the pleasure of feeling her wings beat up and down like an elegant machine. Then she laughed because the moment was too good to let someone like him spoil it with his sparkling personality.

She lifted her voice to reach him. "What's that?" She

pointed at a long, sinuous creature with frilled wings, diving away from them in fear. It was ten feet of silver scales, with wiry arms and back legs that bunched with muscle. In her mind, it was a dragon, albeit a small one. The intelligent eyes faced forward in a black snout covered with slick fur, like an otter. With an indignant squeal, the creature closed its wings and dove, falling like an arrow for several hundred feet before leveling out, casting a baleful glare at Livvy, and then speeding westward.

Garrick said nothing. He didn't even look at Livvy, robbing her of the moment at seeing a beast who had, until recently, been the stuff of legends for her.

Livvy nodded to herself, making an imprint of the feeling that Garrick brought out in her. She didn't like it, but it might be a useful tool when dealing with him in the future. As in, every second from that point forward.

"It's a Renardier," Garrick grunted after a long pause.

"Gee, thanks." Livvy was already tired of his attitude, but her curiosity burned. "Why did it fly away? Isn't everything up here trying to eat us or something?"

His snort was pure disdain, but he answered. "They're predators, but they're more clever than bold. They like to sneak around in the clouds and pick off smaller prey. We don't have anything to fear from them."

Time stretched again, but Livvy savored the silence. With Garrick, less was more. As long he was quiet, he wasn't insulting her or making patronizing noises, and that was something she could live with.

Thin clouds spread above them, casting dappled shadows that raced over their wings as they sped through the changing light of the midmorning sky. It was nearly an hour of quiet, methodical flying before Garrick drifted closer to her and spoke.

"We're close to the first stop. You can't overwork your

chest and wings, so we're going to stop as if you were a child. No, don't glare at me, I know how to fly. You don't, and my parents will wrap me in cords and throw me to the surface if I don't bring you home in one piece."

She opened her mouth for a biting retort, but logic overcame her anger. "Fine." She ground out the single word, then looked forward. An inverted pyramid grew in the distance, glinting in the sun and partially shrouded in thin mist. "Is that—is that our first stop?"

"It is. You need to listen to me now." Livvy felt the anger flare again but swallowed her pride to listen. Garrick's voice was firm, but not his usual jeering tone. When she nodded, he took measure of the distant object in their path. "We're going to land there under poor visibility, on a rocky surface. It's different than Windhook because there isn't an Elemental at the heart of this place, or at least not anything like what we know."

"The Elemental makes it easier to land at Windhook?"

"He does. He's invested in our family, and he's old and kind. This is a different situation. She's been silent for decades, and, even if she cared about our coming and going, she wouldn't help us at all. This is a holy place for us, and everything we do must be with the utmost respect." Garrick sounded like Saiinov for a moment, serious and mature.

"Okay, I'll do my best." Livvy felt a nervous rush at the prospect of the next few minutes.

"You'll do better than that, or the heart of the Columns will hurl you into the sun. It's her sacred duty to protect the names and the Columns. It's how we remember our dead."

"It's a graveyard?" She thought about might happen to the dead. A shiver went through her body, and it wasn't the wind.

"I don't know that word, but I can figure the meaning.

58

Yes, it's where we honor the dead for all to see, and none of us will violate the—it's like what you might call a church. Is that a place for your gods?" Garrick's curiosity seemed genuine, although he was frowning.

"Yes. They're places where some of us go to pray or to have weddings and other celebrations. Sometimes, it's for a funeral."

Garrick's wings began to slow. "Draw back and glide." When she did, he gave a tolerant nod. "We do the same here, but in stone. You'll see. Remember, backwing, feet out, bend your legs. Do *not* lock your knees; it might be the end of you." He dropped suddenly to take the lead, intending to land first and provide a visual map for her to follow. That or he was being petty. She wasn't sure which.

"Got it." Livvy's breath grew short at the sight before her. What had been a vague pyramid hovering in the open sky was now an inverted mountain, its rocky bottom scored with glistening veins of metallic ore. Jagged ridges and outcroppings bulged in a wild array all the way to the sharpened point, from which wispy vines hung to twist in the permanent winds. The surface was fairly smooth and covered with the first living plants Livvy had seen that looked anything like grass or flowers. All over the flat areas, rings of tall, pale stones shone brilliantly in the light of day. *Like Stonehenge, but there must be dozens of them!* Livvy marveled to herself. If names of the dead were inscribed here, then how long had angels been living in the sky? For that matter, just how many angels *were* there?

She interrupted her thoughts as the ground came closer. Garrick landed first with no impact at all; he flexed his legs and tucked his wings in the same motion, leaving him to squint up at her as she began her wobbly descent. Livvy let her body take the lead, feeling her wings cup the air and move back like paddles as she began to slow, then hover a mere step above the soft grasses—

-- And then she stalled, landing on her rump with an inelegant thud. Garrick stood smiling, a look of satisfaction spreading across his face as he savored her incompetence.

"I've seen better." He grinned, and there was little friendly about it.

With great dignity, Livvy stood, folded her wings, and brushed her fingertips over the first real plants she'd seen since arriving at Windhook. If she didn't know that they were miles in the air, it looked like they were at a lush park, albeit one with weird circles of pearly spires strewn across the landscape. She smelled water and realized that a pile of rocks nearby had a tiny waterfall dripping across a mossy surface, filling the air with scents of iron and moss and life. It was almost too much, so she took several deep breaths to calm herself. Whatever happened, she wouldn't cry in front of Garrick no matter how much she missed her parents. And Keiron.

And everything. But the stones were oddly alien, and she had wings. The choice was clear. She could cry, or she could find out why Vasa and Saiinov had brought her to this place in the sky, and that started by learning where she was, and what came next.

"There's water?" She strode confidently to the trickle, holding a hand out to catch the brilliant drops. Holding it to her lips, she found that the taste was sweet and pure, like clouds over grass.

Garrick took a drink as well, using both hands. Livvy noticed that he purposely looked away from her when he spoke, something she'd grown used to during her years with a defective heart. "There is, and fruit trees as well.

We can pick berries on the ridge around the north side, but only if the wind is stable. It's a long fall, and the gusts are powerful enough to make it nearly impossible to get your bearings in the air. More than one angel has been smashed against the underside of this place by an updraft." He grew somber, thinking of someone he might have known. "So we'll look at everything together, and I'll try to teach you some of who you are, now."

"Ok."

Garrick looked shocked as if he'd been expecting a fight. "Do you have questions?" His lip curled into the start of a sneer; it was his natural default.

Livvy exhaled upward at the lock of hair that had broken free to cover her eye. "No, Garrick, not a single one. I'm an angel, with wings, and I'm standing in the middle of a flying graveyard with a jackass who thinks that smirking is the height of personal interaction. What *possible* questions could I have, given that a week ago I was a high school student on a transplant list, hoping for a miracle?" Her brows shot up in disbelief as exhaustion began to seep into her bones. Despite her enormous wings, flying was hard work, and her heart was new. To her.

His reply was measured by the desire to yell back and the realization that what she said was true. For all his life, Garrick had been in a shadow, and now that shadow had changed bodies to come back from the dead and threaten him yet again. He *hated* being wrong, but even more than that, he hated feeling alone, which was the sensation he had when standing before Livvy. She looked at him with a hot stare that verged between promise and threat, and Garrick felt the first tickle of recognition that she was more than just a charity case brought on by his parent's endless conniving. Keiron had been Heartborn, which was rare enough, but to give his heart to this invader was almost more than Garrick could take. He knew there was a reason, but pride and hurt made him look past it to focus on the flashing eyes of a young woman who had something his family needed.

What that was, he couldn't imagine, but even Garrick knew that the world they lived in was gone. Something was coming, and Livvy and Windhook would be at the center of the storm when it broke. With all the control he could muster, he pointed calmly to the nearest circle of pillars. "Each house has a history, and houses are connected through marriage and birth." He began to walk toward the closest column, twenty feet of smooth, pearlescent stone that was part obelisk, part hexagon. It had been shaped by unknown tools until it had six sides that vanished at the narrow tip, which was the width of Livvy's waist. All in all, each column carried more than a simple sense of bulk, there were hints of time and patience as well, even at a distance.

Like the inside of a conch shell, or an oyster. Maybe mother-of-pearl, thought Livvy in wonder as she took the measure of the closest pillar. Everywhere she looked in her new world, there were hints of the ocean as if life had gone from under the sea to the sky in a tumultuous migration. Bitter fear passed through her at the thoughts of her former world being—what? Ruined? Inundated? What could make life leap forward into new forms, and take to the sky to survive? She resolved to look harder, and begin asking questions. From the past, she would understand her future, and it began in the here and now.

Garrick leaned close to inspect the endless lines of chiseled characters that rose up to vanish in the sun, squinting to better see the delicate whorls of writing that told stories of people who had lived, dreamed, and died among the clouds.

Looking at the expanse of greenery, Livvy realized they were alone. "I thought there would be more people here." She cupped her face to shield her eyes as she looked across the scene, losing herself in the loneliness of it all. Despite the vibrant life all around the, there was sadness in every noble stone. They stood on sacred ground, but it was also haunted, or at the very least filled with echoes of sadness from centuries of use.

Garrick pointed to an oddly sculpted swirl of flowers running between two of the nearest monuments. "We're not alone. At least, not entirely. There are caretakers here. It's tradition."

"Oh!" Livvy's exclamation came as the scene clicked into place. What seemed to be random features now came into focus as part of an enormous garden; one that teemed with everything from small waterfalls to sculpted trees. Knowing this changed nothing; she still saw near limitless beauty around them, even if it was done by the hand of angels. "Who does all this? It's an inhuman amount of work." Her tone was openly admiring of the commitment to change a flying mountain into a garden without peer.

"The Savoyards. There are only a few of them, and they're—I guess you might call them religious people. They live here, and will always live here. It's their covenant with the world."

"Are they, umm, angels?" It seemed logical to ask, given the wild diversity of life in the skies.

Garrick frowned but nodded. "Easterners, like Cressa. Dark, almond-shaped eyes, hair black as night, and the only angels I know who consider hard rock to be their home. They fly or climb about with equal ease, and they do not tolerate disrespect of their dominion."

"You said that," Livvy barked, but then softened her next words, thinking of the columns and their names. "I can see why. Are any of them going to talk to us, or is that only if you do something wrong?"

They both leaped up to spread their wings in fear as a voice boomed out behind them. "That is entirely up to you and how you conduct yourselves."

When they landed and turned, Livvy had her sword out, while Garrick held both sword and knife in a ready pose. "You won't need those, friends, and I might caution you to put them away. Someone could get hurt." He was taller than Garrick, with olive skin and Cressa's distinct Eastern features, but masculine and roughened by the wind. His smile was brilliant, creasing his eyes and face in a disarming way. "I'm Sylvain. You are Garrick, of House Windhook?" It was a statement, not a question.

"I am. Have we met, sir?" Garrick responded with care. Sylvain wasn't armed unless you consider the odd tools that hung at his belt, but they could easily be used to harm in the hands of someone capable. Sylvain looked up to the task, despite his winning smile.

"When you were a child, yes. Saiinov brought you here just after your brother was born." The Savoyard looked at a distant stone circle, far off and to their left. It was huddled on a small rise, consisting of five columns all leaning slightly together as in conversation.

"Oh." Livvy's soft exclamation was almost lost to the wind, but Garrick heard it and turned to her, his eyes inviting explanation. "It's just that—did Saiinov carve anything when he was here? Is that who writes the names? The families?"

"On rare occasions, a trusted friend, but that's only if the family has ceased to exist." Sylvain's face darkened with memory. "That happens more than I care to admit, and I'm thankful that it isn't my job to remember. Carrying that much lingering history and sadness would be too much, I think. We leave that to the stones."

"Why?" Garrick asked icily. His eyes were narrow with suspicion, lending him a feral quality.

Livvy started when she realized he was speaking to her. She waited, thinking to lie, but Garrick's eyes were on her like searchlights. He would know anything less than the truth, so she gave it to him like medicine. She wouldn't apologize for her existence.

"Your parents knew that Keiron was going to die. They orchestrated it, just like they wove me into their plans without my knowledge. Keiron knew. He came to me, before my surgery, and walked me through a place where he could set my fears to rest. I think he knew that I had to be stable to accept his heart, and he wanted it to count." Livvy's eyes filled, but no tears fell. Not yet.

"What—place? He wasn't here, so he must have been in your time. I watched him fall to you, to whenever you were. I know it." Garrick's anger rose with each passing second. He'd pushed his brother out of anger, not caring where he landed.

"Maybe that's true, but before he landed, we met. I thought it was real, but now I know it wasn't, or at least not in a sense I know. There were people who knew me and cared for me, and Keiron was there. He—he came to tell me I was loved, and that I could live an actual life with an actual heart. I just didn't know it would be his." The tears streaked her cheeks freely, and Sylvain took her hand. He was incredibly gentle, despite his appearance.

"A harbor," Sylvain said.

"What?" Livvy wiped her nose with one hand, thinking that angels could cry ugly, too.

"Keiron took you to a harbor. It's a place of protection

and magic. They're used by the higher angels, like Heartborn. When they need to transfer their power or lend protection—well, they create a harbor. It's more than a dream and less than reality. Your people have words for such things," Sylvain said, with certainty.

"If it wasn't a dream, he sure fooled me. I smelled the books, and felt the fear when I went in Miss Henatis' room."

"Where you passed through a gate of some kind?" Sylvain asked. He looked a Livvy slyly.

"Yes. . ." She drew the word out while processing the dizzying truths of the past week. So much happened, and so little of it real. Or what she knew to be real.

The ranger patted her arm in sympathy. "It's a big sky, young angel. You'll find that the world you left is much, ah, flatter than this one. We have layers, and lumps." His smile was warm, leaving no doubt as to his regard for the confused young angel before him. Sylvain protected more than just the mountain.

"I feel like every layer is more confusing than the last." Livvy shrugged, trying not to be morose. "I'll learn. I'm learning now." Her smile was hopeful. She looked at Sylvain, who struck her as a natural teacher. "Do you ever leave this place, this mountain?"

Sylvain laughed, his eyes glimmering with good humor. "It would take the act of a god to get us away from here."

"Us? There are many of you?" She asked.

"Enough." He waved at the rolling fields of green. "As you can see, it's a big place. My life's work will never be done."

"What is your work? I'm supposed to teach Livvy about everything in our path. It seems logical to know what you do." Garrick raised his hands in defense of his questions, but Sylvain merely grinned.

"I'm a caretaker."

Garrick sighed in irritation. "Could you elaborate? She's only been here for a few days."

"I thought I did, but since you insist, I'll be happy to for Livvy's sake." Sylvain sat down, crossing and extending his legs in a great show that only made Garrick angrier. Livvy had to stifle a laugh but molded her features to into something like neutral interest. "I tend to this place and the people who come here. Either of those tasks would be far too much for one angel, but we can handle the task because we're made for it. This is our chosen path, and my empathy is such that I can withstand the endless sadness because I can see it for what it is."

"It's love, isn't it?" Livvy asked, but she knew.

"It is indeed. And memory, some of which is bittersweet, but mostly love. My cadre and I know that for every tear shed here, there is a smile, even if it's somewhere between beauty and pain. We keep this place, although, in truth, I would say the stones keep us." He looked around again, and there was joy in his eyes.

After a quiet moment, Sylvain stood. "Come, you'll need water and food. We'll walk the paths to where your family carves their names, and forage on the way. There's much to see."

They made their way delicately along a thin trail that rose and fell with the gentle landscape. It was so much like home that Livvy expected to see park signs or hikers, but there were none. Only the stones intruded on their thoughts, casting shadows as they moved around and through the landscape of monoliths built to the memory of a world from the future. There were some familiar things—Livvy cooed at a butterfly, and thought she heard the *greep* of a small frog as they passed a burbling pool. The flowers were small but numerous, their splashes of color a shout among all the shades of green.

"Here," Sylvain said. They stood before Windhook's stones, listening to the wind. The silence was reverent.

Livvy stepped forward gently, looking upward. From her distance, the stones were luminous, shading from blue to gray and white with thin ribbons of roseate colors between. Only the names were uniform, their neat lettering scoring the stone white, like a clean wound. "I can't read this." She'd assumed that since she had a new body, her mind would be renewed as well. It appeared there were limits to the change, a fact that made her groan aloud. Of all the things she expected, learning to read wasn't one of them.

"You can't read?" Garrick practically laughed in her face. Mockery was his drug of choice, right after outright disdain. "We gave up Keiron for an idiot."

Sylvain moved in a flash of color, stopping with a thin knife under Garrick's neck. His voice was a harsh rasp above Garrick's heavy breathing. "You take liberties at a holy place? Your arrogance will get you killed, boy."

"I—sorry."

"Sorry, what?" Sylvain asked, his voice like ice.

"Sorry . . . sir?" Fear dripped from Garrick's reply. He hadn't even seen Sylvain move, let alone pull the wicked blade.

The caretaker nodded, thinking. In a whisper, the knife was gone as he let Garrick fall to the soft grass. "That's better, but I'm still troubled that you believe such behavior is acceptable. Here of all places, you will honor the dead—and their tenders—or you will join them."

Garrick rubbed at his neck, delicately. "I apologize." He looked as if he wanted to say more, but thought better of it.

That inaction earned him a grudging nod from Sylvain. "Perhaps you can learn. I'd suggest you start here." He pointed to the columns, tracing their graceful curve upward.

The air between them hummed with possible violence but faded when Garrick cut his eyes toward the nearest list of names. "I know about this place. More than you do, Livvy. You can hate me, but you can't change the past."

"About what? I'm here, and you better get used to it. I don't know why you think fighting your family is the way to—what *do* you want, anyway?" Livvy looked at Garrick with a mix of fascinated disgust.

Garrick's brow furrowed, but he nothing to say.

"That's what I thought. I've met you before, but with a different name. Mad all the time, entitled, thinking that everyone exists to serve you. I didn't like you then, and I don't like you now." She turned to Sylvain, who'd been watching with delight at her interrogation of the boy. "I came from the . . . I guess you would say the past, just a few days ago. I have his brother's heart, and he hates me for it." She frowned, amending her thoughts. "He hates me for a lot of reasons, and I'm not even sure he knows what they are. I'm supposed to learn about this place and the sky. All of it, really, and I don't know why. Can you help me?"

"Heartborn? And only for a few days?" Sylvain regarded Garrick with open disgust, all hints of kindness vanishing from his face. He stood, holding out a hand to Livyy. When Garrick began to move, he pointed at the ground. "Sit. You'll only serve to detract from what I have to say, and if you interrupt me, I'll be forced to act." His thumb caressed the knobby end of his knife. "I can assure you, that isn't anything you want."

Garrick seethed, but mutely as Livvy and Sylvain began to move away, toward the next circular memorial. It was flanked by a series of small, twisted trees that were like bonsai covered in tiny white flowers.

After several steps, Sylvain took her arm to guide her to a path made from crushed shells, or something nearly like it. "I've been here for most of my life, and if I'm allowed, I'll die here. That doesn't mean I don't know things." He grinned with mischief as they passed close to one of the sculpted trees. Up close, the riot of blooms smelled like oranges as they waved in the light breeze.

"You'll answer anything I ask?" Livvy was hesitant but hopeful.

"I will. My purpose isn't just tending the grove." He smiled again, and this time it was the expression of a sage.

She stopped to look directly into his eyes. One hand went to her chest as she formed the words, wondering what the answer might mean for her life. Perhaps it was better not to know, but that wasn't how she was built. Not anymore. The sun went behind a wispy cloud, cooling the air as Livvy spoke.

"What am I?"

Sylvain stopped moving, then laced his fingers together in thought. A slow smile lifted his face, making him look even more like a kindly teacher. Despite his earlier lesson with the knife, Livvy had never felt safer. He turned to her, tilting his head slowly before uttering a low whistle. The smile returned, brilliant and warm. "Have a seat. This might take a while."

She sat, and as he began to speak, the world around her fell away.

CHAPTER SEVEN:

FOOTHOLD

My eyes!" Marti's voice was high and panicked. Sand swirled around the sisters as the first blast of heat began to punish them. "Shhh, calm yourself. Give me your hands—no, don't fight me, let me clear your eyes with water. You opened them too soon." Brigha seized Marti by the face and began dribbling cool water across her eyes, flicking the clots of grit away with dexterous motions. "In a moment, you can try again. Be careful; the sun is just as intense."

After a series of gasping breaths, Marti opened her eyes. "Oh. Oh!" Before her spread a vast landscape that made her skin leap with fear. As a child of the skies, she was used to open spaces, but the broad river plain stretching away into the distance was wholly alien to her. They'd come to rest on a stone ridge poised above a broad river valley. As the land fell away, it grew into a rich, green tangle of primitive farms, dotted with two small clusters of mud houses with conical centers. Smoke drifted from a series of small communal fires; there was a sense of purpose about the people who were moving around in the morning sun.

"Where are we?" Marti asked, fighting to regain her nerve. She wouldn't give away her gains with Brigha. Not without an internal fight.

"Someday, this will be a place called Sumeria." Brigha looked around, assessing the rich land. "But not yet. That's why we've come."

Marti sat up, dragging her wings through the gritty soil. She was hot, disoriented, and scared. "If we're in Sumeria, then there are people. When they see our wings, we're dead."

Brigha waved a finger, smiling. "Not quite, sister. We kept our wings for a reason. Only fools endure the horror of losing their wings to become a Moondiver. I selected this place because of what *isn't* here. Look, Marti. A fallow land with people to serve us. A place far simpler than ours, and in need of guidance. We can shape these people to our needs, and take what we will from them."

"I understand the power we can wield here, but to what end? Sorcery doesn't work here unless I misunderstand this hole in my mind." Marti shuddered despite the heat. "I feel empty of power, like I would as a child. Something's missing."

"Is all of it gone?"

Marti considered the question, flexing something unseen in a test of her latent sorcerous skill. "Almost. There is something of my Scholarship left, although I can't say what." Her small face was streaked with water and grit, leaving her a miserable sight in the brilliant sun. Brigha handed her a fine cloth from her pack after moistening it with water. In quick, economical swipes, Marti cleaned her face to restore some semblance of order, grinning with pleasure as she scrubbed vigorously. She was surprised at how something so trivial could grant her control over emotions that had been on the verge of running wild.

Sumeria, or whatever it was, had shaken her as much as

the trip through the storm. Of that, she recalled little save the brilliant tear in the sky and a sense of weightless tumble as she was thrown from cloud to cloud with her wings wrenched back in pain. Brigha was watching her expectantly when the question came to mind, squatting before her in silence. An arrogant smile played about her older sister's lips, making uncertainty burble upward in Marti. After the recent change in their dynamic, it seemed that Brigha still had some measure of control.

Marti hated the sensation. "I'll only ask this once. Why are we here?" Her eyes flicked dismissively across the people and their huts far below. Whatever Brigha answered, it had to be spectacular. There could be no reason to risk plunging into the past for a life like this. She was unimpressed by what passes for civilization and failed to see what could be valuable to the people who lived in the curious huts made from mud.

"House Windhook," Brigha said, her eyes feral and bright.

Marti sighed. "This isn't the time to be cryptic."

"I'm not. The point of this is House Windhook." Brigha looked smug but relented after Marti's lips drew down in a frown. She needed her, and if the truth was known, they needed each other. It was an uncomfortable emotional place for both of them. "I've been contacted by someone here."

Marti spat laughter like a curse. After a long, slow shake of her head, she composed herself enough to point at Brigha as if she were simple. "We pierced the light of days to complete a plan brought about by a dream? Please tell me you're not that stupid, sister. Vain and petty I can tolerate, but willfully idiotic is"—

"It's not a dream, you fool," Marti snapped. Her eyes shimmered with growing anger.

"Really? I'm listening." Marti gestured broadly with

confident disdain, letting her years of resentment shape the motion. She was already plotting the use of her power to return home and forget that she'd ever been gone. Brigha could rot among the savages, and she could move on as the Lady of Selinus.

"I told you, it was—it *is* a visitation. She's calling to me, and it isn't just some whisper in the night. I've been given details, plans. She knows about Windhook." Brigha's lips were set in a stubborn line.

"Anyone can know about Windhook. They've attacked and overthrown the ruling body of our world. Surely you haven't built the plans for Selinus on something as common as word of our civil war?" Marti rolled her eyes, and for a moment, she seemed younger.

"She also knows about you."

There was no sound other than the hot breeze, then Marti spoke, her voice cautiously curious. "What about me?"

It was Brigha's turn to gloat, but she only did so long enough to destabilize Marti's confidence even further. What she had to say was too important to keep tucked away, despite the delicious nature of knowing things about her dangerous little sister. "She told me you would turn, eventually." With a rueful twist of her lips, she admitted underestimating Marti, a mistake she wouldn't make again. Ignoring enemies was an easy way to die in the clouds, and Brigha was a seasoned fighter who knew that your first mistake was often your last.

"Turn? I—fine. I'll grant you that, although only someone as arrogant as you could fail to see what was happening in your house. I don't exist to serve you, and I never will. But that's still a bit vague for my tastes. Anyone who knows our family could send a message through your dream state. In the world of Scholars, it's child's play."

"She also told me that you perfected something called the Augur, and when I saw it, I was to bring it here. To this exact place, through that specific storm, and without delay. She told me you would be resistant, but eventually convinced because of my ability to describe your plans in detail. Would you like to hear them? They're quite brutal, even for our people." When Marti stayed silent, she went on, this time with a cheerful grin. "You've already decided to abandon me here, but you can't figure out how to cast your spell since your sorcerous power is in question. Let me put that fear to rest, your magic is effective enough to make you a goddess here, just as my basic skills will do for me. You are, at this moment, wondering how to take control of Selinus without proof of my death, which is troubling since you don't like uncertainty. You see, dear sister, you enjoy stability, and my goals take that away from you. Are you convinced, or should I continue?"

Marti was still as she processed the possibility that Brigha was truthful. "Anyone could say that about me. It's hardly an insight. It's more like guesses that are"—

"What was the name of the other Moondiver?"

"What?" Marti asked, uneasy. The question was both vague and specific, depending on the context.

"I asked you to give me the name of the angel who wrote of their attempt at building a bridge between worlds. The one who failed but left detailed notes that thrill your darkened little heart with whispers of power and godhood? The story you found on some forgotten shell that inspired you to challenge me for control of Selinus, and then the skies beyond. You didn't suddenly grow a spine; you were pushed, just as I was. The distinction is that your secret growth involves my demise and abandonment, while my plans are for Selinus to replace Windhook as the dominant power in the sky now that Sliver is broken. It may take a century, but it can be done. Now, I ask you for the final time--am I being clear?" Brigha leaned forward, intensely waiting for her sister to respond.

Marti sat as if she'd been struck dumb. Her mind was a whirlwind of fearful denial, but the look on Brigha's face revealed that any lies would be regarded as an act of war. Marti's confidence evaporated like a fog, leaving her to face a sister who was skilled in the art of killing. She was also furious, armed, and on territory she knew better than the disoriented Marti.

The truth was overwhelming in proximity, and Marti knew that there was nowhere to go but forward. Carefully, she considered her words, running a hand through the sweat coating her forehead. Her hand came away damp and gritty, eliciting a grimace. "I don't have a name. I only have a reference from another account, recorded at a different time. Whoever they were, their trips have been many."

Brigha nodded thoughtfully, weighing the truth of her sister's confession. "You say a reference. Meaning?"

"I found message shells from a Watershaper named Barca. He was curious, like me."

"What house? I've never heard of—was it a woman? A man?" Brigha said the name under her breath, trying the unusual syllables like a new wine.

"Carthage, in a group of houses known as Orion, and it was a man. From what I can tell, he's been dead for more than three centuries. I only discovered his existence because I've been doing my research, outside the house."

"That would explain the windburn on your cheeks." Brigha shook her head in grudging admiration. "How often have you been gone?"

Marti touched her face reflexively. "Often enough.

Mostly when you were here, but others times as well. I only needed a few hours to get there. And back."

"Where is *there*?" Brigha calculated speed and distance with ease but could think of nothing like a library near Selinus.

"There is a whirlpool to the east, you know of it?"

Brigha's shock was genuine. No one went near the whirlpools, for reasons of safety and tradition. They were idly turning dead spaces in the air, filled with floating carcasses, trash, and unknown dangers that claimed angels every year. A whirlpool was the last resting place for massive animals whose bodies filled with noxious gas, leaving them to drift across the sky until they were pulled into the invisible eddies. To enter such places was ill-advised; to do so alone was pure stupidity.

"Don't be an idiot." Brigha's retort was scalding. Every angel knew the locations of storms, and whirlpools, and other dangers that marred the perfection of the breathtaking blue. There were maps, updated constantly, and angels who ignored them could end up missing. It was a dangerous business to live among the clouds.

"I'll take that as a yes." Marti gathered her thoughts under the sun's furnace, deciding how best to explain her unusual source of information. She spread her fingers wide on thighs that were sweating heavily under the flexible armor. The world was alien to her body, not just her senses. "It began with a message. A shell, rather. You sent me petty word of some plans you had last year; I believe it was just before you began your visits down here." She waved at the rolling landscape around them, enormous and fearfully different to her angelic senses. "I threw the shell into the sky"—

"And it fell into the unknown. Tell me something I don't know. It's hot, and we should be on the move."

Marti's lips curled in a half-smile. "You're not entirely wrong. Most shells do fall, but not all of them. The one you sent me floated away on a thermal, in a slow tumble. Naturally, I flew after it, and I noticed something curious. It was an older shell, well worn by hands, and scrawled almost white with marks."

"I remember it now. We had no means to get you a message just before I went—well, here. I found an old shell being used as a toy by some children. I thought it felt light." Brigha's arrogance softened, if only for a moment.

"Exactly. As the shells age, gas builds in their inner chambers, and some of them float due to the decay of some inner creature, or their remains. They're like the corpse of a Windbeast that's far too large to do anything other than plummet into the deep below Selinus, yet it may drift for months. I reasoned that if one shell could float, then so would hundreds, even thousands. And I knew just where to look." Marti's triumph twisted her features into something closer to Brigha. Malice and vanity merged to make them recognizable as sisters, a fact not lost on Brigha, who regarded her younger sibling with a flat gaze.

The silence stretched between them until the weight of it made Brigha speak. "And to think, for all these years we could have been gathering information." She tutted like an old aunt, then asked, "Does anyone else know this?"

"Not in our area, and certainly not that I've found. I began making discreet inquiries about purchasing well-used shells. I lied, saying that I considered opening my messenger service now that the Crescent Council had been shattered."

"Clever. Plausible, too, although the demise of the council isn't complete. Sliver still flies, as do many of the

Houses brawling for their chance to resume control over the empire." Brigha kneaded the back of her neck, thinking. "In theory, we could know everything that's ever been sent by shell, but I'm more concerned with what you know about this place." The wind began to pick up, spraying grit in their eyes as the sisters watched an oncoming storm boiling upwards across the river valley.

Shielding her eyes, Marti nodded in agreement. "We'll need to shelter from this, and then I can tell you what matters most." As the wind began to rise, they stood, using their superb eyesight to spot a cave less than a minute's flight away on a hardscrabble ridge of barren rock. Marti snapped her wings open, letting the air begin lifting her from the ground as Brigha did the same. "When it's quiet, I'll tell you about a place called Babylon."

CHAPTER EIGHT:

RIPPLES

Vasa drew her finger through the water of the scrying pool, watching the tiny wake spread in a series of ripples.

"How many times have we been here, in this place and moment?" Saiinov asked, his rich baritone echoing through the wide spaces of the central chamber. Windhook was an airy place, with high ceilings and fabrics that snapped during the moments when breezes reached the inner sanctum. He gazed at his wife in love and admiration, wondering what their next decision might bring as the sun began to rise once again

"Too many, dear heart." Vasa sighed with resignation, making Saiinov look at her in alarm. Vasa was many things, but tired was no one of them. He lifted a brow at her as she flicked water from her fingertips, watching the droplets scatter before drawing a deep breath and holding it. "I think we move forward with all of it and begin consideration of what happens to Livvy afterward. She's strong, but she will need direction. It wouldn't do to let her think that she was called to serve without a destination in mind. She's too smart to be left to her own devices, let alone think that our intention was to sacrifice her to some greater cause."

"Like Keiron?" His voice was soft like he feared chasing

away a ghost.

A tiny, decisive nod was her only motion as she exhaled in a quiet rush. "She won't understand the distinction, only that we need her. I'll take the lead. I think she will prove more valuable as both Scholar and Skywatcher. We know she has the ability, but I'll need her first. I can encourage her mind to unfold and accept all of the possibilities before her. That leaves our first step with Livvy as a member of our family. Where do we go?"

Saiinov tapped a foot against the rim of the pool, his eyes unfocused and distant. "I think we find the armorer first, and then, you begin training Livvy. She's the missing element between past and present. How close can we get her to the armorer? He's been silent for years. He may be dead. Or, he moved from his outpost. " Livvy was a known quantity, but she could not be a warrior without special considerations. Since they upset the balance in Sliver, there were precious few artisans to call on, and armor was an absolute must. That left a source in the north whom they had not spoken to in decades, and even when he'd been working, the armorer was notoriously shy. Whether or not he was willing or able to fill their needs was unknown, just like nearly everything else in their lives.

"Send Habira? She can be persuasive, and she knows Livvy' body size and strengths." Vasa grinned, thinking of her eldest daughter's ability to strike fear into the most stalwart opponents.

"Indeed." Saiinov's laugh was filled with pride. Habira was truly his own. "She'll need the usual array of incentives at her disposal. Coin, spells. Perhaps a promise of future considerations?" Windhook would rebuild their world, and they would need strong people to fill the ranks. The armorer, whoever it might be, could be a powerful ally.

"Just as I was thinking. I'll ready a shell and pack for her when she wakes." Habira was sleeping off the effects of near-constant patrols in and around their group of houses. The instability of war made for little rest, and long hours in the sky. "Are we asking too much of our children?" Vasa reached up to take Saiinov's hand, her eyes dark with worry.

"I don't know. Do they seem older to you? Other than the twins, of course," he added with a wry grin. Vesta and Banu had been mature since childhood, often shocking their parents with the behaviors of far older angels. He made a note to pay special attention to Habira's state of mind after she woke. He hated to think that his children were being consumed like resources due to a war that could determine the end of all things.

Or, it might be the rebirth of their world. It was still undecided, and every decision mattered, especially those that could protect the members of their family for the enduring future. The armorer was one such thing, a detail in the wider fabric of plans so knotty that only Vasa and Saiinov could grasp their true nature.

"Not older, but maybe resigned." Vasa looked thoughtfully into the pool, shuffling memories of her children.

"As am I." He cocked his head to listen as the sounds of Habira rising drifted down the hall. She would need time to shake the sleep from her mind before they inundated her with the oncoming journey. "Shall I do the honors?"

Vasa grimaced. "Please. You know how she is before breakfast." Habira was best left alone for a while after rising. It was family lore that she had the personality of a stinging insect before wine and breakfast, a fact that only the unwise chose to ignore.

Saiinov was both wise and prudent. "I'll get her

breakfast. We can discuss the plan after an appropriate period of, ahh, recovery from her slumber."

Now it was Vasa's laugh ringing through the chamber. "That's why I love you, dear. You know which battles to fight."

"I know when to fight." He kissed her, then turned to the kitchen, chuckling softly. "And when to bring wine."

CHAPTER NINE:

EVOCATION

"Your world came apart in a series of four events, known together as the *Evocation*, and before you ask, no. I don't know what caused it, but there are Scholars who have their suspicions. We hear many things from visitors. Angels tend to be talkative while enduring their grief, and despite the beauty of this place, there remains sadness to be dealt with." Sylvain was speaking casually, his legs outstretched on the grass. For someone describing the end of the world, he seemed remarkably calm. When he saw the stricken look on Livvy's face, he reached out to take her hand. "My apologies, Livvy. I didn't mean to seem callous about such things." What was ancient history to him meant something quite different to the young woman watching him, her face ashen at the thought of an entire world—filled with her people—coming to an end.

"It's just that"—she stopped, unsure what to say. Did she miss her family? Of course. It was a deep, resonant ache in her new heart that never faded. She woke with the hurt, she slept with the hurt, and it crept into her dreams as an unwelcome chill. "They all died?" There was a universe of pain in her question.

"No, child. Not all of them." Sylvain's smile was bittersweet, his tone like a muttered prayer. "Some of us

84

came here."

"How?" Livvy's face was streaked with tears rolling down blotchy skin. She was flushed with hurt and loss.

"Ahh. That's where it gets interesting. There were four levels of the Evocation, although I can't say how or when it happened. That is a question for Vasa. Scholars have found and guarded our secret past for this very reason because feeling the loss of an entire world is too much for any one soul to bear."

The light of discovery burst through Livvy's tears. Even the silent, brooding Garrick turned to look at them from his position a few feet away. "Four? As in four kinds of whatever I am? Heartborn?"

"And the Windborn, and Lightborn, and Cloudborn. Four new things, new souls. Four types of people who took to the skies to change into something the world had never seen, hopefully for the good of all." He inclined his head politely, smiling. "And here you are. A young woman with wings and the heart of a boy who saved her, wondering where she fits in over the next years. And centuries."

"Centuries? But I don't want to live forever!" Livvy all but shouted.

"Oh, there's no risk of that, I can assure you. There is danger aplenty here, and you'll do well to remember that." Sylvain's brow furrowed in disapproval at Livvy's outburst. For his part, he was truthful, even if it meant explaining the harsh realities of angelic life.

"So everyone keeps telling me." Even to her ears, she sounded peevish. "Sorry. I get overwhelmed."

"Every minute." Garrick's sour quip was met with a glare from Sylvain, who waggled a finger in warning. Chastened, he turned away and pretended to look at the nearest rocks, saving some measure of his dignity. He was clearly smarting from the earlier lesson in humility, a fact that sat quite nicely with Livvy. She had no need for his arrogance but every need for his cooperation. As to information, Sylvain was a storehouse of knowledge, and what he didn't know, the other members of Windhook did. Livvy found herself wondering at the nature of Vasa's mind. It must be like the inner chambers of a shell, she reasoned, an elegant room filled with secrets. As to Saiinov, she still didn't understand his duality. He could be martial and rigid, but soft when it came to his family. She was left with no other option than playing along and absorbing in the world around her. She may be new to the skies, but Livvy understood an opportunity when it faced her. Absorb and adapt; that was her new path. Seize chances when they came.

Sylvain was just such a chance.

He began speaking, albeit in a gentler way. "As I was saying, you'll have to ask Scholars for more detail, but I know we came from a place deep in time, and far away. The Evocation was an awakening of all things legendary"—

"Even the dragons?" Livvy asked, brightly. To the angels, they were Windbeasts, but Livvy was a child of humanity. She knew what they were called in a thousand languages of people who were now long gone. Demons, dragons, monsters—all of the myths, come to life, flying free, and gloriously alive when the bones of her world were somewhere underfoot in a land that not even the bravest angels considering visiting. Why, she had no idea, adding that question to the growing list of things she needed to understand. For now, she was happy to know that her heart was no accident, and Keiron's sacrifice had a plan, however opaque it might be.

"You mean the Windbeasts? Yes. Even them, in all of

their color and variety. Fang and claw—and mind! Never forget that the beasts among the clouds are clever, or wicked, or both. Rarely, they're merely curious, but it's best to go through the sky thinking that anything you encounter is a possible threat." He gave Garrick a long, measured look before moving on. "Even those things that look friendly. Do you understand?"

She nodded because she did. His words were plain, his meaning clear. "We fly on to a place called Electra. Is it far?"

"The outpost? Too far to leave now." He squinted into the ending light of a long day, its rusty glow casting shadows on the planes of his face. "You'll stay here tonight and take wing at dawn. Electra is a long flight, and you'll want to be in the best possible condition when you arrive. There's only one possible stop between here and there, a small aerie that travelers use as a rest. It's unoccupied but has nets filled with water."

"We can rest at Electra? Why do we need to be prepared, and for what?" Livvy's innocence burbled forth, eliciting a cough from Garrick.

Sylvain smiled, his teeth bright in the growing dusk. "Your body may be tired, but your mind must be sharp. You're going to meet the merchants of Electra, and they make their living from angels who need things." He grew serious, and Livvy noticed the first stars beginning to gleam overhead. In the sky, night fell with a velvet hush. "I can only give you advice as to your conduct, Livvy, and it is to protect your back, for there are blades everywhere in Electra, and they are sharp and quiet."

CHAPTER TEN:

PATHFINDER

The storm blew itself out, leaving the desert air sparkling but exhausted. Only dull puffs of hot wind mustered across the sand-swept landscape falling away from the cave that had given them shelter.

"That was new." Marti swiped fine grit from her face and neck, brushing vigorously at herself in short, desperate strokes. A sandstorm was completely alien to angels, and the aftereffects left Marti and Brigha with a sense of otherness. They were exhausted after huddling inside the shallow cave for what seemed like a day, but the sun had not set, leaving them to conclude that their travel had altered their sense of time.

Stepping out into to clear, both sisters flexed their wings, snapping them outward to clean their feathers of dust and debris. At its peak, the storm had been too loud for them to speak, a howling vortex of punishing wind and dust that scoured at exposed surfaces with relentless fury. To the distant south, clouds the color of old bruises were retreating, taking the angry winds away to menace unseen people and lands.

Brigha didn't care. She narrowed her eyes in the remaining sun, looking for evidence of habitation or roads; anything that would lead them out of the wilds and into contact with the people she knew to live nearby. It was best if she said little, as the Marti was too smart to accept a lie that they were wandering without purpose. Brigha knew exactly what she wanted; it was only the details that had yet to reveal themselves to her endless lust for power. Here, she could be a goddess, a fury of wing and feather who would shape legends and inspire people to serve her in the manner she deserved.

But for Marti, it could be done in the open. Brigha grimaced at the thought of sharing power but quelled the thought lest the intuition of her sister tipped her secret plans. Even a stray look could be interpreted by the clever girl, so she shaped her features into something like grim determination and interest, leaving the plotting to rest in the back of her mind, safe from the probing glances of Marti and her growing power. It was a balancing act, but she could do it. She would because her life would be spent as something more than the mistress of a minor house in the crowded skies among warring angels.

She would be a queen.

Marti spoke. "I think we should"—

"You should probably drink something first. It wouldn't do for you to overheat." The man stood behind them, shading his eyes in the glare. He was tall but stooped, dressed in loose fitting pants and a tunic of rough spun wool that was cheerfully striped in bright colors. On his chest rested a small stone amulet held in place around his neck with a fiber cord. The skull was nearly black with age or handling, and two horns curled close to the domed forehead. The features were light, even feminine, with the lips pulled up in a furtive smile. There was whimsy in the face, despite it being something akin to the symbol of death incarnate, which it was.

As to the man, he was nut brown from the sun, with a long, mobile face and black hair arranged in carefully oiled curls. A simple headband of copper held his hair in place, and he held a hardwood staff with ease, waving amiably at the sisters with his free right hand. Eyes that were black and friendly regarded the angels as if they were the most natural thing in the world, a fact not lost on Brigha, who snapped her weapon out in a silvery hiss. His appearance wasn't nearly as troubling as the fact that he spoke their language without a hint of accent, but she could address that momentarily.

"You walk quietly, friend." Brigha's voice was low with menace.

"It is my land. Or, rather, my homeland. As to your magnificence, I can only guess why you're here, though I'm known as a lucky man. It seems fitting that goddesses would reveal themselves to me. I have led a pious life, save for some minor sins when I was younger and of hotter blood." He looked unduly pleased with his fortune, then lifted a brow of inquiry at Marti. "Your sister?"

"How did you know?" Marti snapped, losing what little comfort she had when dealing with someone who was supposed to run in fear. At least, that's what she'd expected.

"I did not, although legends suggest that families live"— He pointed the staff upward, toward the sun. "Up there. For security. Family is most important, and, though you do not favor each other, I thought it logical."

"We are. Your name?" Brigha asked, infusing her words with a haughtiness that she'd been practicing for years.

He took no offense, merely bowing from the neck with mild amusement. "Arad, and I am at your service, goddesses."

Marti tilted her head at the man as she took his measure once again. For someone standing in the presence of what he thought were gods, he was remarkably calm. To her cynical mind, that meant he was either intelligent or devious. Possibly both. Thus, he was suspect. She hid this conclusion with her next question.

"Do you live nearby?" Marti watched him closely for any signs he might be lying, but his smile was wide and easy.

"Indeed I do. If I may serve, I'll lead you to my home, and village. It's near the river, just down the plain." He pointed with his chin to a smudged area of green near the winding mirror of a small river. Wisps of smoke from a central fire rose in the air before being shredded by the erratic breeze. There were obvious fields, and what looked like beasts of burden, although Marti couldn't be sure. She'd never seen a horse or ox, only read second-hand accounts of their existence, and even those had been spotty.

"We shall," Brigha allowed, stepping in front of her sister without a glance. Their struggle was still undecided, in her mind. "Arad, what is your position in this place?"

He answered without hesitation. "I serve the goddess, naturally." He looked meaningfully at his brightly colored tunic. "We all do, or at least those of us who wish to live. She's quite generous, even kind, but her will is not to be questioned. Only the goddess can know her plan for our people. And this place."

They began walking down the declination in careful steps. The piled sand was loose, leading to several missteps on the part of the angels, who would have preferred flying. As they walked, Arad continued to speak, pointing out the farms and small buildings that grew closer as they lost elevation. Overall, there was a general sense of order despite the moderate damage from the recent storm. Small trees and shrubs began to appear, then irrigation ditches and a riot of green in thin strips.

Humanity had overcome the desert, leading to a prosperous setting filled with industrious sights. It was a far cry from the desolation of their original landing, and they were only a short distance away.

"What are those?" Marti's eye caught on a grove of trees that groaned with fruit. There were small animals underneath their spiky fronds being tended by children who directed the bleating animals with high, piping voices and the occasional poke of a stick.

"Ahh, those are dates. Quite delicious, and among the most important things we grow." Arad's smile was proud.

"Why? Are they valuable?" Brigha asked, ever on the hunt for material gain.

"Of course, lady. They are food, but also because they can be used to make a powerful wine that is most prized by traders and nobility." Arad gestured to two men who were peering closely at a tree, inspecting it for some flaw. "Insects are an issue, and the farmers are most protective of their groves." He delivered this in the tone of someone who was a born teacher. One of the men waved, paused to goggle at the angels before quickly looking away. The other man shied as well, never averting his eyes from the ground as they passed. Marti cut her eyes at Brigha, who noted the event with great interest. Either the men had been beaten for insolence before, or they were fearful of Arad; there could be no other explanation for avoiding the arrival of two angels.

"You serve a goddess?" Marti asked, turning the conversation towards her needs. If there were competition, she would know who and where they were. She had no plans for walking through a desert to be struck with another angel's sword. Moondivers weren't unheard of, and it might be that others were reaching into the past since the fall of Sliver.

"No, lady. I serve *the* goddess," Arad said. There was no

hiding his smugness; he enjoyed some position of importance under a being he regarded as divine. That was a problem for Marti, and Brigha, too, although how far ahead she was thinking was anyone's guess. Brigha's mind drifted toward the tactical, not strategic. Her anger could cloud the long view, leaving both sisters in a position of weakness. If they weren't unified, they could be taken down as individuals. As distasteful as it seemed, a working partnership was the only way they could succeed in the depths of this strange past.

"Would you tell us about her? Is she of our people?" Brigha's question was as deferential as she could be. Marti smiled inwardly; it seemed that even her brutish sister could use a honeyed tongue when it suited her.

An animal honked in greeting at them as they passed over a small bridge, the water running clear beneath them in a ditch with stone walls.

"What is that beast?" asked Brigha. It was unlike anything known in their world, with tall ears and a long face. Slender limbs held up a solid looking body that ended in a tail constantly flicking at the pestilent flies.

"A donkey. Quite harmless, and useful. That one is a friendly example. They can be rather headstrong." Arad waved to the girl nudging the beast forward toward another grove of trees in the distance. Her youthful voice was a sing-song of trills and laughter as the donkey made its grudging way along the beaten path, but not before cropping a mouthful of flowers to chew. "We use animals a great deal--and the land. Both can be harsh partners, as you've just witnessed. When the rain falls, it's a magical place, but if it doesn't, well . . . " He let his voice trail away with the unspoken truth of a hard land. There was life but only as long as the water flowed over a place that succeeded based on the whims of fickle nature.

Angels used sorcery to move and craft clouds into useful things. There was precious little weather the Watershapers could not move, change, or eliminate completely. The storm that brought Marti and Brigha to the past was a rarity; a thing of raw power on a scope that made sorcery irrelevant. Angels were powerful, but they weren't gods.

At least, not in the sky. But in the past, they were more than enough to be considered some a type of god. Or goddess.

In the village proper, people were interested but wary. There was an odd silence, save the bleats of animals and children, neither of whom understood the nature of the winged beings walking through the dust. Arad led the sisters directly to a large home tucked behind a screen of brush. It was mud and brick, like the others, but with the veneer of wealth that set it apart from every other home nearby.

"Stop right here." Brigha's voice cracked with authority, making Arad turn in mild alarm. She'd been reasonable, up to a point, but that moment was past. With near martial intensity, she walked before the man and stood, eye to eye. She was tall, if not taller than he was, and she let her eyes bathe him in radiant disdain for a long moment before she spoke. The hot breeze ruffled her hair and wings, setting the otherness of her into visible motion. She was a warrior and an angel of incredible power, and, if Marti wouldn't spring into action, then she would.

"Who *are* you?" Brigha's voice was cold with barely contained anger. She took a further half step toward Arad until her face was inches away. Silently, Marti judged her performance from the side. It was an act she'd seen many times before, but in this instance, she greeted it with complete approval.

"I told you, lady, I am"—

Her hand cracked against Arad's cheek like a thunderclap, staggering him into a sideways lurch as he fought to maintain consciousness. Failing that, he took a knee as the powerful blow finished short-circuiting his nervous system, taking his legs away in a wilting tumble. Through bleary eyes, he looked up into the sun, where the angel loomed over him expectantly.

"Well?" Brigha asked in a raspy whisper. She had many flavors of anger to be used as tools; it was her nature to implement both smiles and curses as a means of achieving her goals. Right then, she was on the verge of truly losing her temper in a volcanic outburst, which Marti had seen happen exactly once. The angel on the receiving end of that tirade was now a distant memory, most likely bones on the hideous landscape below where angels feared to tread. Every limb in Brigha's body quivered with potential energy, ready to be unleashed on the oily, slithering Arad if he displeased her in any way. Around them, the village had grown deathly still. Not one face showed among the houses and fields as if the people had fled before the fury of an oncoming storm. They were right to do so, for it's always the common people who are collateral damage when the gods lose their temper.

Brigha let the man recover his senses before continuing her interrogation. "You should think carefully before answering my next question, as there are only three potential answers, and thus, three outcomes." When he nodded gingerly, she allowed him a tiny, vicious smile. "Good. Now, think carefully. Have you ever seen me before?"

Instantly, he shook his head, but slowly. "No, lady."

Her grip on his tunic lessened, but only just. "Naturally.

This is my first trip to your specific area, although I concede it's possible that you've heard of me, if only from a distant source. Given the superstitious nature of these people, that might even be true. Do you know why I asked you this?"

This time, his answer was slower, even deliberate. He'd lost control of the situation and was on shifting sands. It was a position that suited him poorly, given the worried twist to his lips. "No, lady?"

She examined the palm of her hand, idly, as if looking for damage done from the blow she'd leveled at his cheek. Finding none, she looked satisfied, then said in a casual voice, "If I've never been here before, and my sister has cast no spell, would you care to explain why you're speaking my language?"

Arad sat, stupefied. He'd clearly given the matter no thought until that second, and the implications troubled him. Either he was hiding something, or he was a pawn in the service of a being far more powerful than he'd originally estimated. Arad was a survivor.

He was also the ultimate opportunist. Slimy, but likable, and always one step ahead of problematic things like justice or morals. He enjoyed a certain kind of lifestyle, and serving the goddess allowed him to indulge that level of comfort without dirtying his hands among the farmers and their endless battle against the soil. For the first time in his adult life, Arad had no answer and knew it could very well get him killed.

Or worse.

He squared his shoulders as best he could before looking up into Brigha's searing gaze. The world fell away underneath him just then as she leaned down. He noticed that she was intensely beautiful, even in her rage. That bothered him as much as being hit. In his world, beauty was often a sign of danger.

Brigha was both.

After a long moment, Arad decided that saying nothing was the only reasonable decision. The silence stretched between them into a heavy, awkward thing, broken only when Brigha reached down to caress his cheek. It was tender as if she regretted the unsavory act of striking him. Her green eyes were lit from within, red hair lifted by a rare breeze that broke the tension between them, if only slightly. He noticed many things with her being so close, not the least of which was the disgust she worked to hide from him.

He was scared. Not alarmed, but genuinely, deeply fearful of these winged women and what they might do. He'd given everything to the goddess in hopes of—well, everything in return. He was a greedy man, with lust and weakness as his constant companions. At that moment, he needed the goddess to save him, because the angels were asking questions he could not answer.

"Lady," he began, "I do not know." He lowered his eyes in respect. He'd been honest, and humble, both of which sat uneasily on his tongue. For a moment, Brigha considered his words; then she did something he never expected.

She laughed.

Marti joined in, a rolling peal that punished Arad like a wayward street child being mocked by the rich passing by. With each musical noise, he felt smaller. They were laughing at him. At his lack of understanding, his transparent desires, and, lastly, at the common mud huts around them. The worst part was that he knew it. He understood it all because he'd done the same thing only days earlier when he'd last walked through the town, a sneer of superiority on his face as his confidence brimmed over into toxic joy.

Marti squatted next to him, her eyes brimmed with tears of hilarity at his expense. He felt sick, but powerless, which made him feel even sicker. The spiral of shame hammered him downward until the angels fell silent, wiping their eyes and finally regaining control. In moments, both of the sisters wore like expressions of stern disgust, but when Brigha hesitated to speak, she left the way open for her grasping sister.

Marti wasted no time. "Tell me of your goddess." It occurred to her that Arad might be a valuable asset, rather than a mere social climber who sought to be the king of a valley filled with farms, flies, and date palms. She rocked back on her heels, feathers spreading across the dusty ground like a cloak made of snow.

Arad's eyes lit from within. Boasting was something that came naturally to him, like breathing, and he saw the question as a means to buy time before he plotted his next action. "But of course, if it pleases you." He sat down, crossing his legs in an easy motion. He might be fearful of the angels, but he would not be uncomfortable. Spinning a tale required pacing, and ease of delivery both of which were impossible if he cowered in fear. After a swift series of adjustments, he gave a respectable glance downward and pointed to the west. "She arrived from the west, on foot, though she had wings to rival yours, if I may say so."

"When?" Marti asked, and at Brigha's silent urging adding, "describe her wings. In detail."

Arad looked at the sun, calculating. "Before the early rains. She's been here for three moons and then some, but she's not here all the time. She comes and goes at her pleasure, and the only explanation I have been given is that she lives in many realms. I always know when she is coming because of the sky. A small storm will arrive, like a column of summer rains. It descends to near the ground, and she—she appears." He grunted involuntarily at the recollection, leaving no doubt that her method of travel left him in fear. "As to her wings, they are the color of a starless sky. Wherever she goes, there is a cool wind, as if she brings the chill of the night with her. After her first appearance, she issued an order that I should never sleep in her presence if I wished to see another day."

"Black wings, but shaped like mine? Like ours?" Brigha asked.

"Yes. Almost identical, save their color. And"— He broke off, chewing at the inner part of his cheek.

"And what? Don't be coy; this is not a negotiation. You cannot afford to hold back information from us. We are here. She is not. Do you see the facts before you?" Brigha snapped, angry. When her blood was hot, she spoke more like a tyrant and less like the lady of a house. This was one such moment.

He reached his conclusion, closed his eyes, and whispered. "You smell of sunlight and rain."

Marti drew back, her eyes narrowed in suspicion. "Yes?" She could only conclude that their scent had meaning, which was oddly animalistic. She revised her opinion of the man further downward, taking another look around at their crude surroundings. To be fair, it was a village of glorified mud huts. His reaction was to be expected. "What of it?"

Arad swallowed in fear, and the sisters realized it had nothing to do with them. For the first time since they'd arrived, the hint of risk pricked at their senses, rendering them mute as he spoke the words that explained the danger surrounding them. Or, if he was truthful, a danger that would approach them from the west.

His throat bobbed nervously, but a brief shake of his head helped to stiffen his resolve. His eyes snapped upward to stare at Brigha, then settle on Marti. There was no waver in his voice and no hint of a lie. "Her wings smell of death itself."

CHAPTER ELEVEN:

ELECTRA

Livvy felt an overpowering urge to pray as they took flight in the early morning air. Dawn was well past as the day began to fill with color. Wind began to form around them as they stood on a grassy shelf before the eternal blue sky, its raw depth sprawling away beyond the edge of their senses. Sylvain had been good as his word, bringing them a small pack of food and water, but then he left. Being a caretaker was more than just a title. He had work to do, and after wishing them well, he'd slipped a small shell into Livvy's hand with the muttered instruction that if she ever needed him, she should send it to the skies, and he would answer.

She took it as more of a kind gesture rather than a promise of help, remembering how adamant Sylvain had been about it taking an act of the gods to make him leave. The Columns of the Lost were many, as were the needs of the angels who came to visit. Their souls would need comforting, and the land had to be cared for in a myriad of ways unknown to her. Still, she felt her spirits buoy knowing that someone cared enough to give her hope.

Garrick spread his wings in a magnificent gleam of white. "Today, we reach Electra, and there are considerations as to how we'll approach."

"Is it dangerous?" From what she'd heard, it was a

trading post. That meant, in her mind, that their presence was welcome. Given the recent upheaval caused by Windhook, perhaps she should have considered the fact that other opinions might exist. She made a mental not to give due thought to other avenues. Doing so might save her life, especially if Garrick was going to be tight-jawed about the reality of her new world.

"To us? No. We will be welcomed in, but there's a stiff defense surrounding Electra, and they have a *very* specific set of rules for how we should conduct ourselves. It wouldn't do to get killed because of you making a stupid mistake." He grinned sourly at her, flexing his wings again in preparation for flight.

"You mean like insulting the dead and having a knife at your throat? That kind of mistake?" She smiled sweetly at him, watching his cheeks flush with anger. If he were going to regress into some idiotic state, she would be only too happy to help him along. She could find her way in the enormous skies. Somehow.

"Whatever. Just try to keep up. When we get to the outer ring of defense, you're going to have weapons trained on you. Don't do anything dumb until we're cleared," he said. He was still angry, but doing his best to control it. She knew that he feared his parents, and failure for him would be nothing short of catastrophic. He didn't have any other siblings to protect him from their wrath.

"Stop right there. What *kind* of defense? Animals? Monsters? A plant that wants to eat me? And, for the love of heaven, *why*?" All seemed probable to her, based on what she'd seen so far, though she couldn't fathom what was so valuable that it required multiple rings of dense.

Garrick shook his head in anger. "Because they sell everything that the Moondivers retrieve. Items that you couldn't begin to imagine, and worth more than your and my life put together," he ground out in disgust, and, at that moment, Livvy hated him a little bit. She hoped that someday, somehow she would see his arrogance shredded and tossed to the winds, although who would do it she had no idea. He was handsome and sculpted from dreams. If only his interior were as flawless as his exterior, he might begin to approach the perfection that Keiron wielded effortlessly. She broke from her reverie to find him staring at her, a look of pity on his face. Somehow, that was even worse than his outright scorn.

He gestured into the distance. "There will be two rings of defense, and you'd better pay attention. The first will be battle angels under the command of Lockhart, a serious angel without a drop of humor in his blood. He runs the mercenaries from House Spindrift, and they'll be armed with bows. Giant bows with arrows longer than your leg. The Spearwoods can shoot us at a range beyond anything you could imagine, and if you're hit, you *will* die. The arrows are poisoned if you don't bleed to death first." He looked down, adding, "Or fall to the surface."

She was quiet, weighing whether or not to tell him about modern weapons that could go from one end of the globe to the other. Better to let him cling to his truth, rather than lose time and effort convincing him of something he might see as a grand lie. "What about the second ring?" she asked.

"Even more lethal. Those are the Corvids, of House Altair, and they won't bother with the niceties of asking us if we belong. We're either announced by signal from the outer ring, or we die by their enthusiastic use of twin swords. It's simple." His tone left no room for interpretation.

"Fair enough. Why are they so keen on killing? Is it

their leader?"

He sighed in disgust. He wanted to leave, and she kept asking questions. "Their leader is Maev, and she isn't what you might expect. Since we're arriving from the west, I'll guarantee she will be present to see us through to the surface of Electra."

"Because there are rogue armies in our direction, or because that's where House Windhook is located?"

"Both, and you will hold your tongue in Maev's presence. I'm telling you, we *must* pass through without incident. It can affect the prices we pay once we're in the markets," he warned.

Livvy nodded, understanding. To be a problem customer from the beginning meant that they would be at the mercy of whoever was doing the selling. That just made sense. As to Garrick's fear of the unseen Maev, it made no sense. If she was a professional soldier, why would the Corvid ring be any different than the Spearwoods? "Has Maev ever harmed you? Or your family?" Livvy scratched absently at her cheek, wondering who this angel could be to strike such fear into the arrogant Garrick.

"No, but I know a threat when I see it. She might look like a, a"—he hesitated, waving his hand around vaguely as he searched for a description before sighing in frustration. "She smiles a lot, and she carries a moonstone around her neck that always had a full charge of light within. She can kill with that stone, like any Scholar, but she's just so cheerful about it. You meet her and feel like she's your best friend, and get lulled into a sense of peace."

"So she's pretty?"

"Wait—I—how did you know?" He looked at her suspiciously.

"Because arrogant jerks always think pretty girls in

charge are on the verge of something destructive. You're used to getting your way, so when you meet your opposite, it scares you." Livvy folded her arms with satisfaction, savoring the silence enfolding Garrick.

"Whatever, just spread your arms wide when you see them? I'll see them first, and let you know."

"Not a chance." Livvy's tone was mulish, her jaw set in stone.

"What? You don't have a choice." He was stunned by her disagreement. She was supposed to listen, not ask questions, no matter how legitimate they were.

"Yes, I do. It's my life, and I'm not flying up to some ring of death angels or whatever they are without understanding the system. I'm not kidding. If you're screwing around with the truth and withholding something, I'll pluck you like a chicken without a second thought." Her eyes sizzled with threat.

Garrick took a long look at her before asking, "What's a chicken?"

For the first time in days, Livvy laughed with abandon. "It's a bird that you do not want to be," she said, withholding details on purpose. Let him stew. She could keep her secrets, even if it were something as bland as the nature of a chicken. "Are we ready?"

He gave her a searching look before she saw the powerful muscles in his legs bunch. "We are. To the wind, now." He leaped.

She bent her knees, then exploded upward with speed and grace that would have been unthinkable only days before, but this was the new Livvy. A body honed for battle, and flight, and a mind that was only now beginning to fill with the possibilities of the world before her. She breathed deeply, heart thumping in seamless rhythm with her muscles as the land fell away beneath her. In seconds, they were streaking away from the slowly turning mountain; their eyes narrowed as the sun began to split the sky before them. It was a kind of beauty she thought he would never live to see, and now it was commonplace.

"Whatever happens, please don't let me forget," Livvy swore an oath to herself as they began to wheel away, climbing into a thermal that Garrick detected. She realized she felt it too, tweaking her wings to catch the bloom of air that pulled them forward like a rushing tide.

In the distance, the shadow of something enormous and scaled slid into a lower cloud, then vanished from sight. Livvy shuddered, thinking that Garrick was the least of her concerns. It was a place of beauty, and unvarnished danger. She would never forget that, either.

Before her, the sky opened wide, filled with the unknown and her future.

CHAPTER TWELVE:

REVELATION

*H*abira landed at Windhook with a jaunty step, folding her wings tidily before entering the cool inner sanctum of the home. "Storm to the south, but nothing major."

I know. I have told the family.

"Thank you, Windhook." Habira gave a cheerful wave along with her thanks. The Elemental living within their house was old, mannerly, and silent. When it decided to speak, the family made certain to give thanks. Elementals lived at a slower pace, with fewer worries and general interaction with the wider world. They were a contemplative lot, having time on their side to consider that which was best for the house and family, which had always been the prime concern of each Elemental that honored a particular clan with their presence. In the case of Windhook, the Elemental had arrived by some unknown signal on the day they took possession of the immense structure that would become House Windhook. Since Elementals had no physical body, travel was more or less at their whim. The fact that their Elemental chose to guard and live with them was an honor that the family did not take lightly. On more than one occasion, its stentorian voice had boomed out to warn the family of impending danger. It was loyal, aware, and always watching. Those qualities were priceless in the skies, where death was in every direction at all times.

Habira made a mental note to speak to Windhook, whose Elemental pacing could draw out a discussion over hours. She'd had conversations of incredible complexity about clouds, or weather, or animals in the skies—all of which were major concerns for the family, and thus, of importance to the magical being who acted as the guardian of their house. A little relaxation with Windhook could go a long way; there was a soothing quality to conversations with the being.

Habira called to her parents before walking into the central space, where the scrying pool held sway. "Mother? Father?"

There was silence, which wasn't unusual. It was a big place, made for comfort, privacy, and defense. She wound her way across the enormous floor to an archway that led to a smaller aerie on the leeward side. Her parents were there, sitting in chairs, watching a flock of distant birds. They looked up when she approached, their faces both graven with thought.

"Habira. Sit." Vasa smiled to take the sting from her order, while Saiinov merely grinned at his eldest daughter. He'd loved her since the moment she arrived, and pride radiated from his every motion as he watched her sit. She was a Skywatcher in her full glory, and an obvious choice for the legacy he hoped to leave behind. What that might be, he had no idea. Their action against Sliver had been tantamount to civil war, but Habira was a fighter to the very bone. She of all his children would rise to the fight.

"Is all well?" Habira asked with some hesitation.

"It is. We are—your father and I are reaching a conclusion about something that's beyond our normal scope." Vasa looked almost dreamy, her face muted with distant considerations. It was a face she used when the enormity of magical concerns consumed her from within, like a thoughtful dream of things that were barely known. Or unknowable.

After a long pause in which nothing moved save the wind, Habira spoke. "Is it an issue for Scholars?"

Vasa's face lit from within. "You always were quick to assess the problem." Now it was her turn to beam with pride. Habira might be a master with the blade, but she was equally facile with her mind.

"And should I know what troubles you?" Habira lifted a brow in imitation of her father. They were truly alike in so many ways, right down to their playful sense of humor, even in the face of an unknown threat.

Vasa nodded, but in a slow, exaggerated manner. With a rustle, she exhaled the tension surrounding her thoughts, clearing the mechanism of her mind to explain herself. Habira deserved a crisp, linear tale, and they might not have time for more given the unstable nature of the skies around them. Vasa sipped the wine near her hand, its fluted glass balanced on a slender table carved from the rib of an unknown flying creature. The glass clinked with finality as she put it down, like a bell signaling that she should start.

"Have you ever heard of mythical weapons?" Saiinov asked.

"Heard of them? Certainly. I don't know that they're real. All of our swords and knives are magical in some way. It seems rather like greed to suggest that there are blades floating about that can render anyone powerless against the wielder." Habira's sword was old but perfectly balanced. A working blade, so to speak, and not meant to be admired unless by the user. Most of the Skywatchers favored plain blades with keen edges. It was part of being a warrior that one's tools would be functional rather than ornamental.

In the field of battle, gems and inscriptions didn't cut down the enemy. Blades did.

"That is true. There are magical items across our realm, but the best weapons are made for use, not to be waved around like a bauble." Saiinov folded his hands, looking to Vasa for the next part of the narrative. She obliged.

"I've made it my life's work to do two things. The first is raising my children to be complete angels of impeccable character." Vasa paused, revealing her mild doubts as to whether she'd been successful. "The second purpose I am called to is the preservation and use of our past. There are two kinds of Moondivers in this world; one who does research and one who pierces the light of days to fall backward into the past. Often, the second kind of Moondivers are people for whom profit and power drive their every move. Either way, the past is wild and deep, wholly filled with the unknown. But each time I find signs of our former world, it opens a small window into what once was." She sipped her wine again, slowly. "And what can be again."

Habira narrowed her eyes. She knew when her mother was hiding something. Everything about the moment told her that Vasa was wrestling with something outside her normal experiences. She respected her mother more than anything in the skies, so she sat quietly, waiting for all to be revealed.

"When you were a child, I found a—a book, you might say. It was something only rumored to exist, but once it was in my hands, I knew it to be real," Vasa murmured. Her voice was low with remembrance, and a touch of awe.

"Where was it?" Habira asked. Her parents were known

to cover enormous swaths of the sky in search of answers, or allies, or even material things that Windhook needed to thrive. The endless days of seeing them come and go with the dawn blurred into a long smudge of memory that began when she'd been little, and continued well into her early adulthood. It was only the birth of Keiron that truly kept her parents close to home, as if they knew their time with him would be short. They were correct, a fact that Habira still found unsettling.

"In a house that has since fallen, on the western edge of the Seven Sisters. The lady of the house had been a Scholar until her death during a hunt. She was the glue of the family, and they came apart at the seams in an orgy of greed and fighting. As it turns out, she was most secretive, too. I entered the house at night, long after it was abandoned to sink and fall into the maelstrom below. The noises were—it was horrid. Like a long, slow torture. Cracks and moans, and voices whispering through the chambers as I made my way down the frigid halls. There were bones within, either of beast or of man. I couldn't be certain. I was stepping into a massive grave of my free will, a fact that I still consider to be one of my poorest decisions."

"I still disapprove. You take unwarranted risks, love." Saiinov beetled his brow at Vasa, only partially in jest. The fear under his expression was real as he recalled the anxious wait while she prowled the dusty halls, wondering if the house would come apart and trap his wife in the slow fall to her death. It had been a tense night, made worse by the screams of Windbeasts who sensed that the end was near for the once proud structure. That meant food, if there were any unfortunate souls stuck within the house as it came apart. Predators often took the easy route to their next meal, so they were content to wait. Their presence had been like a knife at the throat, making a long night trickle by even more slowly, each second filled with the weight of an inescapable dread.

Vasa admitted, "For an angel with child, I admit that it may have been unwise, but it was necessary that I continue to evolve as a Scholar. I regret nothing, save the fact that I should have gone sooner, especially when I found the book." She sipped her wine, moistening lips gone dry with the telling. "There was a bulge in the wall, thinned by time and chipped with wear. It retracted within to reveal a small space, empty except for a small, hidebound book. I knew instantly that it was something rare, but it wasn't until I'd read it through twice that I truly grasped what I had come upon." Vasa reached into her robe and withdrew a small book with two colored hide covers. One was a lurid red, the other, a deep blue so dark it verged into blackness. There was power within the small volume, for even at a distance Habira could sense the age. Vasa held it out to her daughter, who took it with reverence.

"What is it? Other than magnificent." Habira stared at the small book with a fevered look. The exterior was decorated in a fine, spidery scrawl, black on the red and white on the blue. It was a language Habira had neither seen nor imagined, and she considered herself a person of learning despite her preference for settling issues with a length of magical steel.

"It a language thought to be long dead, known as Greek. I only deciphered it through a combination of sorcery and luck—do you know that angels still speak it? In the rogue armies?" Vasa asked.

"I've never heard of it before, although I don't know everything about each faction in the south. They're notoriously hostile to outliers, even if we do mean them no harm." Habira had been in several armed conflicts with various factions of the rogue armies, each incident being an airborne fight that left no doubt as to the intentions of the enemy. They were, as a group, small to medium mercenary forces who specialized in piracy, raiding, and the odd bit of assassination if there was something to be gained. They lived in the wild southern skies, and precious few angels who met them lived to tell the tale. They spoke with odd accents and wore militaristic armor that seemed to be designed with function and uniformity in mind, as well as being the only angels she'd ever seen wearing war helmets at all times. Habira left no fewer than three of them dead in her travels, and she regretted none of it. "I may have heard them speak this language, but I honestly couldn't tell you. The symbols mean nothing to me."

"They're an origin tongue of our writing, from the age before we ascended into the sky. The rogue armies fancy themselves as holdovers from the great warrior races of old earth, like the Greek city states or Romans. I'd hazard a guess that's why the only angels you see in the south are dressed for combat at all times." Vasa glanced at Saiinov, who was studying the book from a distance. There was unease on his face at the mere presence of it, a fact that he couldn't hide despite his famous ability to remain stoic in the face of trouble.

Habira concluded that the book *was* trouble and felt a shiver run through her senses at the enormity of that fact. Saiinov was a rock. He was an elegant battering ram of skill and discipline, and for him to hint at something that gave him a sense of unease was wholly new to Habira. Her father was a constant, like the sun and wind, and so was his poise. The wrinkle in his brow made her nervous.

"Why does the language matter?" Habira ran a finger over an inverted vee shape, marveling at the embossed ink. It felt cool and metallic under her touch.

"I can think of many reasons why we should care about the letters, but I'll start with the beginning. It's incredibly old, even for our scale of time. It was hidden for a reason, and it eluded my attempts at understanding for years. When I finally grasped what it was, I felt as if the only reason I succeeded was that the book wanted me to know, as if it was a sentient thing. It even has a name, and it's something I recognize from the deepest past." Vasa licked her lips again before continuing. She was sifting memories that made her openly uneasy. "I've never seen an object that didn't fit within my plans as a Scholar. No amount of sorcery or power have ever instilled fear within me, but this book came close. Actually, it succeeded. After years of study, I feel that I understand the purpose of this thing, and it is something I can't say is meant to be mine. Nor your father's, nor you. There's only one person who can use it, and that's Livvy. Even then, I'm not sure it can be used so much as ridden like a half-wild Windbeast."

"What is the name?" Habira asked. To her, the question sounded small and muted. Fear percolated into her words because of her mother's tone.

"The Book of January. It's written on both interior covers, in different scripts and directions. The book is meant to be read in opposite directions depending on how it's held, and it serves two completely different purposes," Vasa explained as she watched Habira turn the book to and fro. Her daughter regarded the item as if it were faintly poisonous, which was close to the truth.

"Two books, and two languages? Can you read it?" Habira flipped the first pages open on the red half of the book, exposing a clean page with two lines of text on it.

"What is this tongue? I feel like I can almost understand?" She pointed at two lines of text, running a finger delicately over the embossed lettering.

"Latin, and you probably understand more than you realize or at least parts of it. We use some Latin, as well as parts of many other languages to comprise our own. The language of sorcery is entirely different, but for our everyday lives, what you are looking at is the root of our written word," Vasa said. There was reverence in her voice. What they were looking at was the humble beginnings of angelic culture. "That page explains the purpose of the book. It also means that it was made for someone specific, or, at the very least a certain group of people."

"You think it's meant to be read only by Heartborn?" For Habira, it was the only logical conclusion.

Vasa took the book back and held it, letting the substantive weight settle into her hand. When she looked up at her daughter, there was a mix of pleasure and pain in her eyes. Habira had seen that same look once before— when she realized that Keiron was going to be sacrificed to some greater purpose beyond her comprehension. It was an alien, chilly mélange of reasoning that made her mother look like a distant goddess, rather than the loving angel who gave her life. When Vasa cracked the silence between them, it was with an inscrutable tone, flat and carefully tailored.

"I don't think it's only for Heartborn. I think it's specifically for Livvy, and we were meant to give it to her," Vasa revealed.

"How? Why? There have been hundreds of Heartborn, spread all over the skies. And the centuries, too. There are Heartborn who've never left their houses for fear of being seized by another warring faction. They're kept in silken prisons, away from the wind and sun for all their days." Habira shook her head in disgust. She'd heard rumors in her travels, and they disturbed her. Angels were meant to fly, not huddle in the chambers of a house, protected from everything that was bright and good. "You know what happens to them. They go from safe to dead in the blink of an eye, all because they're supposed to save us from—what? Ourselves?" Frustration boiled over into her words. She was a Skywatcher, but that didn't mean she loved death.

Far from it.

Like any soldier of worth, Habira hated the loss of life. To her, glory was in the saving, not the killing, although her enthusiasm for battle often blurred the lines between those two positions. She looked at her father, who understood what she felt and gave her a reassuring nod. He too was an angel of the blade and feared what war could do more than his lust for glory. To Saiinov, inaction was as important as action. It meant that you were in control of your emotions, and thus, your future, and that of your house.

"Yes, we need to be saved, or haven't you been paying attention? Who do you think the victims of the Crescent Council were? I'll answer. Angels. Of all houses, and regions, and tongues. Angels of innocence and guilt, crime and virtue, and even angels who knew nothing of the council, but were drawn into wars from distant skies simply because their lands brushed up against the central region that the council used to control until your father and I put an end to it." Vasa's explanation crackled with authority, making Habira avert her eyes. "We ascended into the skies because of a calamity, and we've been doing our best to ensure that there aren't any angels left to fly. The skies around Sliver and beyond have been in a state of civil war since before I took my first flight, and there has to be a reason for it all, don't you see? There *must* be some greater purpose for Livvy. Otherwise Keiron's death means nothing. That means my life, and your life and your father's life are all forfeit. Meaningless, like dust swept away before a storm, with no record of us ever having lived or fought for something greater than ourselves. The Moondivers go into the past for trinkets, but I went there for answers. It turned out that the most important thing of all was right here, in our own time. That's why this book is so critical. It holds two things for the person meant to read it."

Vasa held out two fingers, grasping one and folding it back, then the other as she spoke. "There are questions and answers. Depending on which direction you being to read, you will see two different stories. One is the past. The other, the future. I don't need to tell you that Livvy is both, so it makes perfect sense to me that she was meant to have it, and we should all hope that something is revealed to her that can save us from this endless cycle of war and regret." There were tears in Vasa's eyes as she took her daughter's hands, imploring her to understand the enormity of the days that lay before them. "Do you understand, child? I have reached the end of my ability. I can go no further, nor can you. Livvy must take this book and find her purpose in the skies, but it won't be without risk. Simply reading and ingesting the answers within might kill her, or leave her sleeping like an infant for the rest of time. It depends on her, and the heart that beats in her chest. Since I happen to know that heart intimately, I believe in her, and the ability to thrive where others might die. Let's hope that she has a path far different from all the other Heartborn, for Livvy cannot give herself once to some minor problem. We need her as a key, as a weapon. As a cure for our sickness, that we might find peace, be it in this world or the one before." She had pointedly avoided saying anything about a world after the one they knew, leading Habira to conclude that there wouldn't be anything else. They saved what was now, or they would cease to exist, plain and simple.

Wind rustled past them as they sat, waiting for the impact of Vasa's speech to dissipate. After a moment, Habira dipped her head in acceptance of a thing that was beyond her understanding.

"How can I help?" It was a simple question, loaded with meaning. She was a good daughter, and loyal. She would trust in her mother and look to the immediate needs of the family.

"We need to assemble every tool for war and more. I can't do it all, nor can your father. Garrick is receiving his education while teaching Livvy, and the twins are recruiting houses to our cause. We've sent them to House Lixa in hopes of turning Matriarch Torga and her gaggle of daughters to our aid."

Habira snorted. Torga was a sour presence made worse by her numerous children, all of whom seemed to take being sullen as their sole purpose in life. There were no less than six daughters, all of them Watershapers who preferred their company over any others. In spite of their dull, resentful personalities, each daughter was a genius at their chosen task. There were less than two score Watershapers in their region, and two of those were the twins. Vasa clearly had plans for the use of weather, rain, and water, even if Habira couldn't guess what those might be.

She silently wished Vesta and Banu well, for they'd need all of the luck in the skies to pry that family out of their house to render aid for Windhook. House Lixa was near the center of Orion, a sprawling conglomerate of houses to the west of the Seven Sisters. A minor house, Lixa enjoyed safety due to the proximity with Kemet, Ur, and Gondar, three massive trade houses that comprised the belt of Orion. Each of the Clinch Houses, as they were known, had their large squads of fighters who enforced their trade policy across the region. They were warlike but largely fair, leaving conquest to the Crescent Council. The Orion houses preferred profit to outright war but weren't above the odd incursion if it led to material gains.

"Of all the houses in Orion, why them? They're notoriously bad friends on their best day," Habira said. She was charitable to give the denizens of Lixa that much.

Vasa answered by flicking water droplets from the condensation on her glass. They struck Habira, making her flinch like a child who is being forced to bathe after a long day at play. "Watershapers aren't just for steering clouds toward floating groves of berries or greens, or even sending storms away from houses on feast days." Since there was precious little real land to be had, food was taken from the hunt, or in the case of almost everything else, vicious plants that drifted through the skies producing edibles that comprised the bulk of angelic diets. The plants weren't without their defenses, so keeping them in ordered areas was an absolute necessity for harvesting.

Watershapers used powerful sorcery to create farms in the air, making order out of chaos by nudging spiraling colonies of plants into serried rows. In turn, the plants could be picked without fear of angels being wrapped tightly in the aggressive, hungry vines. Watershapers could also condense clouds into ponds, and rain into streams, forcing the liquid water to dance to their tune in whatever way was most beneficial to a sky filled with angels who loved food and wine far too much to allow the system to falter. Just as with any society, the farmers were critical, as were the magicians who brought the storm under control for the betterment of everyone.

"I see," Habira said, and she did. Of all angels, Watershapers feared no one. Their mastery of the skies was nearly godlike.

If they were good enough. The twins were, and so were all the dour daughters of House Lixa. The attempt to recruit them made perfect sense, now that she had a moment to consider the implications. She should have known to trust her parents, who were always three steps ahead of the world when it came to planning the moves of House Windhook

"I'm glad you do, daughter of mine." Saiinov tipped her glass in her direction, a slow smile growing on his angular features. "You'll be wondering where we're about to send you, right?"

"It occurred to me." Habira stood, facing both parents with a inquisitive tilt to her head.

Saiinov produced a small hide bag, its contents clinking softly. "There is a kind of Windbeast, a rather small, rotund creature, which hunts in and out of the groves to the south. Looks somewhat like a blue globe, with short wings and stumpy legs. Quite comical in appearance. You know them?"

"The pond budgies? Sure. They're everywhere near any large body of water or cloud bank. Always plunging in and out like drunken fools. I think they eat—pond creatures? The fishy things that dart in and out of the water?" Habira grunted as her thoughts came to a stop. "You know, I'm not sure exactly what it is they eat. Or why they don't drown while they're hunting. They're in the floating globules of water more than they're out."

She'd seen the comical antics of the budgies as they plunged to and fro in the random bodies of water that roamed the skies. Where there were no farms, water ran free, or merely dispersed into elemental mists and storms. It was a semi-magical effect that had always existed, as far as she knew. The budgies seemed to fit right in following the runaway ponds or puddles as they tumbled through the sky on their eternally awkward journey.

Vasa beamed. "You're right; they don't drown, which brings us to the reason we're sending you to the Seven Sisters. It's time that we, House Windhook, became farmers of a sort, and you're going to begin acquiring our gear. You know Heike, the daughter of Teobald?"

"The girl who calls the Windbeasts? I've heard of her, but we've only seen each other in passing at the Hunter's Clinch." Habira narrowed her eyes in mild suspicion. "What do you have in mind for me, mother?" She lifted a brow, trying to place the tumblers of whatever scheme Vasa was unfolding. Heike was a herder of Windbeasts, but beyond that, Habira knew little of the girl save that she was Theobald's oldest child.

"Take that bag, and travel with her to their secondary outpost. When she asks you what we need, tell her six. You may have to wait a day, but only until you're confident that she can deliver," Vasa warned.

"She's untrustworthy?" Habira asked, her curiosity piqued. Using an unreliable source for anything seemed beneath her parents, given their demand for results.

"No, not necessarily," Saiinov began. He spread his hands, indicating uncertainty. "Heike is an artist, a dreamer. She's more likely to lose herself in the project, and act surprised when she sees you standing there, hours later. Souls like hers are rare, and require protection—which she has by relation, given the fact that Theobald loves his children more than anything in the sky."

"Money included," Vasa quipped.

"Money included," Saiinov agreed. "Theobald's outpost and all of the scalawags who pass through is the lesser threat, though, given Heike's ability to call the beasts. She can live and craft in perfect safety because, at her call, the sky will fill with Windbeasts." He shook his head, smiling. "It's a short trip to the surface if you raise your hand to Heike. Handle her well, daughter, and remember to specify that we need six."

"All right. Six Windbeasts?" Habira looked puzzled. Even for her parents, this was cryptic.

Saiinov laughed, a low rumble that offset his wife's bright tones. "No, child. Six garments made for a very particular purpose. You're going to bring us the means to defeat a storm without magic because make no mistake, a storm is coming." He grew serious, looking askance at Vasa, who steepled fingers to lips as she considered telling her daughter more. Or not.

She chose more.

"This is not your only task, daughter of mine." Vasa looked askance at Saiinov, who watched his daughter. Her world was about to get slightly bigger, and he wanted to know how she would react. "You will leave one artist, only to keep going. Your next stop is—less certain. Do you remember when we told you the story of the armorer and his particular personality?" It had been years since that word had been spoken inside the walls of Windhook, as rare as actually sighting the angel who made the finest fighting armor anywhere. Reclusive, angry, and notoriously unfriendly, the armorer labored in obscurity, away from the society and influence of a culture that regarded him as nothing more than a gifted annoyance.

"I do." *Past the open skies of the belt to the space between. A lonely house, begrimed and ill-favored,* Habira recalled, thinking of the specific place she would find the lonely, bitter creature and his tools.

"Sorcery will not always win in the coming days." Vasa looked down, into the ineffable depths of the sky. "We came from the water, but we cannot survive in it. That changes now, or our future will be far less happy than what we've known. Go."

Habira went. There were things her parents knew that surpassed magic, a fact that often left her chill with fear. She flexed her wings and leaped into the sky, turning away into the open skies. The elemental voice of Windhook bade her goodbye, reverberating in her mind.

Many of us have come from the sea. Someday, you may know this.

Into the future, she flew.

CHAPTER THIRTEEN:

RING OF FIRE

They'd flown for hours in a silent rhythm, occasionally broken when he would explain what a passing animal or feature was in a terse voice. There had been distant dragons and fleeting glimpses of the hunt, all at a speed that made Livvy glad she had wings. The idea of being stuck on the ground when such animals were around triggered the echoes of her human self that lingered somewhere under her consciousness. With each passing length of sky, Livvy came to understand that the air around her might seem empty, but it was filled with potential danger. She touched the hilt of her sword for reassurance but dropped it when she saw the knowing smirk on Garrick's face.

Let him be bold and stupid. I prefer to be alive. She resigned herself to a long period of acclimatizing to the wonders and fears all around. It wasn't the first time she would feel self-conscious, nor would it be the last. The difference was that now, she was miles and centuries from everything she'd known, and thrust into a family who seemed hell bent on razing their society to the ground.

Not that she disagreed with them, especially after listening to what life had been like under the warm care of the Crescent Council. Livvy's derisive snort broke her from a reverie just as Garrick pointed ahead, slowing his forward airspeed. She matched it without thinking, beat for beat. She was learning.

"Ahead and up, do you see them? They're dark spots at this distance," he said in a neutral tone.

Livvy did, but it wasn't what she expected. The defense of Electra wasn't arranged in a ring, but a moving grid of angels spread over an enormous distance. To her eyes, they resembled a widely spread murmur of starlings, moving together in silent accord. "Where's Electra?" she asked, changing her focus to the space behind the angels of house Spindrift.

Her words were no sooner in the wind before light hit the expanse of a huge structure, well behind the dancing motes of defensive angels. It was camouflaged to match the sky, a pale, shifting miasma of swirling blues and grays that gleamed faintly like the interior of a shell just plucked from the ocean. Even at their distance, Electra was easily twenty times or more the size of Windhook, and there seemed to be smaller houses or outposts orbiting at a discreet distance, like the moons of Saturn. Until that view, Livvy hadn't understood the word outpost. Now she did, and her thoughts began to drift toward wondering what could be so important that it needed protection of this degree.

"Slowly, arms spread, Livvy." Garrick rose to a vertical hover, holding his hands out in the universal gesture of peace. Livvy followed suit without comment, mindful of the serious look Garrick wore. If he considered the situation worth his full attention, then she would emulate his every move. His ego was enormous, but apparently not beyond understanding the need for obeying rules in certain arenas. Electra was already a wonder if it was enough to humble Garrick, even if only for a moment.

Three shapes broke away from the patrolling angels, winging toward them with astonishing speed. When Livvy gasped at their approach, Garrick hissed to get her attention.

"They're using sorcery to close on us. It's fine. They do it for everyone. It's some kind of spell that only works for them, and only close to Electra." He fell silent as the angels swooped toward them like blurs, their wings cutting the air with ruthless efficiency. They were tall, clad in unadorned battle armor of matte gray, and all had both sword and war bow at the ready. The recurve bows were enormous, spanning the entire length of their bodies and bound with metallic rings around the grip. Runes of an unknown language glowed softly on the sights, casting a muted blue light on the hand of each warrior, who all looked fully capable of putting several huge arrows into Livvy or Garrick without a second thought. An air of potential violence hung between the five angels, who all winged in place as they took one another's measure. They were all pale, muscled, and nearly asexual with their hair tucked up under skullcaps of silver-chased hide.

The middle angel spoke first, her voice a menacing growl. "I'm patrol leader Willets. Who do you seek?"

Garrick bowed at the waist, his wings never slowing their measured beat. "Garrick of House Windhook. We fly for trade with Teobald, and ask succor as well."

At the mention of Windhook, all three defenders tensed, their gloved hands tightening on the war bows. Speaking again, Willets lifted a brow, her expression lightening somewhat. "Windhook, eh? I think I know why Lockhart tells us to keep our eyes west." A wry smile broke the impassive face of the angel on the left, his eyes crinkling at the opaque comment.

"Why does Lockhart say that?" Livvy asked. She leveled

her chin at the trio, though her nerves flickered with uncertainty.

"Aren't you bold for someone new to the wing?" Willets gave her a measured look, lingering over her wings for an uncomfortable beat. "Tomack, correct me if I'm wrong, but aren't angels born rather small?"

The angel to Willets' right nodded, his eyes never leaving Livvy. "This is true. I noticed she flies much like a child, even at a distance. Up close, it seems as if she's stolen the wings not a day ago, and is learning her way through the air with each passing beat." He tilted his head, appraising Livvy further. She bristled at the memory of doctors doing the same thing to her, back when she was in a different place, with a different heart.

"I did not *steal* these wings. As you might notice, they're attached to my body." She flapped them hard enough that the ends cracked together, making her wince with pain. "If you're through sizing me up, I'm getting tired and would like to go on. My heart is new, not my wings."

"The Heartborn?" Willets asked, and there was genuine shock in her voice. She was prepared for conflict, not revelation. Then Tomack and the silent Luta both stared, but their hands around bow grips relaxed, as did their body language. "As I said, Lockhart told us to keep our eyes west. I suspect he didn't think this was something we might see."

"And what might that be?" Livvy asked, drawing herself up even further. Damn their bows and arrows; she was tired. Hungry and thirsty, too, but she'd fall through the clouds before admitting that to Garrick or anyone else, for that matter.

Willets laughed again, and this time it was one of open admiration. "I'll let Maev inform you of that. We're just grunts, keeping the skies clear for pay. You may pass." She turned to create a gap between the triad of guardians, waving Livvy forward. "Straight ahead until the uniforms turn red, and you see the glimmer of gems. Do *not* deviate or linger. Maev won't like to be kept waiting, even for someone as unique as a Heartborn."

"Um. Who is Maev?" Livvy asked, more meekly than she intended. Garrick hissed at her again, but she waved him off.

All three battle angels laughed at that, subsiding only when Livvy gave them a hard glare. It was Luta who answered the question, his light voice at odds with the most martial bearing of the three. "She is the queen witch of the guard, and you will answer to her." He looked Livvy over again, but with curiosity, not pity. "Or your voyage ends before you ever set foot on Electra."

CHAPTER FOURTEEN:

CHOOSING

Brigha winced at the flavor of the thin, sour beer. "You say this is the best in the valley?" Her tone was dubious, but Arad responded with a dip of his chin. Shrugging, Marti drank from her wide clay cup, avoiding the straw provided. Her face darkened at the taste, but she was too thirsty to stop. The heat was unrelenting, as was the dust and grit. In the hours since Arad's explanation of his master, there had been precious little activity around them. For the most part, they'd been left alone, save a pair of curious children who had investigated Brigha's wings with the relentless curiosity of youth.

A pulse of cool air hit Marti's face, leaving her gasping with pleasure. It was the first relief she'd felt since their descent, and she turned her face into the glorious breeze, letting it wash over her in a welcome rush. "Do you feel that, Brigha? It's"—

"My master is here," Arad announced without ceremony. He knelt to the ground immediately and touched his forehead to the earth, arms splayed out in a show of complete submission. The wind picked up, blowing leaves and odd bits of sand about in a tempest. The air went from hot to frigid in seconds as a column of dense fog descended from a blinding point in the sky. It thickened at the base until the mist was opaque, save a dark shape that moved within. A specter began to take shape in the small, intense storm, even as the upper edges of the column faded into nothingness, leaving clear air and a single, dark figure standing a short distance away.

It was an angel, her wings so black they drank light from the sky, shifting into the ultraviolet spectrum in waves that were impossible to follow with normal sight. She was tall, pale, and radiating an arrogant menace that came from within, for her exterior was comprised of a classic, if severe, beauty.

The angel stepped forward without hesitation, opening a palm toward Arad. Her eyes were black to the rim, cheekbones high and sharp, and ebon hair cut close like a warrior maiden. Two swords dangled from a belt made of silver links encircling her narrow waist, though the only weapon she held was a small scepter of black ivory, unadorned save a skull at the crown. The eyes were inlaid with stones that gleamed with the hidden promise of wickedness, and the jaw hung slack in an eternal scream. She wore battle armor of scarlet and black, but her feet were bare, as were her long, pale hands. Around her neck hung a pendant carved from bone, its leering face drawn down in a frown of patient mockery. When she stopped before Marti and Brigha, Arad dared to lift his eyes up at her terrible beauty, a look of ecstasy on his long, servile face.

"Master, these women are from the sky. They seek your council." He concluded his brief speech with a series of bows from the neck down, resuming a completely passive position in the dirt. To the sisters, it was a disgusting display of weakness, earning a pair of sneers from them as they regarded Arad like an insect.

"Are they?" The goddess' voice was as crisp and chill as

the wind that guided her to earth, each word clipped to the point of insult. She fixed a stare on Brigha, and then Marti, her eyes sliding from one sister to the other as she took their collective measure. Her face was an impassive wall, revealing nothing of her conclusions.

For the first time in a century, Brigha began to feel uncertain. As to Marti's emotional state, she cared little, but a furtive glance revealed her sister was experiencing a similar state of disquiet. Inwardly, Brigha smiled. Let the little snot twist in her fear. She would regain her composure and take command of the scene, for her journey had not been taken to end in a state of emotional surrender, even if it was to an apparent goddess.

Brigha drew herself up in an attitude of imperious disdain. "I am Brigha, founder of House Windhook"—

"I know who you are," the goddess interrupted.

The silence stretched, broken only by the braying of a distant animal being urged to work. Other than that lone noise, the world was quiet, either from fear or respect. Perhaps both, given the weaponized malignancy of the dark angel's presence.

It was the bookish Marti who thought to ask why, giving shape to a fear that twisted in her stomach like a chill worm. "You sent for us?"

Again, the silence reigned, but this time the goddess let a flicker of amusement play across her lips. It was the first normal behavior she'd allowed, and then it was gone, replaced by the stern perfection of her sneer. "Indeed I did, although you seem blissfully unaware of being called. One might think it an indication of your shortcomings, or if I'm direct, your wanton stupidity."

Brigha twitched at the slur, while Marti stood mute, years of abuse at the hands of her sister granting her a serenity in the face of open insult. She'd learned to react later, after absorbing the outbursts of a sibling who had both power and poor impulse control. The goddess took note of their contrast, nodding her approval.

"The younger one knows. See how she waits, Brigha? It would behoove you to take her counsel in this matter. Rarely does one gain anything from an outburst unless it's designed to send a message. Remember that when I use my more strident expressions to drive a point home."

"Who are you?" Brigha asked, her cheeks flushing with anger. She was unused to being spoken to like a child, and it made her bristle.

"A reasonable question, but not relevant at this moment. A better question might be to ask why you've been summoned to this place." She looked around, eyes taking in the valley, the huts, and all of the primitive elements of the deep past. "Arad stated that I live in many realms, and although he's little more than a beast, he is not incorrect. I am the constant, the end of all things, and I am eternal. I am everywhere and always waiting, and I am the last visitor in the pitiful lives of these creatures who exist only to feed my glorious darkness." The goddess swelled with pride at her litany of boasts, reveling in the existence of something that Brigha and Marti could not understand. "I selected this place simply because it is nowhere, albeit close to the ground where I will build my temple."

"You want us to open a window." Marti's quiet statement hung between them, shattering the fevered look on the goddess' face. She was rewarded with a smile for her efforts. It was a bright and terrible thing, out of place and time in every way.

"Aren't you clever? I wondered which of you would be first to discern your purpose here. It's been quite an effort to seed my plans into your time. Angels are quite resistant to building an empire that is not in their name." She tutted at that, then turned to Marti as a teacher to pupil. "Why do you say window? Aren't you here? Isn't that evidence enough that free movement between our worlds is possible?"

"It is, but not for you," Marti stated. Her words were flat with certainty.

The goddess laughed. "I knew you were smart, but I had no idea—let's just say you shine brightest in your house. Your sister is used to bathing in accolades, but that isn't any indication of brilliance." At Brigha's complaint, the goddess waved airily. "You're confusing persuasion with intelligence. I can assure you, Brigha, in your case the two are quite different."

Brigha's voice dropped low with menace. "Tell me, *goddess*, what is your plan to secure our help, since you obviously need it?"

"Ahh, the heart of it all. Well enough, let's get down to business, as the moderns say." She began to pace in front of the sisters, slowly, her hand clasped together in a pose of thoughtful serenity, the scepter now tucked under one arm like the crop of a lecturing general. "I've been claiming souls for longer than your species has existed. You may think of yourselves as ancient, but you're a relative newcomer to the world, the last resort of humanity if you will."

"You mean since the birth of skies?" Marti mocked.

"A common lie. Your kind has not always been at flight, Marti. In fact, your kind was little more than relics of a time so far gone that the stories of your wings were regarded as pure fantasy. Of course, I knew the truth, but then, I've been everywhere for much longer than your fanciful little species. I'll admit you're pretty, and lustful in battle, but as builders, you have precious little insight or desire. You ride the houses around in endless orbits, and few of you ever think to ask where it all came from." She raised a finger, smiling coldly. "Or where you're all going."

"I take it you're going to tell us the history or our people, or are we to guess? Regardless, it's tedious." Brigha tried to sound bored, but there was interest in her voice. She had just enough vanity to crave the stories of where she came from if only to add to her glory.

"You're partially right. This *is* tedious." The goddess turned, her smile deepening into a leer. It curled the angles of her face into a beautiful nightmare, and the look in her eyes was deep and unknowable. Both sisters went rigid at the sight of those black eyes regarding them like prey, reacting with senses that were beyond anything ever seen in a human. In silent accord, Marti and Brigha smoothly drew their swords, letting them dangle easily, their glimmering blades an implied threat. They said nothing, letting the hot wind blow around them in a gritty embrace.

The goddess snapped her swords out in a blur, parrying Brigha and striking her across the temple with the pommel of one weapon, the impact yielding a meaty thud. Without stopping, she whirled, striking out and down to pin Marti's blade to the sands. Their eyes met, and for the first time in her like, Marti knew mortality and fear in the same heartbeat. The stench of death spun from the goddess and her wings of black night, a cold radiance adding to the feeling that the creature wielding those terrible swords was anything but alive. With a flicker of motion, the goddess struck, both swords darting forward with the practiced stroke of an ancient killer.

Marti felt the metal slip home, parting her ribs and armor as one in a low hiss. She went rigid with shock, the pain an electric sensation of hot agony that raced through her nerves with the speed of a wildfire. The goddess looked askance to see that Brigha was watching, half sitting and swaying from the force of the earlier blow.

"You asked, and now I will assure that you obey. Look here, and remember, Brigha." The goddess twisted the blades, eliciting a scream of such agony from Marti that birds leaped from a nearby tree to wing away in terror. When Marti slumped to the ground, she hit face first in the dust, wan with the instant transformation of death. The goddess placed a hand over her mouth and closed her eyes in naked ecstasy as the air around them hummed with indefinable magic. Marti's final violation was the loss of her life energy, stolen with a pass of the goddess' long, pallid fingers. Brigha knew, somehow, that her sister's soul had been ripped from her body, to be consumed at the leisure of a monster from beyond time.

"Brigha, look at me." The voice was a command of such power she could not look away. The goddess was glowing with power, a being of such malignant presence that Brigha began to sob, her will broken into dust.

Brigha met her eyes with the hesitancy of someone standing on the edge of death. She said nothing, merely flicking her gaze between the corpse of her sister and the goddess.

"Here is your answer, Brigha. Here is the choice you have." She prodded Marti with a foot, then turned her poisonous gaze back upon Brigha. "Obey, or die."

The goddess waited for her answer. When it came, it was a rusty whisper drowning in fear, just as she liked. "I will obey," said Brigha.

The goddess smiled. She had chosen the right sister.

CHAPTER FIFTEEN:

WITCH QUEEN

*I*n the distance, Livvy saw red.

The Corvids wore lurid crimson armor, banded with strips of silvered hide. They flew in groups of three, unlike the paired Spearwoods of the outer ring, and made no notice of Livvy or Garrick until they were closing in on a gap between the patrols. Seeing them at work, Livvy noted their motions were smooth and efficient, more like a dance than a purposeful defense of the outpost. The only weapons in evidence were long dirks at their belts and a coiled length of rope ending in a looping knot.

From the sun's flare came a tuneful whistling, accompanied by the flapping wings of a modest angel in plain red armor. The only distinction between her and the nearby Corvids was the glint of jewels on her left ear; seven bright points twinkled merrily in the brilliant sunlight.

"The seven sisters," Livvy muttered, admiring the gems as Maev drew close. It could be no one else, as Livvy took stock of the leader for the first time. She was a pretty, smiling angel with pale skin and eyes that hovered between green and blue. Around her clung an air of power at odds with her charming grin, made real by the deferential body language of the other Corvids who were approaching only to hover at a respectful distance.

Maev spoke first, doing away with any dramatic pause to assert command. She demanded their attention simply by her ease, flapping casually as she regarded Livvy and Garrick with a neutral smile. It was a cool, professional look designed to gather information.

"Windhook. Lovely of you to join us. You're to see Theobald, I take it?" Her voice was crisp and young, like her appearance. To Livvy, she sounded like a newscaster, with the inflection of someone who was doing a job with mild interest, but nothing more.

"We are," began Garrick, but Livvy began to break in, her voice bright with curiosity. Maev was clearly not what she'd been expecting, and therefore, interesting. Livvy knew that if she was to learn everything about the skies, it rested on her to do so. That would begin with Maev and the curious nature of a trading outpost so important it required the most fearsome angels she'd seen since arriving in this strange world of angels and war.

Except for Windhook, she thought. Habira and Saiinov were entirely different beings, and Vasa was playing at another game, as far as she was concerned. The twins had a reputation that spanned the sky, and even Garrick had skills. He might not know it, but Livvy thought that underneath the arrogance, there was something more to come.

"You were saying?" Maev asked, snapping Livvy back into the moment. Her penetrating gaze fell like a physical touch, making Livvy miss a beat with her wings.

"Why all of you, here? Is this place under attack?" Livvy asked. It seemed the best question to lead with, as Maev might not reveal trade secrets to an unknown angel from a distant house. Although it seemed to Livvy that Windhook was neither distant nor unknown in the minds of the Corvids.

Maev cocked her head, and it was the most birdlike

137

gesture Livvy had seen from any of the Corvids, who appeared far more sturdy than any crow she'd ever seen. She stifled a laugh before focusing on the witch, who let a smile play at the corners of her lips, making her look even younger. "We've been under attack since the day angels ascended to the skies. Don't you know your history, Heartborn?"

"No, but Garrick was supposed to be my teacher." Her tone was so sour, Maev's face broke into a beaming smile that mocked Garrick's newly sullen attitude. He withdrew under the wattage of that look before cutting his eyes at Livvy with a dark glare of his own.

"I have some knowledge of what it means to take on a new title with little experience. I wasn't always the witch queen, you know." At that, two nearby Corvids snickered. Their comfort around Maev spoke to her quality as a leader. Fear might shape some fighters, but camaraderie bred stronger bonds in times of war.

"I guess we should see Theobald first. I don't mean to offend, but I'm not sure what comes next. All of this is new to me, especially your outpost, and we do have a task. Vasa and Saiinov were clear about that much," Livvy said, letting Garrick off the hook for his refusal to give her more than cursory instructions about the workings of Electra.

"Fly this way. You're permitted free run of the outpost, despite the instability of the skies. The echoes of Windhook's rebellion are being felt here, as well as to the east. I think it'll be some time before any of my patrols draws a relaxing breath." She looked pointedly at the nearest Corvids, who took her hint and bustled off at a brisk pace, their wings carving the air with mechanical efficiency. "Theobald is an acquired taste, just like me, but he runs a clean, safe post. You won't be troubled here, despite the nature of your mission."

"What's that?" Livvy asked before she could stop herself.

Maev looked surprised, then turned her face back into the sun. "War, Livvy. You're here to prepare for war."

CHAPTER SIXTEEN:

SOLITARY

In the distance, a small house hove into sight, its design unusual by any standards. Around the middle of the squat, dim structure gleamed an orange band of light, seeping from the inner recesses of the house which had only one apparent landing. The narrow aerie was split by a single, graceful door, the arc rising and falling as if designed by water. The same light leaked out onto the smooth surface of the unadorned aerie, making Habira wonder if fire had broken out in the house.

She approached with caution, opting to hover at a distance that was farther away than common decorum commanded. Saiinov had been emphatic in his orders; she was to remain respectful to the artisan unless he was openly hostile. If that proved to be the case, she was to leave for Electra immediately. There, she would gather Livvy and Garrick, negotiating with other, lesser crafters who would provide armor for the Heartborn. Under no circumstances was Habira to return home empty-handed, a fact that rang in her ears as she cupped hands to mouth and bellowed at the silent, glowing house.

"Halloo the house!" Her voice rang out in the air, a sharp contrast to the relative silence surrounding her. Only the sound of her wings broke the hypnotic quiet until a gruff voice answered from within the recesses of the armorer's home.

"You'll be wanting to leave, pretty!" It was a man, his words ground out in a bass that sounded rusty and unused.

"Can't do that, sir. My parents have given me explicit instructions, and those begin and end here, with you."

"Who's yer parents?" A shadow appeared at the aerie door. It was an angel darkened with soot and grime, his hands both holding tools of unknown types. One was a long, slender blade, the tip curled inward like a claw. The opposing tool was a hammer with fine points on the head. Both gleamed from use and care.

Progress, thought Habira. Her smile was lost in the growing dim. The day was ending, its light slipping below the horizon with each passing beat of her wings. "Saiinov of House Windhook, although he's not your concern."

"Really? And who would be my concern, then?" He stood in the fading light, a stooped figure of great age. His wings were singed from unseen fires, feet bare, and his arms lined with shiny scars all the way to each elbow.

Habira laughed, expecting this. "My mother. She said you would be difficult, but if worse came to worst, I was to threaten you openly in her name."

This time, the gravelly voice laughed before answering. "Vasa has always been of high spirit. Tell me, is she still as beautiful as ever?"

Habira flapped closer at the unspoken invitation. "She is, although her Scholarship is more important than her beauty. Just ask her."

"You would be her true daughter, then. Always quick to defend family and certain of yourself." He eyed her with grudging respect. "Come on, then. I don't want the fires to die. Something tells me I'll be working throughout the night. And beyond."

"I'm only here for a single set of armor. For a new—

sister, I guess you would say." Habira's feet touched the aerie as he stepped back to allow her room. The surface was warm, almost hot.

"Is there anything special about this sister? Your mother wouldn't send you to me without something in mind. There are dozens of charlatans making armor good enough for a household guard, or a street brawler." He spat with disdain, retreating into the insufferable interior of his house. It was a circular forge with many stations at high heat. The source was unknown, contained in a trough that ran the length of the circular wall, positioned underneath the work areas and hammering tables. There were three cooling baths, sloshing lightly in the motion of the house. The air stank of chemicals and ash and fire, and Habira found herself fighting a cough.

"You live here?" She gasped. It was like the stories of the land below, a place of fire and light.

He placed the tools in his hands carefully on a rack. While the house was dirty, it was not without order. The tools, supplies, and placement spoke to a master at work. "Don't be ridiculous. I live on top, where the air is clear. I only work here." He cast a gimlet eye at her before collapsing into a three-legged stool cut from the bones of a sturdy Windbeast species known as a Dricothere. Metal rings held the chair together, tapped in place with a delicacy that gave an artistic air to the practical piece of furniture. He folded his muscular arms across his chest and settled onto the seat, looking tired but alert. "Well? I know you, and you seem to know me. Now that we've established that, why don't you tell me exactly what Vasa has in mind for our world, or at least what your parents have allowed you to know. I know she's never thought small, nor has your father. If you're here, the only things I can be certain of are not having the armor you'll need."

"What's the other certainty?"

He grunted, a deep noise of satisfaction. "That it's completely necessary. And that, in turn, means I'll most likely do it, despite my general distaste for politics. And angels." He looked thoughtful, then added, "And small talk."

"Thank you, sir. I know the size of what is needed, if not the exact nature," Habira offered. It was as mannerly as she could be, but given the circumstances, it sounded like a masterwork of diplomacy in the sweltering air of his forge.

"Rauta. Call me Rauta, it's what your mother knew me as before I became less sociable," he allowed, standing and moving to a table. In a smooth motion, he unrolled a hide so thin that light shone through it with ease, poising a charred sliver of bone above it in an attitude of hesitant consideration. "This sister of yours, is she new?"

"In a sense." An awkward silence grew while Habira decided how to proceed. "She's a Heartborn, and a Moondiver, and new in her body, so to speak. She's new to all of us, but mostly, to herself."

Rauta's face softened. "New to you, and a Heartborn. Tell me, did the heart in her chest come from one of your family? Is that why she is now, ah, yours?"

A single word. "Yes."

He grunted, a not uncharitable noise between understanding and regret. "You're left with a new angel for whom you have no understanding save that she carries your blood, and your parents will spend anything to protect her?"

Again, a clipped answer. "Yes. Exactly."

He repeatedly nodded, bringing the charred stick down in confident, sweeping motions. For several minutes, his eyes raced over the hide as he drew, delineated, and redressed his earlier mistakes until Habira saw a complex sketch of armor that looked unlike anything she'd ever imagined possible. It was elegant, simple, and composed of panels that would cling to Livvy's vulnerable spots, but give her motion where she needed it. The armor was designed for war, not show, and had a single layer everywhere save the chest.

For that, Rauta created a series of overlapping sections that thickened the area over her heart. The slender shapes rotated around an axis to create a stylized heart shape, the sole nod to artistic showmanship on the entire suit. When Habira grunted in surprise at the elegant shape, the armorer merely smiled, pausing in his work.

"There's no reason it can't be dynamic, as well as functional. I think your new sister will not mind a little flair, given her position." He resumed drawing, filling in the tiny details under each arm to assure a maximum range of motion for swordplay. The resulting suit looked supple and efficient, two factors that would go a long way to assuring Livvy's survival in the event she found herself in personal combat. How she could avoid such action was a mystery to Habira, who was a seasoned veteran of raids and the odd dustup. Being a veteran taught Habira many things, not the least of which was that armor, like swords, was made to be used.

The same could be said of Livvy. All of the elements were being put in place to make her more than a simple brawler, and Windhook was going to considerable lengths to render her inviolate to danger, even though complete safety was a myth.

"You're wondering what she will be," Rauta said. It was a statement, not question, his hands never ceasing their work as he completed details Habira hadn't even know were missing.

"I think I know, but I don't know why."

"Hmm. That's how it always is, before a fight. The planning, and the hopes. All of them are thrown to the surface at the first clash of metal." He shrugged, adding, "Or sorcery. She'll find out what your parents have in mind, but the opposite will be true, as well."

"They don't know what she might be?" Habira asked.

"How can they? She's Heartborn, and not of this place. She has strengths that they can't imagine, but Vasa sees something over the horizon and knows this girl is a key. Yes, a key. I think you should consider her to be something new to us. And herself." He smiled, finishing the sketch with a flourish. "Done. Now, we get to work."

"We? I wouldn't presume to"—Habira began, weakly.

"And you shall not. I'm a master, I won't allow you near my forge," he said, but it was gentle and free of insult. "Do you know why my armor is the best? Because I'm the only angel to ever turn stone into liquid, in a manner of speaking."

"Here? Where do you find the stones? Aren't they rarer than anything else in the skies?" Habira asked, fascinated by the notion that something as unusual as rock could be made into armor. Even sand was considered too valuable to waste on anything trivial, and there were a lot of other materials used to make armor. Hide, bone, and shell were all fashioned into the tools of war, and the animals they came from were plentiful and relatively easy to hunt. It was true that Windbeasts of fearsome variants would kill or maim angels every year, but even that was considered a normal risk. The creatures were both food and sport, as well as raw materials that angels used to make their lives in the sky into something less barbarous.

Rauta shook his head, indicating a bubbling forge pot nearby. "That isn't stone, or at least, not the rocks that make up the word underneath us. I'm talking about osteoliths."

"What?" Habira was intelligent, but the word was completely unknown.

"Pearls, of a sort, but even that term isn't accurate. As certain more aggressive Windbeasts get old and more lethal, their hearing organs grow large, layered stones within. It's a dangerous business, hunting them, but the purity of the osteoliths is like nothing else in the sky. A Scholar from the south perfected the technique for melting them into a fluid that can be poured over molds made from the same material. I do it in layers, over and over, and it cools almost immediately. If my touch is true, then the resulting piece is strong, nearly translucent, and shatterproof. The only reason everyone doesn't clamor for it is because the cost is too high, both in money and blood."

Habira's hand dropped to her sword without a thought. "How many of these stones will you need?"

Rauta's bark of laughter rang within his home despite the constant low roar of the forges. "I appreciate your eagerness to hunt, but it won't be necessary. At least, not yet."

"You've some in reserve then?" She looked around wondering if something of such value would be out in the open. Despite looking tough and capable, Rauta seemed to be alone, and therefore at some degree of risk to raiders.

"Naturally. I don't like to be unprepared, especially in these fractured times." He gave her a wintry smile in recognition of her family's role in the recent upheaval. Standing, he went to the nearest forge, reaching behind it to place a calloused palm on the heat-warped wall. Habira doubted anyone else could stand the temperature that close, so she merely watched in silence, wondering what he was doing. With a hard shove, he pushed with the entirety of his hand.

A flat, delta shaped section of the wall came free in his hand, glimmering bone white where his fingers smudged the accrued grime of time and work. Rauta looked pleased, flipping the stone over in his hands with a surprising delicacy as he withdrew from the heated area over the forge.

"Sometimes, it's best to hide things in plain sight," he offered, placing the osteolith gently onto the flat table where Habira stood. "I would let it cool for a moment before your inspection." At Habira's noise of inquiry, he said, "It's all right, you'll want to see what all the fuss is about. It's only natural."

After a quiet moment of admiration, Habira lifted her brows to ask if it was safe yet, feeling oddly relieved when Rauta tilted his head in acquiescence to her request.

The osteolith was like holding magic itself. It was light, yet substantial, and it hummed with the vibrations of the forges as if a living spirit fluttered within. "Oooo. . . it's— is it sorcerous?" There was wonder in her tone. She'd seen many things in her time as a Skywatcher, but nothing like this.

"Possibly. I know the melting point, and how to work it—even where to find them, but as to why they occur in some creatures and not others, I have no idea," he admitted.

"How strong is it?" Habira never took her eyes from the stone, rapt with attention as Rauta began wiping the stone clean. It was pearlescent, with tiny ridges serrated in regular patterns like the waves on a body of water. She'd seen such things when the Watershapers turned their streams and ponds into the wind to irrigate passing copses of plants.

Without stopping his ministrations, he answered in a

voice that bordered on reverence. "Stronger than any metal or bone. I've seen the armor survive a direct cloud strike from lightning that would kill a Daggerall."

Habira made a sound of appreciation. No one hunted Daggerall unless they wanted to die. They were huge, toothy, and faster than almost anything in the sky. Other than their red coloring, they gave little warning before an attack. Thankfully, they were rare and seemed confined to the southernmost skies. At the thought of them, she wondered aloud, "Do the Daggerall have these, ah, stones?"

Rauta stopped working, looking at her through narrowed eyes. "They might. Might not, too, but none of the angels I know have ever come back except one."

"Did they live?" She was curious. It would be a feat worth telling, to survive that kind of hunt.

He began polishing the stone again, turning it over to reveal the sooty back. "Not for long, and I doubt she would have wanted to live any longer. Her name was Solveig, and she was one of the most feared Skywatchers ever to ply the northern ranges." He lightly emphasized the past tense, making Habira inexplicably saddened by the loss of an angel who had once been brave and vibrant.

With a final swipe, he removed the last of the grime. What lay beneath was a wonder.

"It's stunning." There was open awe in Habira's comment. The osteolith was unearthly in its beauty, a thing of light and whorls that defied the eye. It was all colors, and none, and then, purely white, sometimes in the same instant. The ridges cast sublime blue shadows on either side of their lined presence, creating a rolling look of darkness and light that threw the entire stone into living relief.

"It's even more beautiful when I've worked it," said

Rauta, and there was no bragging in his statement, only fact. He looked down with a proprietary gaze, turning the stone slightly to gauge how he would best use the raw material. It was the look of a master before his canvas, and Habira knew it well. She'd seen her father do the same thing when choosing a sword or at that moment before her mother selected a spell while in the throes of truly transcendental magic.

"May I watch?" Habira's voice was low, respectful. She couldn't break contact with the stone, so mesmerizing was the dance of light within.

"Of course. In fact, I'll need you here every step of the way. There's some residual fluidity after each layer is cast, and you'll need to direct me as to the size of your sister. It would be better if she were here, but since she isn't, I'll need every bit of your help to render this in a perfect fit before the shell is set."

Habira closed her eyes, thinking about Livvy's slender frame and awkward gait. When she opened them, they were bright with memory. "I can see her."

Rauta smiled, then clapped his hands together in anticipation of a masterwork. "Then, by all means, Windhook, let us begin."

CHAPTER SEVENTEEN:

NATURAL DEFENSES

Where Windhook had an aerie, Electra had a pier. It was a miracle of engineering, a long spar of bony material polished to a high sheen by the contact of endless feet, goods, and ships. Several small windships bobbed at anchor, unguarded and open to the sky. Angels cycled through landing and leaving in a blur, their wings roiling the air around Electra into a tempestuous scene of barely controlled mayhem.

Livvy smiled, a wide, brilliant look of unbridled joy. Electra was wondrously alive, unlike the stately interior of Windhook, or the open reverence of Sylvain's mountain. It was the closest thing she'd seen to normalcy if one considered an airborne market of angels and their flying ships to be normal. For now, she did, letting the buzz of activity wash over her in a welcome tangle of noise.

"We don't need to check in or anything?" she asked. With a neat backwing, she landed next to Garrick on the only clear point of the pier, a slight widening about a third of the way from Electra proper. The outpost walls were riddled with windows, from which angels called out to new arrivals, adding to the fray.

"Maev is our permission, but I'm sure Theobald will meet us." He spoke in a disinterested mutter, weaving his way through the chaos to an open area marked by a high, overhead arch. It was a breezeway into Electra, too wide to be crowded and open enough to show a bright, airy space inside. There were vines and flowers growing along the rim of the door, their color a bright punctuation to the uniform pearlescent blue of the walls.

"Ever met him? Theobald?" Livvy dodged a rolling cart heaped with animal hides, tanned to a modest green color. Scales dotted the hides, which looked to Livvy as if they'd come from the back of an alligator or some other toothy creature.

Garrick shook his head. "No. Heard he's rather loud but harmless. That didn't come from my parents, by the way."

His amendment was lost in the booming call of an angel who parted the crowd while making his way towards them, his booted feet pounding the floor with singular intensity.

Livvy drew up, stunned. From that moment on, there would be loud, and then there would be Theobald. He drew up before them, a massive angel with the carriage of a dockworker and the hands to match. He was tall, far taller than Livvy or Keiron, broad chested, thick-limbed and muscled to the point of being noticeable, a rarity for angels. His enormous hands were held out to the sides, thick palms open in welcome. Theobald's skin was the color of strong tea, his nose long, and his teeth whiter than the light of stars. He was smiling, which crinkled the skin around eyes that were nearly colorless, although Livvy could only see one, as the other was covered by a dangling shock of silver hair. In each ear, the merchant had a single green stone larger than Livvy's fingertip, the light within gleaming with verdant cheer. He wore a plain woven shirt that strained to contain his chest and shoulders, open at the throat to reveal a necklace of seven bright points. His pants were for work, he was barefoot and on the balls of feet, rocking in the perpetual motion of someone who actively shapes their life during every waking moment. Planting his feet in a broad base, Theobald looked at neither of them but lifted his chin slightly as his eyes drooped closed. After a moment, his face turned unerringly to Livvy, and he held out a giant, calloused hand to her in greeting.

"Theobald, and I've been expecting you." His smile deepened, threatening to hide his eyes entirely. His voice was a mellow tenor, perfectly matched to his outward good cheer.

"Livvy. I'm new here."

Theobald's laughter came from his belly before exploding outward in a storm of merriment. When he finally regained control, wiping his eyes, he wagged a finger at her in friendly admonition. "You must warn me before such honesty next time. Of course, you're new here, Livvy. I wouldn't have met you if that weren't the case. As you can see by the general chaos, I'm far too busy to greet every brigand who graces my outpost with a haul of pilfered goods." With a deferential nod that also seemed dismissive, he acknowledged Garrick briefly, before returning his attention to Livvy.

It was an uncomfortable thing to be pinned by a look from Theobald, and Livvy squirmed slightly under the relentless, bland expression he directed at her. Before the space between them could fill with anything more than a long pause, a young woman walked up, placing a possessive hand on Theobald's shoulder. "Dad? The Hunter's Clinch is threatening to close up early if we don't get rid of the pests. They're all complaining about losing product to a mysterious beastie that's too fast for them to catch." She finished with a laugh, leaving little doubt as to her opinion of the efforts being levered against the unknown creature. At the dawn of womanhood, the girl was tall and willowy, with Theobald's brilliant smile and long nose, but where his hair was white, hers was blacker than a moonless night, falling in curls to languish past her shoulders. Her eyes matched her hair, but with flecks of gold swimming within the black, bright with good humor and intellect. There was no doubt she was Theobald's daughter, save the different color of their eyes. It was in that moment Livvy realized he was blind, though she saw no walking stick to guide his steps.

"I can tell by the silence that you've figured out my eyes are merely here for beauty, Livvy. Fear not, friend. I know my home, and every inch of this outpost is as easy to navigate as it is for you." He grinned to take any challenge from his words, leaving no doubt as to his disposition. He was a being at the peak of his life, in his space, and he wanted for nothing, let alone the pity of a Heartborn. Only days earlier, Livvy had been regarded by many as too broken to experience life in all its fullness, a fact that enraged her to tears on more days than not.

Her new heart was more than life; it was a rebirth into a body built for things other than quiet study and reflection. For Livvy, the shining confidence of Theobald was a refutation of her doubts, and she found herself smiling at the girl for that reason and so much more.

"Danila, and, yes, I'm his. I help here, but he runs the place fine with or without me. That's why I've got so much free time, right dad?" She cocked her head at him, grinning with conspiracy.

"I can tell you've plans for doing little or nothing today, daughter of mine?" He mocked her lightly, but there was an ocean of love underneath that he couldn't hide.

"We," began Garrick, "have a great deal to do, if it's alright with you. I was instructed that we go to the Hunter's Clinch and begin gathering supplies immediately. It's not a holiday," he finished. An air of self-importance clung to him like his father's clothes. It neither fit nor looked right, and he knew it.

It was Danila who chose that moment to become something Livvy had been looking for since the moment Garrick opened his perfect mouth filled with ugly words. Smiling sweetly, she sized him up in a slow, lingering gaze that made his cheeks flush with rising anger. After taking her time, she raised a finger, waggling it in a perfect impersonation of her father's earlier gesture. Garrick seemed on the verge of exploding, fighting to control his emotions with an inner core that Livvy found surprising, if not comforting.

"You may walk with me to the Clinch, and while we're there, we can see if the complaint about pests is legitimate." She let her eyes slide down him again, then smiled with a hint of satisfaction. "Something tells me you'll know your kind when you see them."

Theobald burst out laughing again, sending Garrick into another sputtering paroxysm of anger. "Oh, she's measured you well enough, lad. I was told you're the difficult one in your house, but"—He put a huge hand on Danila's head in a gesture of such tenderness, if seemed impossible for someone his size. "I think you've met your match. No, let me amend that-- I know you have. I've seen her break down stronger wills than yours, so you may as well get used to doing things her way from now on if you expect to return home with what you need."

"Is that a threat?" Garrick asked, his voice cracking with the effort to seem menacing. Theolbald didn't flinch, despite the stupidity of challenging him in his outpost.

Rather, he drew his face into something like the mask of a politician who's decided to play nice. The effect was chilling. It didn't match his nature, nor did he seem to like it.

"Not at all. I deal with numbers and facts, as well as personalities. Let me save you some time, young angel. You're going to be enraged by Danila's mockery of you and your arrogance, but here's something no one else has told you up until this moment. You have it coming. Oh, I know of your haughty ways, and your beauty—yes, don't interrupt me, I can abide many things, but lies are not one of them. I'm blind, not stupid, and even in your voice, I can hear the ease with which you've lived your life as a column of anger, daring the world around you to disagree." He addressed Livvy, slyly. "Do you concur?"

"That's about right." She folded her arms while glaring at Garrick with narrowed eyes. She didn't understand their mission, but she knew that Theolbald could make or break it. Garrick wasn't just stupid; he was selfish. Being scalded in public by Theobald could help Windhook in ways the arrogant boy couldn't begin to imagine if only he could swallow his foolish pride.

"Ah, then we're in agreement. Attend my daughter's wishes, and we will help Windhook pull the skies away from an unholy war. Yes, that's why you're here, and yes, that's why you will be a dutiful son and prowl the Clinch while listening to Danila as she goes about her business. You must rest today, for you leave tomorrow." Theobald pointed unerringly to the north. "There. You must go there, but not far. We'll gather the other things you need, but as to that? You must go yourself."

"Leaving? We just got here," Livvy protested, but it was weak. She knew so little of what they were doing, and her chest hurt. She had muscles in her back that were new and painful things, making her wish, however slightly, for the days that she hadn't been expected to do anything more strenuous than eating cookies and listening to her mom's music collection. Flying was magnificent, but it was also hard work.

Theobald made a gesture of conciliation. "True, and that's why you must rest tonight. Tomorrow, you'll fly a short distance outside the rings, into the wild skies of the north. That's where Heike spins, and herds. Trust me. You'll want to be at your absolute best when you meet her, it's a sight"—he broke off, listening. "Arms! To arms!" His bellow was instantly obeyed, as every angel on the pier spun, brandishing a variety of weapons in a blur of steel so smooth that it seemed choreographed.

Livvy's pulse raced as her hand dropped to her sword, drawing the longsword with a muscle memory she didn't recognize. *Angel bodies are made for war, not play,* she thought. To her continued surprise, the blade felt natural in her hand, though she knew there was much to learn. Garrick was faster still, his motion more feline than angel as he drew, presented his side, and rocked slightly on the balls of his feet in one single movement. Had he not been so repulsive inside, Livvy would have found him beautiful, but she knew him too well for that kind of appeasement.

Streaking toward the pier came a dragon. There was no other word for the thing, though Livvy knew it would have a clever name meant to describe its qualities or history. To her, the long, muscular beast was a red terror. Its scales were fine, the mouth huge and crammed with needle teeth, and night-black claws that curled inward like a predatory bird's, but on a scale beyond anything earth had seen in a long time. The broad, membranous wings were folded back to allow the dive as the creature fell like an arrow toward the middle of the pier, where a group of angels was loading a windship with massive racks of smoked meat.

That's when Livvy noticed the beast's right eye. It was swollen, barely visible, and weeping fluid backward in the face of the vicious wind as it dove downward. She saw other wounds, too—a gash along the left forearm, a broken section of fangs, and a tear near the ribs. This was an animal who had fought recently and lost. Badly. It was starving, or desperate, and now, it was headed in a near suicidal arc to steal food from beings who were armed and prepared to repulse exactly this kind of attack.

Livvy screamed, a raw, disorganized blast of sound with no form as she leaped forward, trying to wave off the ranks of angels who surged forward to meet the creature in battle. There were grim faces, but little fear, even on those angels closest to the giant ranks of food that had drawn the wounded animal into its streaking dive.

She wasn't fast enough. No fewer than a dozen angels met the Windbeast, dodging to the side and raking the animal with long, deep cuts of sword and spear, drawing a piteous cry from the creature as it smashed against the decking in a glancing blow before sliding off, dead, to fall downward into the open blue maw of the unforgiving sky.

"They killed it," Livvy gasped. Her heart hammered against her ribs in a beat that threatened to make her faint. She dropped to a knee, placing one hand on the smooth pier as her sword fell in a forgotten rattle of unfulfilled promise. She'd drawn it, yes, but to use it on a starving animal was a prospect that shook her to the core. Livvy was kind. She was a person of questions, not actions, and in a flashing moment of color and danger, she knew that the time for questions had passed.

Danila came to her, a short spear in one hand and a

worried look on the dark beauty of her face. "It was a Lindworm. They usually don't"—

"It was wounded. Did you see?" Livvy gasped.

Danila merely nodded. "They fight in the sky. Sometimes, they lose to a rival. They don't usually attack, but"—she let the word trail away into the wind. With the attack ended, angels swiftly recovered their senses after a moment of jocular congratulations; then the pier became a hive of activity once more.

"Is it always like this?" Livvy's face was like stone. A cold knot of something new settled inside her, and she wasn't sure she liked it.

"The killing, or Electra?" Danila helped her to stand. She was strong, and Livvy staggered as she rose.

"Neither." Planting her feet, the sway of the pier went away or became normal. Livvy couldn't tell which. Pointing into the sky with her sword, she sheathed the weapon and said, "All of it. The sky. Life. Here."

Danila made a noise of understanding, then slipped her arm under Livvy's, steering her toward Garrick and her father. "Sometimes, it's a lot worse."

CHAPTER EIGHTEEN:

MANEUVERS

"There was always going to be a time when we were needed for something other than sorcery," Banu explained to her twin, Vesta. Cressa stood watching, her eyes switching back and forth between them as they discussed a sort of grand tour for recruitment among the houses Windhook traded with. She was mildly disconcerted by just *how* much the sisters were alike, right down to the small, economical gestures they both made when speaking. Both sisters were of medium height, with dark hair and angular features. They clearly favored Saiinov, but where he was masculine, they were fine drawn and elegant. Their gray eyes flickered with intelligence, and both were prone to pulling their full lips to one side as they thought, which was often. When they smiled, it was a transformative event, taking years off their lives as the expression turned them from serious Watershapers into the picture of youth. Where their mother was regal, they were serious, with a subtle charisma as natural as gravity.

Cressa rubbed her eyes, still adjusting to the presence of two identical angels speaking virtually in unison. They shared a nearly inexhaustible knowledge of weather, magic, and the skies, leading to entire sentences in which Cressa felt that she understood one word in three. When they spoke of other things, they both slipped into an easygoing conversation, sounding much more like angels in their early years.

"Are you sure I should be here?" Cressa asked, interrupting their ongoing discussion of which flight path would bring them into contact with the most houses in a short time. Even as a Flyer, she had to confess that they knew how to plan a route.

The twins turned to blink at her like owls before Vesta asked, "Why wouldn't you?"

Cressa glanced at the shading of her wings, identifying her to everyone as a murderer. "Blightwings aren't exactly welcome at the table everywhere, you know." How they could be so obtuse was beyond her, but Cressa tried to be pleasant. She cared too much for the fates of Windhook to do otherwise.

Now Banu spoke in a matter-of-fact way, her expression never changing. "If anyone makes you feel unwelcome, we will drown their house in the sky and strike them from our list, then." She gave a tiny shrug as if this was the only logical conclusion to Cressa being slighted in any way. Vesta grinned in agreement, looking up at the taller angel with bemused certainty.

"Ah, well. I appreciate your, um, vigor in my defense, but it's alright. I'm used to it. Being overlooked. Or judged, because of these," Cressa said with a flick of her wings, though in truth she hated every second of the snide comments, or dismissive glances. Sometimes, there was outright fear at her appearance, as if she could lash out and kill again at any second. It gnawed at her, daily. Her face gave away the sadness she felt, prompting Vesta to put a kind hand on her shoulder.

"We weren't bluffing about defending you. Mother and father consider you a part of the house, as I'm sure you're aware by this point. We're growing, as a family, and that means we trust you. I heard your story from them, and to be honest, I would have done the same thing. Children shouldn't be thrown into the sky like trash," Vesta said.

"Ever," added Banu. Her lips were a thin line.

Cressa had been forced from her home due to the Eastern policy of selling titles. When her eldest sister decided that she was in charge of their family fortune, a fight ensued, and Cressa killed Belora to save her life. House Carillon had been broken into parts and sold off, to be forgotten along with Cressa and the entire family. It was her greatest shame and her finest hour, braided together into a work of darkness and light that would forever define her. She was a survivor, a criminal, and something new under the protection of Windhook and the world they were crafting. The Crescent Council's domination was gone, but what that left was uncertain save one thing.

Cressa was free.

She was also under the watchful eye of two powerful Watershapers, who took a firm interest in her role at Windhook. It was a consideration she would add to the mix as she moved forward, no longer a mere Flyer, and yet not anything else. The entire world was a place of transition, and no one felt it as keenly as Cressa. She only spoke after considering her options, which were new to her. Up until only recently, she hadn't been able to choose anything for herself.

She liked the sensation.

With a sheepish smile, she asked the twins the only thing she could. "What do you want me to do?"

"I think the question is where, not what," answered Vesta.

"You're a symbol of the new skies, Cressa, but we're

taking you with us for more than just decoration. Your story is important, and we mean to let you speak on your behalf," Banu added.

"What will I say?" Cressa's brow furrowed in confusion. She was still young, and commanding a room seemed beyond her.

"The truth, and only the truth. We're going after the heart of angelic civilization, to appeal for their help, and you're going to be a part of it. We—our parents, our family—want you to speak to the people of every house we fly to, in hopes that we can present them with multiple views of what we hope to achieve," Banu stated. She was neither grand nor humble, but quietly confident with her facts.

Vesta adjusted her feet as the aerie shifted in the wind. They all stood in the open space, looking out over clear skies that were brilliant with light. It was late morning, and the only clouds were a line to the north, barely visible on the horizon. Sun set the cloud tops on fire in a distant warning. Vesta took note of their drift, ever watchful. After replanting her feet, she pulled a small piece of hide from a pocket in her armor. It bore a simple line drawing of the greater houses to the north and east, a small section of known sky but still enormous in depth and scope.

"We're going straight to those most likely to help," Vesta explained, drawing her finger across the huge groupings of houses that comprised Orion and the lesser leagues around them. "There are needs other than simple fighters. We need information, observers, and supplies. We're entering a new era in which the old alliances won't work. In fact, they'll do us immeasurable harm. This will be the war for eternity, not merely control of the skies by a grasping hand."

Banu nodded, agreeing with her sister's view of the

coming fight. "We'll also approach those houses who are capable of understanding the threat to all of us. Insular houses are worthless to us, and might only serve to slow us down. Better we use our time in the air wisely, and separate the houses who cannot look to a future without the Crescent Council."

"When I was a Flyer, I always brought bad news. What's to stop them from ignoring us?" Cressa asked. Even though she'd been a messenger for only a short time, the Crescent Council's representatives were rarely welcome.

The twins smiled, rich with conspiracy.

"Leave that to us," Banu said.

CHAPTER NINETEEN:

OBSESSION

*H*ouse Valuri was dark.

It was also still. An alarm began to fizz in Saiinov's warrior blood, just as Vasa began drawing upon a sorcerous defense when her instincts prickled with fear. The house, small but graceful, spun in a lazy orbit, its walls ranging from dark blue to gray in the low light of dusk. The crenelated top glowed rusty orange as the sun's last touch began to angle away and up, slipping into the darkness that grew among the spray of brilliant stars.

"I'm going in," Saiinov announced without hesitation. Vasa gave a terse nod, showing him her hands, which were cocked in a position that would allow her to dispense something nasty at a moment's notice.

"I'll be outside the aerie. Call out if there's trouble." She began to wing around the lazy orb of Valuri, coming to a hover outside the dark opening of the landing space. It was bare, just as the windows. There was no light, and as close to a complete silence as she'd ever heard in the sky.

As a mother, Vasa was a veteran of long nights, but none in her past were longer than the moment of silence that followed Saiinov's plunge into the dark interior of a house that felt like a grave. Squaring her shoulders to regain focus, she waited.

He called out as her pulse began to rise, his voice

controlled, but rough with emotion. "Come in, love. Our daughter is here." His words were grim, but not mournful. She knew Prista was alive, at least. With a single gliding motion, Vasa slid through the air and stepped feather-light onto the aerie, letting her inertia carry her inward to the hidden spaces where Saiinov waited.

Her breath left in a gasp when her eyes adjusted to the low light.

"What- where is she?" Vasa croaked.

"Here. Come to her." Saiinov's voice was behind the main central column, its smooth structure spreading into the ceiling with organic whorls. He'd found a small lantern of sorcerous nature, its husk casting a cool blue light over their daughter, who lay supine in Saiinov's lap. She looked like a child, her gown torn and filthy, wings clotted with dirt and skin so pale that Vasa immediately put a hand on her face to verify that she was alive.

She breathed, slowly but deeply. Her skin was cool but living, a roadmap of neglect and something else. Vasa knew this look, the scene—all of it. It was mania, or as she knew it, spellsickness.

Scholars were susceptible to fits of research so intense that the world itself fell away, leading them into a whirling descent of lust, power, and discovery. That tendency was a prime reason that there were few Scholars of note who lived alone, or at the very least, without an elemental in their house. They would dive into their work to the point that their bodies broke down in a sea of neglect, filled with the eternal desire to understand more and more, often at the cost of their lives. Prista had always been a serious, if loving, child, but her eruption into this kind of decay was an utter shock to Vasa.

Saiinov's reaction revealed he was less confused by the

situation. "She'll survive, I think. She's malnourished and spellsick, but this is nothing we can't fix, dear heart. Help me"—

His words died in a look of puzzlement. Following his gaze, Vasa looked into the gloom.

From floor to ceiling and beyond, message shells, scraps of hide, and unknown items were stuck to the main wall, curving away into the outer loop of the home. At first glance, it looked like a child had run amok, sticking unrelated items at random points around the wall, over and over. There, chaos reigned, but only for the first moment of their glances.

It was a story. Rather, it was *the* story of how life and death had come to the skies after the Evocation. It was complex, violent, hopeful, and unfinished, and it sent a chill of raw fear through both Vasa and Saiinov once they understood what they were seeing.

Lifting his daughter with ease, Saiinov followed Vasa to the nearest edge of the wall, watching silently as she trailed her fingertips from one line of objects to the next. There was order in the madness, as the oldest items gave way to newer looking shells and scrolls, all splayed out in the low light. The narrative was simple to follow, even for someone seeing it for the first time.

Underneath all of it was the history of death.

"How long has she been at this, do you think?" Vasa asked, her voice pained with the weight of leadership and motherhood at once. Saiinov shifted Prista to rest her over his shoulder, like a child. She stirred, coughing lightly.

"What's that? You can tell us, Prista. We are here." Saiinov's voice as a rumble in the empty house, his soothing words low and kind.

"Since the first day." Their daughter's voice was a coarse whisper, brittle to their ears.

"Months, then. And she's clearly been all over the skies. This can't have come from just one area." Vasa pointed to a misshapen hide, embossed with an unmistakable scene of war. "This could be anywhere, or anytime, really, but when you see the houses ringed around—a mountain? Could it be the columns?" The drawing was elegant, even vivid in detail. A bulky shape muscled through the clouds, pouring enemies up into the open skies where angels waited to meet them in aerial combat. There were individual fights as well as walls of sorcery being hurled into larger groups, sending some of the victims plummeting through toward the land below. It nearly pulsed with violence and danger, unsettling Vasa and Saiinov alike simply based on the scale of the battle.

He stepped closer to look, tilting his head away from Prista, who seemed to have slipped back into unconsciousness. "I don't recognize any of these beings. Or magic, for that matter. Who is this, a general? A Skywatcher?" At the base of the drawing, a single creature with wings of solid black held both hands aloft, calling lightning upward in a spiral that raked the avenging ranks of angels. "Could it be a Blightwing?"

Cressa was a Blightwing, a convicted killer, and thus her wings were shaded to black. The angel directing the assault before them had large, solid black wings that looked enhanced in both size and shape. There was something unnatural about the entire representation, although one thing was abundantly clear. The scene was meant to convey death, just as the embossed hide next to it, and the painted shell past that—all the way down the wall in a uniform story of unending chaos.

The same figure—tall, winged, and lethal—was present in a variety of the items Prista pinned to the wall. With a thoughtful look, Vasa pried several free, tucking them in her bag in a manner that bespoke her state of disquiet.

There was something fundamentally wrong with what Prista had saved, and bringing it to Windhook was, at best, an unknown. Angels died because of the unknown, so it was with some trepidation that she patted the bag as if reassuring herself that the items were harmless. What they chronicled was clearly something dangerous, and that meant that they had to nurse their daughter to life to grasp what caused her degradation to the brink of sanity and death.

"Will Valuri survive if we take her?" Saiinov asked, moving easily to the aerie. He'd carried heavier loads through the air, and his daughter would be no challenge. There are no limits to what a parent can do in the name of their children, so he stepped confidently to the ledge, letting the wind begin lifting his wings as he adjusted a flying strap around Prista's torso. With gentle pressure, he cinched her to him while Vasa looked on, checking the connections to make certain there was no chance of failure.

Vasa looked back at the darkened house. "I think we need it to, for her sake. And ours, in the case that we need additional information from what she's done here." With a wave and a word, Vasa sent columns of sorcery twisting across every opening of the house, sealing it off from anyone, save the members of Windhook. "It's safe for now. Home, then?"

"Home." With a leap, Saiinov surged skyward, his daughter silent and pale beneath him as the dark disquiet of House Valuri quickly fell away. "We let her heal, and then we find out what scared her into the void."

Vasa pressed her lips into a thin line. "I know who did it. As to what it is, I intend to find out."

They flew on, as the need for answers grew with each sweep of their wings.

CHAPTER TWENTY:

SHEPHERD

" Stop pacing! If you cause me to err, I'll tell my father you tried to kiss me," Danila said to Garrick, her eyes twinkling with pure mischief. With a look of disgust, he stalked off to another room in the capacious home where Theobald and Danila lived and worked. She was busily setting Livvy's hair into a complicated triple braid that some angels of Electra seemed to favor, chatting away about the general purpose, characters, and happenings within the Hunter's Clinch. From what Livvy could surmise, there were honest traders, bad traders, and then there were the Orions, who seemed to pursue material goods with a single-minded purpose that verged into religion. Their appetite for anything and everything was a constant churn for their standing forces, as well as the need for officers to look superior in the face of competition.

"So, Maev is the most normal among them?" Livvy asked, tilting her head obediently as Danila pushed her to one side. She had no idea what was happening back there, but then again, she wasn't going to argue. It was a rare feeling to have a friend, especially in the exotic future that was her reality.

"Oh, sure. She's sneaky good at keeping her people in line, but for the most part, it's nearly impossible to become a Corvid without a family connection."

Livvy chuckled. "Some things never change."

Danila stopped her ministrations, peering around to eye Livvy with a half-smile. "It was this way where you're from?" She avoided asking where that might be, making Livvy thankful for the ability to avoid a long, uncomfortable conversation sprinkled with words she still couldn't bring herself to say.

"Mmm-hmm. Always who you know, not what."

"You *do* know how Electra works, then," Danila laughed, resuming her task. Her hands fluttered about like brown birds, graceful and constantly in motion. After a final tug and some minor adjustments, she nodded with finality, a gesture that Livvy could sense behind her. "Take a look," Danila said, holding up a small mirror.

"Oh!" Livvy's exclamation was short and joyous. Her hair was now in three thick braids, coming together at the end to make the shape of a violin. Somehow, they stayed in place, glossy under the gentle lanterns gleaming along the walls of Danila's main chamber.

"There's more to it than being pretty, you know. Just like so many things we do here on Electra," Danila said, her smile brilliant.

"Let me guess, something to do with not getting dragged into the clouds by a monster that wants to eat me, but can only get my hair?"

"And here I thought you were new to this place." Danila stuck her tongue out, then laughed, as the two angels rose from the cushions where they'd been sitting. The entire home had the feel of a plush camp, rather than castle. It was sparsely furnished, but comfortable, and only cluttered in the kitchen and main sitting rooms, which were clearly used for entertaining. There seemed to be no separation of business and life, which fit what Livvy had seen of Theobald. His management style was built on accessibility, not elitism, and it was obviously working.

On her initial tour of their home, Livvy marveled at the hanging gardens than ran from hall to kitchen to room, vines and bushes fat with berries and unknown fruits. The smell of life was rich, sharp, and clean, like the first rays of sun after a morning storm. Everything was curved, with few edges. In a flash of recognition, Livvy saw that the entire home was designed for Theobald, both in safety and using his working senses, be it sound or smell. It was quiet but alive in a way that Windhook was not, nor could ever be. There was simply no substitute for the bustle of commerce and life, all crowding into one nexus of color and light, shadows and scents.

"Time to eat, and then we'll walk the Clinch. Or we can nibble on the way. Maybe you'll see something you'd like there?" Danila asked.

"I—sure." Livvy balked, but only for a moment, remembering that Saiinov had slipped her a pouch filled with what passed for money here in the skies. To Livvy, the opaque disks were somewhere between fish scales and wind chimes, and she couldn't decide which. There were markings on each, denoting a value in a language that hovered in the neighborhood of a child's looping scrawl. She'd have to rely on Danila to see she wasn't shortchanged, though anyone trying to challenge the daughter of Theobald struck Livvy as being incredibly stupid. Still, she was thankful for her new friend, even if it did make her feel less certain of what role she was meant to play. After a moment of reflection, Livvy decided that she could follow Danila's lead, but keep her eyes open just the same. There were secrets in the sky, even in the brightest places. Of that, she was certain.

The Clinch arrived well before they saw it. Noises, both

garrulous and industrial greeted Livvy's earth trained hearing, a pastiche of voices and movement that was as alien to her as the dragon who'd slid into the depths earlier. Angels were an industrious lot, she decided, watching them hoist and talk and barter in a dizzying array of transactions that seemed to move to and fro like a school of fish, but winged and punctuated with a raucous energy, unlike anything Livvy had known. Her house, while loving, had been relatively sedate, even taking on a museum-like hush late at night, when there would be no sound save the turning of pages from books being read by small lamps. Theobald's outpost was the complete opposite of everything Livvy knew, but that didn't mean she was scared or nervous. Rather, she let the wave of sound and warmth envelop her as Danila led her by the arm into a courtyard with high, gossamer spires surrounding it. Pennants snapped smartly at the higher altitudes, their colors a spectrum of decrees as to who sold what and where, all of it perfectly sensible to the angels in the know, who lived and worked within the environs of Electra.

"What's that smell?" Livvy's stomach growled perceptibly even over the din. Something delicious was nearby; of that she was certain. It was somewhere between roasted nuts and browning sugar, a combination that set her mouth to watering without so much as asking her permission. She closed her eyes involuntarily, nose up like a tracking hound. A goofy grin split her face as she thought about how she must look, but she couldn't bring herself to care.

"Starshine. I want some too." Danila was already pulling her toward a stall built around an enormous kettle of some kind, where the proprietor busily stirred some rattling concoction against the vaguely metallic kettle

walls. The starshine, a name Livvy found positively
enchanting, rang like brawling pennies as it caromed
around the conical innards of what she decided was the
world's largest wok. With each stroke of her enormous
paddle, the angel in charge would turn the starshine up
and over, a constant flipping that yielded a toasting
aroma so intense Livvy nearly groaned. "I know. It tastes
better than it smells, too," Danila confided, holding up
two fingers to the cook, who grinned over her should
while finishing the current batch with a flourish.

"What's it made out of?" Livvy asked, leaning forward
to see the bins where the uncooked goodies were kept.

"'Stashios and stem syrup, with some spices for good
measure. Browns when they heat it, and no one does it
better than Tusa here. Right?"

Tusa leaned back from the cooking bowl, her brow
dripping sweat as she laid the paddle over one shoulder
with a practiced motion. "At this age, I'm beyond flattery,
Danni." She'd clearly known Danila for some time,
addressing her in the tone of a favored auntie. "Who's
your friend?"

"Livvy. From Windhook. Dad's having me show her
around before she goes to Heike tomorrow, thought we
might grab a bite of the best," Danila said without an
ounce of guile.

"Windhook? You were there, at the council?" Tusa
asked, eyes wide with respect. Livvy decided to count her
among those who thought life was better without the
council's heavy hand and filed that fact away.

"No, sorry. I'm a—recent arrival?" A light grimace, the
very face of a young girl who was uncertain about how to
deliver bad news. She still hadn't acclimated to the idea
that people would accept her, regardless of her origin.

Tusa gave a decisive nod in the manner of all cooks

when they judge someone worthy of their food. "Two cones, then, and you'll only pay for the one. I'll not hear otherwise, despite the fact that I know you're cheering me as an old sop right now, Danni." She filled two cones made from something like rice paper, but stippled, the starshine nearly spilling over each brim. With a saucy wink, she handed the one that was slightly fuller to Livvy. "Don't want her getting used to taking advantage of me."

"I would *never*," Danila started, her words failing as she tossed the first handful of piping hot starshine into her mouth. To supplant her protest, she widened her eyes into innocent globes, only to be rebuffed by a wagging finger from Tusa's free hand.

"You would, and you will again. Off you go, scamp, and you're welcome back anytime, Livvy." Tusa's smile was luminous as she began scooping more nuts and spices into the wok, or kettle, or whatever it was.

Livvy inhaled deeply, feeling her mouth begin watering anew at the hints of unknown spices and sugar. She took a handful of starshine and began to chew, closing her eyes to make a memory of the first time she would eat, for pleasure, with a friend. It was delicious—like Christmas and candy and unseen holidays, all toasted and hot, each bite better than the last.

"Well?" Danila, friendly but impatient.

They'd only gone a few steps, letting the chaos flow around them like a river. "I feel like I have something in my teeth, and grease on my face, and"—

"And what?" Danila laughed, looking into Livvy's cone, now almost empty.

"And I think we need some more." Her face lit from within, joy breaking out in the unbound way that good food and friends can create.

"There's a lot more to see. Ever heard of a plum cake?"

Danila asked, taking the lead again as they dodged four angels carrying a carved log of some sort.

A rib bone, Livvy thought, alarm percolating somewhere in her hindbrain as they passed the quartet, exhorting each other to hold it aloft in good natured banter. "That looks like the front of a ship, sort of."

"It is. Probably being taken to a house, where they're putting a bigger windship together. They assemble offsite, but most of the trade deals go through here," Danila explained.

"You said Heike is a herder? Does she herd things that would have a bone that big?" Livvy watched the magnificent carving disappear around a corner, still held high by the determined angels carrying it to points unknown.

"Oh, no. Not even close. That was from—you know I'm not sure. There was no maker's mark on it, so it could be one of a dozen beasts but fairly easy to hunt. You won't see anything that size around Heike's part of the sky. My sister is quite vigorous in her control. She has responsibilities, both to her house and her beasts."

"She keeps the dangerous creatures away?" Livvy asked, hopeful. She liked the idea of a sky without dragons, or whatever they were called. At least until she could swing her sword with a little more authority, and if she was honest, maybe not ever then.

Danila laughed, a series of musical notes that matched her perfectly. "She doesn't have to. Her beasts will. They're *much* larger."

Livvy dreamed.

Or maybe it was real. It began with Keiron's simple words. *I am here, Livvy. I am close. Always.*

Somehow, she knew tears were spilling down her

cheeks, even as she slept. He was close, yes, she could tell that was real but had no idea how such a thing was possible. Then, even in the depths of her sleep, she felt the rustle of her wings and laughed, or smiled; maybe both. If she had glorious wings, then anything was possible, even the boy who loved her reaching out to speak across a place she could feel but not see.

Did she love him, still? She felt . . . an ache? Yes, that was it. A pain, deep and bittersweet, memory inlaid with moments of joy and hurt, from his kiss to his leaving. All of it wrapped tightly around her heart, not constricting, but never truly letting go, either. That was fine with her, decided the girl who dreamed, wondering how many tears could spill before she woke.

"Livvy, wake up," Danila said, her voice low and urgent.

It was that curious gray before dawn, a time that was neither day nor night, but something indefinable, a doorway between that which was, and what is coming. Livvy opened her eyes to it, groggy with sleep. Her cheeks were wet, and she flushed with shame. "Sorry, what?" Her voice and sight were both bleary with sleep.

"You were crying, but then you smiled as I reached to wake you. What troubles your sleep?" Danila's enormous eyes were dark with worry.

"I was, um, dreaming," Livvy offered, but with hesitation. How could she explain Keiron? Patient, gentle Keiron, who held her hand and watched her struggle to breathe, knowing all along his own heart would end the war for life that Livvy fought for seventeen long, painful years. She liked Danila but wasn't sure she could bring herself to share that yet. Keiron seemed so close, still. What if the pressure of others knowing pushed him away, to wherever he might be if that was even real?

Danila gave a knowing look, taking her hand. "It's okay.

Sometimes, our dreams aren't meant for others." She pulled playfully at Livvy's arm, looking toward the kitchen. "Breakfast. I'll raise that lout so you don't have to," she said, but there was something playful in her tone, rather than resignation.

"I'm sure he can't wait to see you." Standing, Livvy felt the sadness draining away, but still wiped her face. The tears were part of the dream. They, too, were for her, but looking at the friendly smile of Danila, she thought that sharing the truth might feel good, filing the decision away for a later time. For now, she had to focus on the next day and the flight. Dealing with Garrick and the skies was burden enough, though if Livvy were any judge, he would have his hands full with Danila.

After washing and dressing at a basin made from what appeared to be a single, gigantic fish scale, Livvy walked into the wide open space in the heart of Theobald's home. Brightly colored bowls filled with fruit, grains, and other general breakfast food awaited her, as did a tall carafe of juice, its pallid glass dripping with condensation.

"Good morning," Theobald boomed, throwing her a saucy wink and striding out of the room with great purpose. "Can't stay, more's the pity. I'll see you off at the pier." He waved, jocular and brisk, before vanishing through a passage to leave Livvy, Danila, and a perplexed Garrick standing around the table.

"You should eat. Travel packs are ready, and you'll need to catch air before the sun is high. Heike isn't far, but there's a low bank of clouds we didn't anticipate. Might complicate your trip." Danila sat and began helping herself to the spread, piling a plate high with globes of various colors. Livvy noted, yet again, that the angels sure did like berries. Or nuts. Or whatever the array of round things Danila was busily eating, not that it mattered. She

177

was too hungry to pass up a meal, even if the flavors seemed to run to extremes, be it sour or sweet.

"Thank you. Garrick?" Livvy inclined her head politely, offering him a tray, but he looked down, cheeks colored with the blush of emotion. He didn't look angry, just— shy? That was new to Livvy, who regarded him with a side glance as she popped a lurid white berry into her mouth. Its flavor was somewhere between and apple and a potato. She liked it, so she took a spray of them.

"Of course," he mumbled, taking a wide array of items. He might be quiet, but his appetite was in fine order. Without a word, he began to eat in a methodical, cheerless way.

"Are we okay flying over the clouds?" Livvy asked. She didn't know, and it seemed like the best way of finding out what was expected of her if Garrick was surly.

He drank some juice while appearing to give her question serious thought. "Depends on how high the bank rises. All I know is that Heike's place is a three-hour flight, which means we have some leeway if we're airborne soon." He pointedly looked away from Danila, who was busy studying her breakfast.

Something was up, Livvy decided, and it was most likely Danila who'd been the instigator. Judging by the general awkwardness, Livvy surmised that Danila teased Garrick one too many times, realizing that he *was* beautiful. When you played with fire, things could get out of hand. She knew this from experience, given that Keiron's attentions had gone from a curiosity to a wildfire in the blink of an eye. When Keiron held her, she wasn't sure if it was her failing heart or his presence that made her feel like the world was coming apart at her feet. Looking at Garrick and Danila, she saw some of the same—or did she? Livvy had little experience in the laws

178

of attraction, but had spent her whole life as a keen observer of the human condition. Angels, she corrected, but the principle held.

"I hope they're as regal as I imagine," Livvy said, to no one in particular. Her eyes went soft at the thought of magnificent beasts swimming through the sky. Would they be silent, or loud, like a herd? How did Heike do it? She had no idea what to expect, and, in part, was thankful for Garrick's unwillingness to do his job and help her learn. There were some things best left to one's own eyes. This was such a time. She stood as a wave of impatience swept over her, wanting more than anything to see these creatures of the air and sky. By way of standing, Livvy took the lead, finishing the tall glass of clear juice whose flavor fell somewhere between sweet and sour.

"Garrick? If you're ready, then?" She smiled to take the edge from her words, but Livvy's eyes were already moving on as she tried, in vain, to see through the outpost walls and catch a glimpse of Heike and her beautiful creatures.

He froze for an instant, finally turning his head to gape at Livvy. "*We* will be ready when I'm done eating." He tossed a piece of fruit into his mouth, chewing defiantly. It was a childish gesture, made even more ridiculous when the fruit popped, leaking pale green juice down the side of his mouth. With a splutter, he wiped it away, glaring at Livvy but failing to hold the look as a cough shook him, once, then twice.

After noisily clearing his throat, he wheezed, "I liked you better when you were"—

"Obedient? I don't think that's why I'm here, and you'd better start getting used to it. Why do you think that treating people like trash will make anyone care for you? Look around--*no one* is clamoring for your friendship.

I've seen how people look at you here. They tolerate you. They don't welcome you. You know what the saddest thing is? You can't see she thinks that somewhere, deep inside that carcass of yours, there might be something worthy of a person like her." Livvy turned at Danila's intake of breath, smiling ruefully. "Sorry. It just clicked when I saw you avoiding each other here at the table. You're a better person than I am, but who am I to judge? The only love of my life gave me his heart. I'm not exactly an expert."

Garrick stood suddenly, knocking his stool back with a dull clatter. "Who do you think you are? You're nothing. You're a charity case. A *freak*. A savior my parents think is here for our family, and everyone else, but you killed my brother before you could even stretch your wings and fly the length of a cloud. How does that *feel*?" His voice was an icy whisper, so heavy with cruelty that he seemed shocked to have even said such things.

Livvy walked around the table, reaching up to pat his face in a gesture that was tender beyond his worth. "I was wrong, Garrick. It just occurred to me that there's something sadder than your stupidity." She shook her head, looking up into his eyes. They narrowed with suspicion, but he didn't draw away from her touch. "You were sent away so that the Crescent Council wouldn't jail you, and then kill you?"

He made a noise of disdain. "Yes. What of it?"

Livvy let her hand drop, and now her eyes were bright with sadness. Pity raked Garrick, who flinched under the pain of that look. "Do you know, since I've been here no one in your family told me they wanted you back. So, you tell me, brother of mine. How does that *feel*?"

No one spoke. For the first time in his life, Garrick knew what it was to be utterly alone. He wasn't broken, but nearly so, and the years of arrogance and rage left him like an unwelcome guest, flowing in a silent torrent hidden only by his broad palms, covering a face gone spotty with shame. He sat heavily, unmoving save his wings, which lifted and fell with the inner war of a boy trying not to come apart under waves of shame. Grief was like that. It took solid things and made them crack, and Garrick was riddled with a lifetime of flaws, now exposed for the world to see.

Wordlessly, Danila and Livvy flanked him like sentinels charged with his care, their hands on his shoulders with a light touch. One dark, one light, they watched as the shame and self-loathing burrowed out of him, or at least as much of it as he was willing to let go. It was the dismantling of a lifetime, and it would not happen quickly. Time was his friend now.

So was Danila. She leaned down, her lips brushing his cheek. It was a promise, a confirmation of her presence. A gift, and one worth more than anything in the sky, since it could not be bought. It had to be earned, and only by someone of rare character. She saw something in him, a future vision of possibility and hope. Her touch led him to the light, as he turned his face to look up at her, the first tears of his life drying on cheeks that were aflame with regret.

"I'm a coward." His words were flat, devoid of anything. He looked down, reddening again at the hideous admission.

Danila shook her head, the glory of her black hair making a rustling sound in the stillness of the room. "I don't think so, Garrick. This is hard. Cowards don't do things that are hard." She took his hand, squeezing it. Their fingers fit, not perfectly, but well enough. It was something. "You have to help Livvy. And your family. All

181

of us. This is more than your pride."

He was quiet, finally answering with a nod.

"I need your experience. I need a brother, not an enemy," Livvy said.

Garrick stood, but slowly, as if wounded. In a way, he was. "You can have it. As to the brother, I can only try."

"That's all I'm asking," Livvy answered. She looked up at him now, but he only saw Danila. Things had changed.

"Fly with me, then? Let's go see these dragons." Livvy's smile was impossibly bright.

"I will." He hesitated, reaching for the small pack of food. "Will you be here when we return?" His question to Danila was simple. There was nothing left to hide. "Yes."

"Good." He smiled, and it was the first Livvy remembered seeing. His face transformed from cruel perfection to unfiltered joy. It looked good on him.

Danila smiled, too. "Fly safe. Come back. There are things ahead of you now."

"I'm counting on it," Garrick beamed.

They stepped out onto the family aerie, a small deck hidden away from the bustle of the pier. The wind was sharp, the sun bright. Only low clouds marred the view, well under their feet. "Ready?" He asked.

Livvy nodded, eying the sky with glee. "I am. Let's fly." They both waved to Danila, leaping out into the breathtaking blue. In seconds, the winds took them, and they spiraled away, but, after a few seconds, Garrick couldn't contain his hopeful curiosity. Danila was still there, watching. From a distance, it looked like she was sad to see him go, but that could have been a trick of the light.

CHAPTER TWENTY-ONE:

THE WEAVER

" $\mathcal{G}$s that a House?" Livvy asked, her voice trailing up in confusion. Garrick had led them on their swift, straight flight, high above the impenetrable cloud bank that roiled a thousand feet below. They were circling the strangest thing she'd seen since coming forward into the skies of angels, which meant it was unusual indeed given the bizarre nature of the sky and its denizens.

"It is, but it's purpose built. Or altered, as you might say. I'm told that her ancestors added the rings long ago. Their family has been at this for some time- longer than Windhook has been around, and well before that, I imagine," Garrick said as he began to turn sunward.

The house was medium in size and typical in many respects. Globular, shining, and crowned with the knobs of an ancient conch shell, it ranged in color from a deep rose to bright blue at the top, streaked with pearlescent white in rippling shadows that danced under the glassine surface. There were round windows, covered with fluttering curtains, but where an aerie would have served angels was a massive, open landing, circling the entire house. It reminded Livvy of a giant, round porch, but open to the sky and without any railings.

Odder still were the rings.

Each ring was black as night, roughly elliptical, and

nearly fifty feet across. Some were even larger, going up in size to a monstrous example that was wider than some of the smaller houses Livvy had seen. The rings bristled like a comb, each tine matte black and pointed inward, their shiny material uniformly rigid and roughly the length of an angel's forearm. Before they'd circled a full revolution, Heike appeared at the nearest door, waving cheerily to them.

"Come in! I'm getting ready to call the herd, and you'll not be wanting to jostle with them when they begin their passes," she cried, her rich voice carrying the distance between them with ease.

"Thank you. It's a welcome landing," Garrick said. His manners were a new addition, but one that Livvy liked. Perhaps the possibility of Danila made him consider his words even when not in her presence. That was a good sign, especially for Garrick. He needed something to temper his soul.

"I'm Heike, but you'll be knowing that already. Your sister was here, a rather lethal angel, but polite and kind. She had business elsewhere but leaves you her greeting and wishes for a safe flight home." The introduction was punctuated by a firm handshake and Theobald's brilliant smile. Heike was a true daughter to him, tall, broad, and striking. Her black hair was bound with metallic cords, exposing a face of dark skin, angular cheekbones, and black eyes scored by crow's feet. There was a mirth to her and the kind of solidity that made it plausible that she should call beasts and have them answer.

"Garrick, of Windhook. This is my new sister, Livvy," he said, with only the slightest hesitation.

Flushing, Livvy saw the calculation on Heike's face. It was measured, not sour, and the following smile was just as open as her first. "Livvy. Thank you for seeing us."

"It's my pleasure, truly. Not," Heike said with a grin, "that I'm above making the odd bit of coin. Windhook pays quite well, but my herd would work for free if need be. It's my other efforts that eat at the hours."

"Work? They do work?" Garrick asked, looking around as if expecting to see baskets and tools suitable for a giant Windbeast. There were none.

Heike's cackle was infectious. "Hah! Only if you consider a bunch of lazybones scratching their bums to be work. Which reminds me, sun's getting on a bit, so I'll start the call of victory. It rousts them a bit faster than my less insistent songs, but, in truth, the lazy sots will answer to any kulning that drifts across their ears."

"Kulning?" Livvy asked, feeling the unfamiliar word on her tongue. It was odd but satisfying, hinting at alien things of great age. She turned the syllables over in her mind, once, and then again for effect. The word remained impenetrable, yet inviting.

"Indeed. It's a learned skill, and not just for any fool who can bellow. I've been singing it to them all my life, and we've reached an agreement of sorts. Just wait here until they're present, and then if you wish, you can join them in the air. It's quite a sensation to move among giants, especially when they take a fancy to you."

As she moved off to the edge of the landing, Livvy began to sense something in the air. She'd been in the presence of otherness, or sorcery, whatever it was called— she'd been square in the middle of it repeatedly since joining Windhook. She's even felt the odd, unknown fear of Miss Henatis being nearby, but what began to build around her now was different. It was warm and secretive yet familiar in a way that tickled at the very edges of her awareness.

"She's powerful, although in what way I couldn't tell

you," Garrick admitted. He felt it too. Heike's strength was an inarticulate force that surrounded rather than pressed.

A memory surfaced for Livvy, and she found herself speaking out loud, relating something from a world that was far away. "When I was a kid, my parents took me to a small circus. It had a few animals, but mostly people who did acrobatics, tricks, things like that."

"What's a circus? Like a day fair?" Garrick asked.

"Sounds about right," Livvy agreed. "They had an elephant, a huge male named Otto. I slipped under the rope that kept people back and went up to him. It was— well, it wasn't smart, but I'd never seen anything like him. He was huge, and he watched me with this small, sad eye as I approached him. I touched his tusk, and then my mom grabbed me from behind in that silent panic that parents seem to perfect when danger is immediate and real. The elephant keeper was furious, but in all the noise of me being carried away, Otto never made a move. He just watched me, quiet and noble. That's what this feels like to me, right now. Like Otto is over the horizon, watching us."

"I don't know what an elephant looks like, but I think I understand." Garrick's voice was soft. He was thinking, which revealed a better side of him. "I think she's starting?" At his question, Heike turned around to glance over her shoulder, licking her lips to moisten them. When she turned back, even the wind died for that precious second before something wondrous happens.

"*HEEEE-hoooo-deeee-doot!*" she sang, a piercing cry of ancient music that vibrated the marrow in Livvy's bones. Garrick jumped slightly at the power of her initial call, and Livvy took a small step back, though she smiled in amazement at the raw force of the tune. This was an old song, she could tell. Maybe it was sorcery, but up close, it felt like something from the mists of time. A tradition, so long practiced that the origin and meaning ceased to be known, passing from the hand of fact to legend, and legend to magic.

Heike sang three more lines, allowing the last to end in a plaintive uptick so full of longing that it was like a broken heart had been put into a single note. The sounds caromed about in the air, perhaps meeting an impenetrable barrier in the clouds below only to return to their ears, slightly diffused. Heike looked back over her broad shoulder once again, face alight with news.

"They come."

Livvy felt a frisson of excitement, stepping forward with Garrick to the edge to look down into the thick clouds. At first, she saw little if any motion as the crowd of nimbostratus moved serenely east, their thick, rounded tops a solid wall of unyielding gray, shot through with more ominous black.

Then something began to muscle upward as the clouds bulged, their collective masses being disturbed in one, then two, and then many places, swept up and away in curling sheets of featureless mist.

Heike chuckled, a low noise of satisfaction as her eyes flickered across the changing cloudscape. With a small grin, she turned her head to look directly at an area to the south where the cloud cover grew dark, and then darker still. With an experienced gaze, she began to identify the herd before Livvy could even discern the difference between animal and sky, finally pointing toward the darkest place below them with a long, calloused finger.

"They're here."

Livvy gasped. There were no words to prepare her for what emerged from the clouds, and she found herself thankful that Heike chose to let the herd arrive without fanfare. Garrick stood mute, his mouth open at the majesty of the first beasts that broke free from their blanket of vapor to spiral upward with massive strokes of their fluke-like wings.

"Whales. They're like—like whales, but thinner, and they *fly*," Livvy whispered. Her eyes were moist with tears before the full herd had risen to Heike's call, and she felt herself go weak in the knees. They were magnificent. Slow, regal, enormous, each animal was easily two hundred feet long or more, ranging from midnight blue to emerald green, and covered with a haze of fine down that gave them the appearance of fading in and out of reality. Their wings were two section flukes, broad as a city street and fading to edges of brilliant white, undulating as they cut through the air and propelled the giants forth in silent glory.

Their heads were smoothed, rounded, with small ears and a smirk on their wide, comical mouths. They looked like old men who've just won a game of checkers, their expressive brows lifting and falling as they twisted about to position themselves for entry into the rings. They knew their routine well and seemed genuinely pleased to be called. With two legs and a plump tail that ended in a vertical spade, they made small adjustments to their majestic, elephantine flight, all the while responding to Heike's cooing encouragements with their own deep, resonant songs.

As they neared the rings, Livvy could pick out differences beyond their distinct colors. Some were more gracile with thinner torsos and legs. She decided those were the females, confirming her belief when she noticed a low ridge of horn on the necks of the bigger, darker beasts. They seemed to be in pairs, too, breaking off to form a pinwheel pattern that approached the rings from a single, rotating flight path. Individually, each animal began to backwing and slow their airspeed to a slow drift, hooting in pleasure as they did. It sounded like good-natured bragging, if on a scale that Livvy found mind-boggling. After a closer look at their overall motion, they seemed able to float *and* fly, making Livvy wonder if their ability was sorcerous or biological.

"To your rings, now, you know the spots." Heike was waving them about like an airport director, each animal turning to regard her with a huge, shining eye as they glided past. "Nilakka! I'll not tell you again, slothful wretch. You will go to your ring, and not your sister's. She'll nip your fin again, and you'll complain all summer, which is only fitting if you insist on nudging her with that muzzle of yours. Very good, Pikku. Thank you, dearest. You always were better than that husband of yours, and don't you glare at me, Kallavesi, you know I'm right." Heike kept up her running commentary on their failings or virtues as each animal took a place in the ring of rings, a sight that made Livvy feel insignificant, even invisible. The sensation was not unwelcome.

With great sighs, the beasts began to pass through their respective rings, whose tines scratched lightly through their fur with a low, muttering hiss. The fastest of the herd finished their combing in less than a minute, though two older beats with graying snouts took their own sweet time. Their laconic pace earned them a scolding from Heike, who flew from place to place urging and thanking the herd as they emerged back into open sky. Livvy noticed that each animal would roll out and down in a gentle dive, propelling themselves away from the house with a single massive swipe of their tails. As each beast dove back toward the cloud cover, they sang, a long, hooting note of thanks and amusement.

An hour after Heike began her call, it was over. The air hummed with something like sadness, a sense of completion that was bittersweet. Livvy wondered if she would ever see anything so noble again, then chided herself for thinking like the girl she'd been once before. There were more things in the sky than she could ever imagine, and if she didn't find them, then they would find her. With a slow smile of appreciation, she looked at Heike, who stood with hands on hips and a grin of her own.

"What's next?" Garrick asked. He'd been affected by the spectacle, too. It was evident in his voice.

"We pull the strands from each ring, and I'll show you the loom. The easy part is over; now, I have to earn my coin." Heike took wing, motioning that they should follow. Over the next hour, they went from ring to ring, pulling the long, silken strands left behind by the herd's passage. Each strand was a yard long, much thicker than a human hair, and slippery like the finest silk. The colors ranged across blues and greens, with gray, silver and black in the mix by the time they'd secured every single strand of wool. The yield was a surprise to Livvy and Garrick, who weren't used to thinking of herd animals the size of small houses. Heike has no such limitations as she laughingly gathered the crop to be turned into shearwater cloaks.

"We've enough for an extra cloak," Heike began, giving Livvy and Garrick appraising looks. "Or two, though it might be tight on your shoulders, young Garrick. I think you'll grow yet, but I can always add to the seams at a later date. Yes. I think eight cloaks in total, once all is said and done. In we go, then. It's time for wine, a meal, and then I'll get to work."

"May we help you?" Livvy asked.

"With the loom? Certainly not, girl. I'll let you look, and perhaps watch for a bit, but as to helping? No, I think not. It's a life of work that brought me to the point where I can do this, and moreover, it's my family secret." She grinned to take the sting from her words.

"My apology. Don't know what I was thinking," Livvy admitted with a rueful smile of her own. Some things were best left to experts, and this was one such skill.

"What is the loom made from, Heike?" Garrick asked. His interest was more than polite, and it brought out a kindness in him that had been missing.

"Ahh, an excellent question, and one I can answer without fear of compromising my family tradition," Heike said, moving inside though the broad, open doorway the stood before. The space inside was open, airy, and light, dominated by three of the strangest things Livvy had ever seen.

Along the eastern wall stood Heike's looms, gleaming with care in the light. Ten feet tall, and just as wide, each frame was a series of interlocking grids, held in place by heavier beams that were attached to the wall with straps of cured leather. Looking closer, Livvy realized the looms weren't made of anything she'd ever seen before. The material was smooth, gray, and bent under her touch when she pushed lightly against the nearest piece. "Is this from a Windbeast?" It seemed logical, given the thrifty nature of angels as they eked out a living in the skies. Nothing was wasted, not if a House wanted to excel and not merely survive.

"It is, but not from anything that ever lived here. There were great creatures who circled the sky, feeding on herds of prey that followed the currents," Heike explained. "They would inhale great drafts of air, straining it through their mouths. These"- she tapped the flexible grid closest to her, "are the baleen they discarded during their growth. Angels would follow them for the hunting, saving these out of curiosity. My family was the first to see their true purpose, using four of the baleen to create a loom. I send the thread back and forth with these bone needles." She held up a cane, which Livvy realized was a needle made from some part of a Windbeast.

"The scale of this place boggles my mind," Livvy said, taking a needle from Heike. It was nearly weightless but strong. She pursed her lips as a stray thought burbled to the surface. "Are these creatures still around?" She waved the needle for emphasis.

"The beasts who provided the baleen?" With a mournful shake of her head, Heike said no. "They didn't survive long after the Evocation. I don't know what happened, but I suspect they served a purpose beyond my understanding. Perhaps they made a path for us to survive here and then died, their purpose fulfilled. I don't know. Other than these looms and some rumored talismans in the houses of the wild south, there's neither hide nor hair of them."

It wasn't the first time Livvy had heard of the Evocation. She began thinking of time differently, given the idea that there were animals and conditions no longer in existence. In her mind, that meant there'd been a time of violent transition between the world she knew and the skies around her. Looking at Garrick, she saw he was considering the same thing, a pensive look on his face as his brows knit together in consideration.

"Are those the only creatures who no longer exist, or the only ones you know of?" Garrick asked pointing at the looms for clarification.

"Only them. They were larger than anything in the skies, and now, they're gone. As to the rest of the sky, it seems to have stabilized, or at least it did after the third Evocation. There were three, some say four, you see, and out of it all came—this." Heike waved expansively at the house, and the looms, and her life in general.

Silence ruled while Livvy considered her next question, but she chose to be quiet when Heike clapped her hands together in the universal sign that work was about to begin in earnest.

"May we watch?" Livvy asked. She didn't understand what the cloaks would look like when finished, but the act of creating them felt like something she needed to see.

"For the first one, yes. The others? No, you're to be on your way back to Windhook. There are plans afoot, child, and they involve you being back home, rather than watching me work with my pretties." Heike winked saucily and began filling a circular bin with wool from the herd, her hands moving without pause in a rhythm she knew in her bones.

"How will the cloaks get to Windhook?" Garrick asked, then snapped his fingers. "Don't tell me—Airdancers?"

The Airdancers were elegant, undulating creatures shaped like elongated rays, their sides pulsating with the light of expressive chromatophores as they chattered to each other in the sky. Silent, graceful, and silken in the air, they were secretive creatures who answered to few angels save those of House Windhook. It came as no surprise to Livvy that Heike could enlist their help since Windhook seemed to wield power of that kind as easily as one might breathe.

"Airdancers, indeed. There are quite a few around here who enjoy the company of my herd. They listen quite nicely, once I've given them their share of sour berries and a good song. Quite useful, that lot, and a sight more friendly than most of the beasties who skulk about between here and Electra." As she spoke, her hands flew over the frame, pulling and nudging long strands of wool in a tightening pattern that began to ripple in the light. "Pour the wine and take a seat. When this cloak is underway, I'll see you out. You've time to return to Electra with the full sun, and then on to Windhook." She narrowed her eyes at them before speaking directly to Garrick. "How are her wings holding?"

He gave her question a solid moment of thought before answering. "Good, and getting better. She's fast in the air and slow to turn, but we expected that. Moving in space is always harder than straight flight, but her body lean is good enough that she could fight right now if need be."

Heike gave a decisive nod. "Good. Subtlety can come later, but for now, the most important thing is endurance and a quick initial burst of speed. One never knows when a strategic retreat is in order. Remember that, child. You can't win a fight from the depths of the atmosphere."

"I'll remember," Livvy said, raising a hand to acknowledge the weight of Heike's advice.

"Good. Then let's get on with the weaving, and see you on the currents back to Electra." With a brusque nod, she began to work again, and Livvy wondered if she would ever stop running, even if it were powered by wings and a new heart.

Livvy added a silent prayer as she touched her chest. *Please, whatever happens, let me not be afraid.*

CHAPTER TWENTY-TWO:

THE WINTER BUTTERFLY

𝒯he mood around Windhook's dining table was a pastiche of tension and joy. For the first time, Garrick was engaged, even cheerful, but cognizant of the underlying concerns as unseen forces began nudging his family closer to total war.

That was not to say the welcoming meal was without good humor. Vasa and Saiinov listened to their son give his report, sharing sidelong glances as he omitted or fumbled the parts of the narrative involving Danila. The twins were present, as was Habira, and there were additional guests filtering in and out through the evening. Representatives from a series of minor houses in Orion, the Southern Wilds, and even a lone flyer from the Eastern Reaches who swore the allegiance of her house and their nine available swords. Saiinov had gravely thanked the angel from House Deneb, inviting her to stay in a guest room until she was rested enough to fly to the rally point. He suspected that by the time the night had worn on, there would be several more angels sleeping off the effects of long, hard flights. He didn't worry, as they had plenty of room, and every single warrior mattered.

Previously against the Crescent Council, Windhook forced the issue without any clear allies. Now, they built a coalition of forces both great and small for a war that would, according to Saiinov, reveal itself in due time. To the compulsive planners of Windhook, it was better to prepare for an unseen fight rather than wait to counterpunch, a technique that served them well in every instance thus far.

When the evening began to slow, Prista made her appearance, emerging from the shadowed hall to walk timidly into the light of the central room. Her health was improving, though she remained a wan imitation of her mother. Prista's blonde hair was pulled back to reveal a face that was beautiful, but graven with some hidden weight. Her eyes looked blue in the lamplight, a neat trick that gave her an internal liveliness she'd been missing.

In her hand, she held the Book of January, giving it a measured look before placing it gently on the table in front of Livvy.

"What's that?" Livvy asked, head slightly fuzzed from the effects of her first restful meal. The book was plump, covered in hide, and embossed with things beyond her ability to read. Yet.

"I don't know, exactly, and I suspect my mother doesn't either. It's a spell, of that I'm certain. As to what kind? I couldn't begin to understand. That worries me, and yet it doesn't." She sat, gently, then arranged her hands in a careful way, not looking at anyone. Her eyes were vague as she began to dredge thoughts of sorcery and other distant things. It gave her a dreamy, sad look. "As my mother has no doubt told you, there are answers within that book, but only for the person capable of asking the right questions. I believe that person to be you, if only for the simple fact that you're a child of two worlds, and thus, you can see things that are beyond us. Living here in the skies makes us warlike and tough, but it also inures us to things from the past world."

"You mean I'm too new to be jaded?" Livvy asked, and

her question was tinged with the bitterness of a veteran fighter, eliciting a laugh from Prista. Saiinov and Vasa watched the exchange carefully, sending each other meaningful looks. Clearly, they'd reached some of the same conclusions, but in their usual fashion had kept their own counsel.

"In a manner of speaking, yes, but I prefer the term elastic. It sounds so much more dignified." Prista smiled, revealing even more of the similarities between her and Vasa. It was disarming, and Livvy began to relax. "When you were in Electra, did you see the goods that the Moondivers bring back? From the—I guess we should say the past, or whenever they can go?"

"I don't think so?" Livvy turned to Garrick. "Did we? I think I would have noticed any technology from my world."

He shook his head. "It was there, but we had other concerns. The Moondivers bring back all manner of scraps, but for the most part, they're oddities. Some of them risk their lives for nothing more than baubles." His tone revealed what he thought of that sort of endeavor.

Prista nodded serenely. "They pierce the light of days because they can, not because they have to. As I'm sure you've seen, we can survive here with our wits and inventiveness."

"*Survive*," Livvy repeated the word like a soft curse.

"True, but tell me where life isn't hard?" Saiinov answered.

"It's never really easy, but life here isn't just about surviving. I'm beginning to think it's a refuge—a last ditch effort to continue life without giving in, and doing so here in the skies because the alternative was impossible," Livvy concluded. After seeing the looms, and the inventive need for people like Heike, she began to understand that angels weren't just some trick of evolution. They were an attempt to beat back whatever it was that lay waiting under the clouds, on the bones of her world.

"You sound as if you speak from experience," Vasa told her.

"I do, and you know it." Livvy's hand went to her chest out of sheer habit. "My entire life was surviving from one breath to the next. I recognize a struggle when I see it. All of this? It's more than life in a hostile environment. It's a daily war, and now there's something even worse lurking in our future. I'd like you to tell me what that is. Now." She held up a hand to Vasa, who opened her mouth to protest. "Please don't lie. I'm young, and new here, but I'm not incapable of seeing the furtive glances between you and your husband. You may be used to keeping secrets from the family, but I'm not one of yours. Not yet. You have to prove it to me before I open some unknown artifact and let it scramble my brains, all to further your Gordian plans for changing this world into something unrecognizable." Livvy sat back, leveling a piercing look at everyone in the room.

Prista spoke first, unencumbered by the shame of being caught in a lie of omission. "It's not going to scramble your brain, but you might end up with . . . advantages." Her words were neutral.

"How so? Don't hide the truth, Prista. I can't abide secrets anymore." Livvy was angry but tired. Flying was hard work, but palace intrigue was even harder.

"I don't know. The book isn't for anyone from here, and that means it was meant for you. Whatever happens, it won't be painless, but from my, ahh, research, I believe you will become something different. A new thing, here above the clouds." Prista flushed, embarrassed at the mention of her breakdown despite there being value in that period of madness.

Livvy reached out, picking the book up with a trembling hand. When she spoke again, her voice held a querulous note. "It's heavy. I hoped it wouldn't be heavy." In her experience, important things were heavy, and she'd hoped the entire existence of the book was a mistake or some quirk of fate. As it turned out, only the latter was true.

She ran a thumb over the embossed cover, feeling the details of a face rendered in profile. Looking at Saiinov, she asked him the one question he might not answer. "Does anyone else know about the troubles in the sky? The things that have been happening since I arrived? Or is it just Windhook?"

He never got to answer, because the sound of wings made everyone in the room lay a hand on their weapons. Even Livvy felt herself grab the hilt of her sword, a reaction that seemed far more natural now when compared to the first alien caress of the hide wrapped pommel.

"Two visitors," said Saiinov, visibly relaxing.

He was correct. Two angels emerged from the darkened exterior hallway, their faces hidden with cloaks of black fabric. They rustled lightly with the sounds of excellent armor, but their weapons were silent, bound in scabbards that were tied across back and hip. Without hesitation, both—women, Livvy decided, they were too graceful—the women approached the table, their steps light and confident, and wings folded into relaxed positions of full repose.

As one, they drew back their hoods, eliciting a gasp from everyone except Saiinov, who clearly had ideas of their identity based on something in their bearing.

"I think you'll find us to be welcome guests, once we describe what's happening in a storm far to the east," Maev said, the light catching her jeweled ear with a merry twinkle. She rocked back on her heels, her lips pulled to the side in a smirk.

The second angel leaned into the light even as she dropped something on the table. The object landed with a dry rustle, gleaming in the lamplight like a poisonous fruit.

A scorpion. Dead, but recently alive.

"Which question would you like me to answer first, Windhook? Where I've been, or where I found that— thing?" Factor Utipa asked, her black hair spilling out of the hood to reveal a deep red streak that Saiinov and Vasa hadn't seen since the fall of Sliver.

Moistening her lips, Vasa recovered first. "The scorpion, if you please. I can surmise you've been working with the Corvids and House Altair, in some capacity."

Utipa smiled, and her black eyes glinted with mischief. She looked good for someone who might have been dead and was certainly missing. After the final combat during the Crescent Council's desperate attempt to hold power, she alone had vanished, gone from the skies without a trace.

"You'd be surprised how far I can fly when I'm highly motivated." She looked at Maev with something like thanks, then pointed at the mechanical creature sitting inertly on the table, its carapace smooth and menacing. "I was taught many things by my mother, but the most important lesson was always to be prepared for a sudden move. History teaches us that we can never really get too comfortable, can we?" Utipa moved around the table to stand near Livvy, looking down at her with an inscrutable regard. She was an experienced politician and an obvious survivor. They would have to wait for her to reveal her intentions.

Saiinov folded his arms, sitting back with a sigh of resignation. "If we could move this along, that would save some of the lamplight we're wasting?"

Utipa grew serious. "Understood. The scorpion is from House Selinus, which is now a floating husk, and damn them to the winds," she spat, naked disgust on her face as she related the origins of the oncoming war. "The sister who controlled it is missing. So is everyone else, and that isn't the only issue."

Maev took up the narrative, unfurling a small map and placing it on the table. She quickly put mugs and bowls on the corners to hold it flat, then pointed at the shape of a storm drawn in the southern portion of the hide. "This storm has been in existence long enough to be on trader's maps, but as of two days ago, it's no longer a normal atmospheric condition. If anything, it's grown smaller, but more intense, rotating around an invisible point of sky that cannot be approached by anyone."

"How do you know?" Vasa asked, never taking her eyes from the map.

"Because a half wing of my best long range flyers vanished when they tried to bypass it, and it wasn't due to lightning or beasts." Maev's face darkened with anger. She could not abide the loss of good soldiers for any reason, even something unexpected.

"Sorcerous?" Prista asked.

Maev nodded, slowly. "It has to be, which leads me to my next concern. We ransacked Selinus and found extensive notes on using modified spells to create an artificial corridor for Moondivers. I'm assuming they tried more than once because the maps indicated several failures and *two* successful attempts at bridging the light of days. The first was in a place called Mauritania, if that means anything to you, and was drawn as a kind of vortex. It collapsed after less than a day but lasted long enough that Brigha was able to make several trips to the past. It's obvious that she learned enough to try again, after perfecting or adjusting her method of entry. As for who we're dealing with, it's Brigha who led the house, but it was her sister, Marti, who was the intellect behind this innovation. I don't need to tell you why this worries me, and why it should make you nervous as well."

"You *do* need to tell us, or at least me," Livvy broke in. When Maev fixed her with a chilly stare, she didn't look away. "I'm new here, so I need information, not presumptions."

"Fine. Then see if Lady Vasa can explain this to you in detail later, but for now, understand this—the Evocation that created this world was probably magical. Vasa, do you agree?" Maev asked, her tone like iron.

"I do. It's likely that sorcery is to blame for the end of Livvy's world, but as to how that event could be caused by the future, I have no answer," Vasa confessed.

"I have one." Utipa squared herself to address everyone. "It was the same force that allowed the Crescent Council to seize control of the skies. It was stupidity and greed, married to someone with incredible power. A Scholar, most likely, but possibly someone who was an elite sorcerer in more than one school. Think of a Watershaper who was the most gifted sorcerer in the skies, and you're close to whoever this unknown angel might be."

"How can something that hasn't happened yet change the past?" Livvy asked.

Maev shrugged. It made her look less militant and more natural. "I don't know, but I suspect we're going to find out at some point. Whatever shattered the past has to be present here and now, but we simply haven't identified it. That's why House Selinus must be stopped. They're twisting a storm for reasons I can't begin to imagine, but if our default assumption is that it's a power grab, well— we know how that can go. And they're doing it in the middle of a storm that's been altered to kill without a trace. The most aggressive Houses we've ever known have taken the same path—they leave no trace of their crimes, and therefore have no one to answer to. That kind of subterfuge is the mark of someone doing bad things on a grand scale, and that's why Selinus is at the tip of danger beyond anything I've ever seen since assuming command of the Corvids."

As a seasoned veteran of the skies, Maev had seen blood and war. For her to connect a storm to something worse than the current state of conflict was unnerving, because she held her position of power and respect based on an unflappable will. The angel before them wasn't the laconic, smiling leader who greeted Livvy at the defensive ring outside Electra.

Underneath her calm shell, she was worried, and everyone in the room knew it.

"Magic," Livvy said, and it was more curse than utterance.

Vasa looked to her for an explanation as the room fell silent. Even Maev fixed her with a quizzical look, waiting to understand why the youngest person in the room felt the need to speak.

"Go on, Liv," Cressa urged, it was the first she'd spoken from her place leaning against a column, half shrouded in darkness. Her dark eyes were tilted like a cat's, giving her an inscrutable quality in the shadowed space where she'd been listening to every word of the discussion.

"House Selinus is using a storm to disguise magic so

that they can seize power. They probably had it in mind well before the Crescent Council was—how should we put this?" Livvy looked slyly at Utipa, who watched her with bemused tolerance. "Let's say Windhook asked them to leave." There was general laughter in the room, earning her a wave to continue from Saiinov. "The fall of Sliver left a gap in the power structure, and whoever runs Selinus saw it as an opportunity. They're using unseen magic to control a storm that kills angels without a trace. How's that so far?"

"Accurate," remarked Utipa with a dryness that Livvy couldn't discern between humor and hostility.

She plunged on, working out the detail as she spoke. "If Vasa has taught me anything, it's that the events in the sky are always related. So, this book isn't an accident, and that means I'm not either. My arrival wasn't a hiccup in the history of a world I'm still getting used to. It was more than luck. I know, because my dad was a soldier when he was young, and he told me about why war is never an accident."

"He was? I thought you said he was a teacher or something?" Cressa asked.

"He led two lives, one before I was born, and then the life of a parent. He's a kind, gentle soul, but he understood what it meant to be a soldier. He hated it, but he respected it," Livvy explained, twining her fingers together as she tried to explain the long talks she'd had with her dad, under the tree where they'd buried Keiron. It seemed like another life. It *was* another life or at least a different one, wholly alien to the young woman speaking of things like war and sorcery. Now, she was immersed in something beyond everything she knew to be real, and the feeling that she played a critical role in this world was becoming an inescapable reality.

"He sounds like a true soldier," Saiinov murmured. "We

do the work, but we despise the violence. It would be better not ever to fight, but there are fearful things among us, and our first duty is to our House."

"That's what dad said. He told me that I was his ocean, his sky, everything. He held me while mom slept, and she held me while he watched. They love me more than anything and would die for me. I know this to be true because I know when someone is lying. It's part of growing up with a—with a condition. My parents never lied, at least not intentionally, and even then it was only to protect me from knowing that all of this was real and that, someday, I would have to give them up. But I know there's a lot more than that, isn't there?"

Livvy looked at Vasa expectantly, then turned her accusatory glance to Saiinov, but it was Prista who delivered the truth in her quiet, thin voice.

"The book isn't just questions and answers. It isn't even a spell, or not from any school that I recognize. I think it was put here, just as you were, because the entire world is spinning on an axis around us, and you, and Windhook. Whatever cracked the planet below into fire and death started here, and that means that it can end here, too." Prista stared out into the night, falling silent even as Livvy's wings rustled with nerves. "I have to wonder if we see a foreshock of the Evocation in this little beast," she said, looking at the scorpion thoughtfully. "Still, if Selinus is at fault and they're gone? I can only conclude they've set something in motion that doesn't require their hand to control it, not that they ever could."

"Selinus, you say? Do you have any more sources to ask as to what they might be doing?" Livvy asked. She was fishing for something specific while drawing lazy circles on the cover of the book.

"I have . . . unexplored options that will confirm my

suspicions, but yes. Selinus is where this began," Maev drawled, and there was something dangerous in her tone, like rocks just under the water.

Livvy's face clouded, cleared, and then she smiled like a man at the gallows. "I think you'd better get going then. Maev. You're going to need a lot of help at the edge of that storm, and I'm going to be the one to give it to you. Well, me and about a thousand battle angels, but you get the picture. So, you better get ready."

"Why?" Maev asked, unblinking.

"Because I'll have a lot to say on the other side." Livvy opened the book to the gasps of everyone in the room, releasing a crimson spark that curled around her finger like a serpent. The light bloomed within her hand, firing up through her body with the glow of a dying ember. She cried out, went rigid, and stood up hard enough that her chair flew across the room to shatter against the wall in a splintering crash.

"It's so dark—"

She fell as the world vanished and silence came to take her.

CHAPTER TWENTY-THREE:

REUNION

She knew the smell first. It was old books and paper and carpet, hints of coffee and the cologne of a patron who'd passed by on his way to read the magazines, hanging glossy in their plastic covers.

The sensation was like a bolt of lightning that began in her eye and ended at her chest as memory washed over Livvy, ending in a warm tide.

If I'm here, then he must—

"Turn around, Liv."

She froze, aching to see, but fearing the possibility that it was all a dream made specifically to break the beautiful song of the heart he'd given her.

"It's real. You can turn around," he repeated, soft but insistent.

She began to rotate as the gears of her hope made her eyes, then shoulders, and then her feet begin to move, slowly, and then whirling with a strangled cry as his face came into view. Black hair, black eyes, skin of gold, and a furtive smile that told her she could reach out. He was real.

"Livvy," he said into her hair, crushing her to him in arms that were the one true thing she missed while living with the angels. He smelled right, he felt right—she wobbled in his grip, her knees gone watery at his touch.

She had no wings. His arms were tight to her body as they withdrew only far enough to come together in a kiss that went from hesitant to crushing in the flash of a memory. It was everything she'd wanted, and the world went bleary from her tears when they surfaced, far from slaking their thirst for each other. The kiss was enough, and could never be enough. Even as she looked at him, studying the planes of his face, she knew that the Library wasn't real and Keiron was still gone.

"Why here?" she asked, and the balance of her pain hung on that one question.

He shrugged, looking for the words. "It was where you were born, and it seemed like the right place to continue."

A tiny frown creased her brow. "Continue what?" Their hands intertwined, their feet touching. Her eyes flickered across his face, drinking in details.

"Let's sit, in our alcove. There are things we need to say." He waved, and they were in the small area where they'd first kissed. The feelings of their inchoate attraction rushed back, leaving her warm with memory. Outside the windows, there was sun, instead of the brooding clouds that had marked each day during her first visit to Keiron's construction of pure will. As one, they sat with their knees touching.

Between them, there was only the Book of January, the vague space beyond them fuzzed into bland shelves and walls a few feet away. Their world was small now but filled with each other. Reluctantly, Livvy felt her eyes pulled to the latent menace of Vasa's discovery, feeling her breath catch at the first good look of what she knew would be her undoing.

The Book of January lay open, its vellum pages bright and clear save for some bold, small print. Every word was drawn with ink the color of midnight, the letters somehow difficult to see from a direct glance.

"I'd rather not touch that again," she confessed.

"You don't have to. That's why you brought me here." He grinned, and the boy in him came back. "It's your purpose, Liv. It's what you are meant for, and that continues through the book. You know what it is?"

"A spell?"

He shook his head. "More than that, just like you are more than a girl, who became Heartborn. Tell me what you're feeling, okay? Let all of this go away." He snapped his fingers, and they sat in a circle of warm light, the Library a distant memory. Leaning forward, he was inches away. There were flecks of gold in them she'd never seen before, and she wondered if they were stars or just part of some dream.

"Tell me how you feel." His invitation was gentle but clear.

The question hung between them, a vague menace that threatened the perfection of their golden circle. Livvy closed her eyes, opening them only when he touched her wrist.

"Keiron, I'm scared." With those words, she opened the truth to his light, only to have him lean even closer.

"I know. Why? Is it this?" He pointed to the book, where the outline of a crescent moon began to emerge on the page. Shy at first, it took shape in bold, hidden strokes, the ink a perfect match of the silver moon rising in the east, even at that moment.

"What?" But the spell wasn't done, she saw, because whatever unseen hand drew the moon began a complex design just above the canted angle of the waxing crescent. Keiron said nothing, and the silence between them was total. In swift, decisive marks, the delicate sketch filled in from mere lines, to shades, and finally, with a flourish, the last burst of color flooded the page. Spilling from somewhere else, the gold and silver gave depth and shadow to something Livvy had only read in the stories of her childhood.

A crown.

"Do you understand?" Keiron asked, his voice as distant as a passing cloud.

"A moon? A crown? I can't *rule* anything, let alone some distant rock. This is—it's cruel, even for sorcery." Her disgusted tone told Keiron what concerns she had about the art of magic and its practitioners.

"Livvy." One word, and a yawning pit of possibility within it. Keiron took her hands again. They shook in his. Whatever he was going to say, she didn't want to hear. She wanted to go home, and not just to Windhook. Home, even if it meant no wings and no breath. Fighting to live, but in a place where she belonged and *far* away from being anything other than herself.

"No." Her answer. Flat, brittle. Honest.

He changed tack. "What do you think of my family?"

Her eyes went round, but she answered. There was nothing else to do, not there in the depths of a spell that told her lies among terrible truths. "I don't trust your parents, but I understand them. Habira is kind but dangerous. The twins are immersed in their work and only look for the relationship between magic and power. As for Prista? She might be broken forever."

"And Garrick?"

She smiled, a small thing, but real. "He's in love, but he doesn't know it. I think he'll be fine if he survives."

"I'm happy to know that someone has pushed him to grow. I never could." He spoke without regret.

"I've loved watching it happen. He speaks kindly now— not always, but he knows there's a world outside himself.

I won't tell him this, but I'm proud of him."

"I *definitely* would avoid saying that to him," he advised.

She coughed with laughter. "Don't I know it. I think he'd regress just from the sheer spite of knowing that someone likes him. Someone other than Danila, that is, which will play out in its own time." She began toying with his fingers, sensing that their time was running out. "I'm just a girl, you know, but now I have wings and a heart." Her face began to close up, weighted by the distance between her former life and the here and now.

"You were never *just* a girl, Liv." He took her hands, looking down. His golden skin. Hers, pale. They fit. "Do you know how long seventeen years can be?"

A spark of anger flared in her but burned out when she saw his face. It was open, serious. He loved her and was looking for something.

"I know exactly how long it is. Every breath, every missed heartbeat. Watching mom and dad sick with worry, looking down at me and telling me to breathe in and out, like a song." She began to cry, not from the pain, but because of what they had endured. They lived it with her, and then they were brave enough to let her go, just like Vasa and Saiinov had been with the boy who held her hands as if he was made for it.

"Do you feel guilty? You shouldn't," he assured her.

She shook her head, freeing the hair on her neck to move as if alive. The air around them seemed to swirl, though she couldn't be sure if the effect was real. "I did, for a long time. My dad broke down once and told me how they cared for me in ways I didn't even realize. I found out he had been a soldier and asked him if it was scary. I think I was ten or so?" She smiled, full of sweet admiration for the man who had held her, pointing at birds and clouds every night in their back yard. "Dad was quiet, and the room got cold from my question. He told me that war had been nothing to him because being my father made him understand what real danger was, real fear. Terror, naked and raw, coming like a thief in the night to steal my breath and then my life. By extension, *his* breath, *mom's* life. He said waiting for my heartbeat to stabilize was the longest night of his life, crammed into a span of minutes. His hands shook while he explained all this, a scene of me on the kitchen table, lungs heaving and face too pale to be alive. I would want to cry but couldn't, and he swore that, if he could have given me his own heart right then, he would've done it without a second thought. He lived for me, and mom, and together, somehow, they dragged me through the years, creating a cautious girl who counted her steps and breaths and wondered if today was the day we got the call for a heart."

She cried freely now, a steady spill of tears too powerful for her to resist. The past had her now, a stream of memory flashing past, wicked with pain and echoing loss. When she lifted her eyes to him, they were bleary but grounded. She held on through the force of will alone, and in her, Keiron saw what the book knew. There was greatness in Livvy, and his heart belonged to her in ways both real and spiritual.

"I'm so sorry you had to endure that." He didn't know what else to say.

"It's not me, you understand? It was them. I could leave at any moment if my heart gave out, but they would've lived on, and now I'm here. How is that fair?" She coughed again then covered her mouth in horror as the words settled in her mind.

"It's alright, Liv. I would do it again." His assurances did nothing to mute the realization that she complained to her heart donor about loss and pain. "I mean it. Just like your parents, no thought, no hesitation. There's no doubt in my mind that I did what I was meant for, and that you'll do the same." Their foreheads were touching, but his skin felt cool. She was losing him, or the book was losing control of the illusion. She chose to believe the latter because anything else was too much.

"I feel like an imposter with—with your family, and these wings. The sword. All of it, it's unnatural. I love books, and my cat, and sitting with my parents under the tree, feeding the fish. I'm not built to be a queen or a warrior born from the light of a moon I can't touch. It's not real, Keiron. None of it is real to me, and it might not ever be."

He noticed her tears were drying into freckled tracks, hints of a storm that had passed them by. "Is this real?" He touched her heart. The beat was strong, quickening slightly under his fingertips to reveal a desire for so much more than stolen kisses in a room made of dreams. She could deny it, but that would be a lie. Livvy didn't lie, and she wouldn't start now, not with so much at stake.

"Yes." Her answer was low. Steady.

"Then *that* can be real, too," he stated, pointing to the drawing, now slick with color and light. The book seemed to pulse with life, sensing that she was beginning to understand.

She waited, thinking, and when she spoke, her voice was that of a woman, not a girl. The dam within Livvy broke, letting her potential rush downstream to crash through the blockades that had kept her quiet and still for all those years.

"There's going to be a war, and it's between my world and yours—ours," she corrected, eliciting a grin from Keiron "I know there will be spells, and death. I know there will be falling angels." She inhaled, letting the breath trickle through her nose to clear her head.

"Many falling angels," he growled.

"Will I see you again?" She watched him, still conditioned to look for the lie, but there was nothing but hope and love in his mood.

"Maybe. If you ever find a spare heart, call for me. I can always find wings." His smile was sly but sweet. There was a possibility if only time and sorcery were theirs to rule. In a way, he liked her chances because the aspect of Keiron that sat before her could see more than reality. He saw potential in a long, winding ribbon through places and events she couldn't begin to imagine.

Livvy leaned forward, kissing him with an aching tenderness that was all things wrapped up in a goodbye. It was a kiss filled with promise and ending, and he knew it. If they met again, it would be due to Livvy finding a way to change time itself, and she wasn't going to rule it out. He was worth it. *They* were worth it.

She took his hands again. "I can fly, but I don't know how to do the one thing I need right now."

"Anything." He meant it.

Her eyes went dark, thinking of what lay ahead. "Tell me how to fight."

CHAPTER TWENTY-FOUR:

ARCHITECT OF THE SKY

*B*righa watched as the goddess paced, hands clasped behind her back. While she spoke to Brigha, she would free one hand to punctuate a statement, pointing or cutting the air with confident motions as she drove home ideas and needs for the upcoming invasion, or what was shaping up to be more of like total war. She kept the scepter behind her back, favoring her pale hand to do the work of emphasizing her vision for the world of angels.

And it was most certainly war.

As the plan began to unfold, Brigha quailed, thinking that her arrogance had been wholly misplaced in the face of this unknown being. Her goals—a dominant house, then perhaps control of the sky- all paled in comparison to what the goddess believed to be a foregone conclusion. They walked through the valley, scattering peasants like leaves before an oncoming storm, followed by Arad at a respectful distance. Even he sensed that great changes were at hand, choosing not to utter one sound over the next hour as they wound their way ever lower into the remains of a great lake. In the dim past, the waters had once lapped at the edges of the valley. Now, only a small stream flowed, though it was nearly deep enough to cover an ox that crossed just to the north, its great head tossing in irritation at the inconvenient bounty of running water.

At a vague point, the soil turned to muck, and Brigha noticed an array of holes, small tools, and the odd stack of dun-colored mud, piled in strange shards. The goddess took note of the scene with a bemused expression, waiting before what could only be a row of primitive kilns.

"How much protection will you need to create and keep the corridor between worlds safe and open?" The goddess didn't look at Brigha, forcing the angel to acknowledge her inferior status. It was a small thing, but to the vain Brigha, it was a deep cut at her ample pride. The knowing smirk on the goddess' lips revealed that she knew it too. Bringing the prideful to heel was her specialty, and her experience in the matter was vast.

"Opening the corridor, as you call it, is simple. Keeping it open in a permanent state is going to be a challenge." Now it was Brigha's turn to smile, a wintry display of teeth that had nothing friendly about it.

"What do you need?" The goddess sounded deceptively neutral, perhaps even caring.

"If anything happens to me, the spell collapses. Our sorcery doesn't work extant of our living spirit. In short, if you kill me, everything you've planned will tumble in a firestorm of magical energy and howling wind. This *place* will be inundated with rains, and lightning will scorch the soil down to rock. I should add that if the storm is allowed to rage unabated, not even you will escape its fury." Brigha finished with a smug twist of her mouth, watching the serene face of the goddess for a reaction.

"So, you'll need to be protected. Cosseted, even, and at any cost." The goddess waved a hand at approaching workers, led by the relentless oily cheer of Arad. He nodded once in understanding and began directing the column of slender, harried men onto the edge of the mud flats. Without pause, they began filling primitive molds, shaping the mass of globular muck with their hands in a practiced motion brought about by years of repetitive labor.

"What are they doing?" Brigha asked, a note of uncertainty pressing into her voice. She didn't like the men or their inscrutable task. She hated the valley and everything in it, but she feared the goddess, who refused to acknowledge the fact that a dead Brigha was little more than an invitation to disaster.

"They're a test crew. Now that I know what we need, I'll begin recruiting other, more suitable groups of workers for my vision. This is an old place, filled with people who know the old ways. Those men are brick makers, and their work has only begun. Walk with me. I've something to show you." The goddess moved off toward the lowest point of the area, a wide, flat section of land that was suspiciously clear of life. When she stopped, Brigha looked around with suspicion. There was nothing to see, and therefore, nothing to infer regarding whatever machinations the evil being had in mind.

"I won't live in the mud, so you can stop this plan right now if you think I'll capitulate to your wishes. I'll die first." Brigha's jaw was set, her eyes flashing. In the moments since they'd begun their little stroll, her mind had gone from fear to resolve. She wouldn't allow the goddess to force her into the dirt like a common beast, and any hope of returning to the skies of her future were fading like water through sand. Now, she could only hope to negotiate the best position in what looked to be an eternal war- a conflict she was losing, but only for the time being. She could bide her days, or years if need be, but, eventually, Brigha trusted that her natural vindictiveness would win out. First, she would find a way to twist the goddess to her purpose and win her freedom. After that, she could concern herself with the skies around House Selinus, if it still rode the winds when she broke free to return. A warm rush of possibility filled her mind, and for the first time since her sister had been cut down, Brigha laughed.

"Is this funny to you, angel?" The goddess watched her with eyes as flat as any serpent's, their black centers matte and unreadable.

Brigha's smile faded, but her spirit remained buoyed. Somehow, she would survive. "No, but there is merit to be found here. It's up to me," she said, jabbing herself with a thumb, "to discover it in the midst of this muck. I'm sure it's here somewhere." Wiping her hands together, she reached in for the shell that would open the door between places, and presumably, the chance she needed to defeat the implacable angel with wings that smelled of death.

"I can assure you, it is. In fact, you're standing on it. This is the spot where you'll crack the sky and give me my door. Right here, right now. Begin." To emphasize her point, the goddess placed her scepter under Brigha's chin, lifting her eyes so that their gazes met. The scepter felt colder than anything Brigha had ever known, a chill so rabid that in seconds, her teeth chattered uncontrollably.

She made her decision, choosing to fight another day, and in a means that would allow her a chance at victory. There was no doubt she would taste steel if she drew on the goddess, so with a small, vague nod, Brigha withdrew the spiral cowrie and lifted it high overhead. The punishing sun caught at the silver ribbons running inward, setting a brilliant light up and out from the shell like a penumbra of silver mist, surging skyward in an ever-narrowing beam.

Brigha furrowed her brow with effort. What had been

TERRY MAGGERT

simple in her skies was now a massive drain of her power, locking her legs in place as if she were in the thrall of a summer storm. Sweat began to bead on her skin almost immediately, and in less than a minute, rivulets of perspiration sluiced down her cheeks to stain her armor dark with the color of labor. Her muscles protested, shaking under the intensity of an effort that married magic and will together on the battlefield of her body. Her hair began to lift, forming a halo of gossamer ribbons that moved like a school of fish, darting about according the pressure of unseen forces that made the very ground around them begin to hum with latent energy.

"I—I cannot--" she began, but the goddess stepped forward with a skin of wine, opening the stopper and tipping the cold liquid to Brigha's mouth. In utter shock, she drank without thinking, licking her lips and nodding thanks before realizing to whom she gave gratitude. There was no time for a frown, and her muscles couldn't have shifted even if she'd wanted them to. Every fiber of her body was tensed like the strings on a loom, taut and growing tighter to that place where they sing just before breaking.

With a tortured cry, Brigha lifted from her feet, boots barely scraping the wet earth. A beam of light shot forth to crack the sky open in a wound of pale golden light, with red and blue sparks dancing along the hideous opening in a show of wild power that was never meant to be used.

Brigha remained still, humming with energy and locked in her awkward position as she held the shell aloft like a statue paying homage to an unseen goddess of the sky.

It was as she feared. The power was too great, and she would be trapped in the feedback loop between *now* and *then* unless the goddess—or anyone—could knock her free of the spell's grip.

"Perfect," cooed the goddess, taking a short spear from one of the men who encircled Brigha. The soldiers close to hand were better fed, with clean tunics and expressions of competence on their dark faces. With a smile, the goddess drove the spear through Brigha's foot, pinning her to the ground like a collector might save a butterfly. Silently, one of the men handed the goddess a second spear, allowing her to repeat the strike in the other foot. Before Brigha could cry out, a leather thong was wrapped around her mouth, silencing her even as she battled against the spell that could burn her alive if she faltered in the slightest. It had been a risk on the part of the goddess, but one she needed to take.

Brigha could not be allowed free motion at any cost. Such a thing was now impossible, courtesy of the two spears that held her fast in the mud. The light of her spell shone forth into the heavens, brilliant and true. The door held.

The goddess kicked at a loose rock, turning slowly to assess the scene once again. She pointed down, at the base of Brigha's feet.

"Begin here, and don't delay. I expect the walls to be higher than my head by sundown. You'll leave a shaft of light wide enough to reach the ground. I want a clear line of sight from the earth to sky at all times, and if necessary, have those oafs build the walls like a cone. Let me be clear, lest I have to soak the earth with blood. There *must* be a line between the angel and the storm at all times." The goddess' voice boomed with authority as she pointed at Arad and the other men, who began kicking and lashing furiously at the columns of slaves arriving under similar treatment from men in leather chest pieces. The overseers were brutal figures carrying whips they clearly knew how to use.

"How high will we go, my lady?" It was Arad, eyes downcast but smiling. He was convinced he'd thrown his lot in with the winning side. To a weasel like him, it was the assurance of a life he'd only dreamed of, if he could stay alive in the presence of the goddess.

She looked out over the plains of endless mud, envisioning a tower of such height that it split the heavens. It would have to be enormous to protect her pet under any circumstances. To close the corridor was not an option, and for the first time in centuries, the goddess smiled with genuine joy. There was endless work to be done, and plenty of hands to do it.

Looking upward, she spoke without looking at the sniveling Arad. "Until we block the sun, or reach their skies. Whatever comes first."

CHAPTER TWENTY-FIVE:

RISING

" Liv?" The voice was urgent, worried. She tried to process who or what they wanted, but the world kept pulsing in and out like a distant siren. Through gritted teeth and will, she made everything center, grow calm, and hold fast.

Shaking with the effort, Livvy opened her eyes. It was Cressa, but she wasn't alone. All of Windhook stood over her, their faces pale with worry. Saiinov reached out to touch her forehead as if he expected her to implode. When he saw she was warm and dry, he smiled.

"I'm not going to shatter, you know." Livvy sounded peevish, even to herself.

"I didn't expect you to. We're simply glad to have you back." He looked meaningfully over his shoulder, where the Book of January sat on the table. It was open, pages down. Discarded.

"How long?" Livvy's head felt clear if a bit sore.

"Ten minutes. Not long, but too long for some of us," Vasa said, coming into view above. Livvy realized she was prone, on the floor.

"Help me up," she directed, and grasping hands gently lifted her to a sitting position. Her head swam, but only briefly, and someone thrust a glass of wine into her hand. She sipped cautiously before turning her head in a gentle motion. "It's still attached, so I must be alive. This is good," she added, draining the glass and putting her hands on the floor. She felt more stable by the second, and it was welcome.

Every face watched her now, bursting with questions. Before anyone could speak, she looked at Maev and Utipa. In a voice that crackled with authority, Livvy addressed them, not as betters or even equals. Livvy told them what she could do, and what she might be. There were frowns and doubts on the faces of everyone save Cressa, who seemed to grasp that Livvy's arrival, like Keiron's sacrifice, had been no accident.

In clear points, Livvy explained what the Book of January meant to her and Windhook. She made certain to be clear that the spell had been lying in wait for a vessel, much like Keiron's heart, and that only an alignment of the stars brought her here, where she could help the people of her present.

And her future.

Livvy felt herself growing with each sentence, letting the pulsating confidence radiate outward as her heart kept the beat of a girl who was more than a mere blood daughter. She spoke to them as potential allies during the next phase of her life, an undefined idea sparked by a spell, a moon, and a crown. When she finished, there was only one thing left to say.

"You understand that I cannot tell Saiinov and Habira how to fight, or how Vasa should use the depths of a magical power beyond my comprehension? I'm a glorified mechanic, and I'm here to facilitate, not dominate. I saw—possibilities, while in the grip of the book's magic. Nothing more. Utipa, how long did your council rule? Maev, how many swords answer to you?" These were rhetorical questions, but well placed. They illuminated the changes brought about by Livvy's immersion in the Book of January, leaving the room quiet with contemplation while she continued working out the details of her experience.

When Livvy stood, there was none of the awkwardness she'd endured with her wings during the first days after her arrival. She was born to them now, just as Windhook was an irreversible part of her life, no matter what the coming fight might bring.

""I thank you for your generosity with regard to my expertise, daughter." Saiinov's rumbling demur covered his laughter, but the smile he wore was nothing short of brilliant. "However, as a Skywatcher, I'd be remiss if I didn't ascertain your value to Windhook and the skies in general. You're a new thing, Livvy, born of the moon and my own son's heart. That means you're valuable in ways we cannot understand." He straightened, and Livvy saw the general in him once again. When he took Vasa's hand, Livvy experienced a flash of uncertainty as to how she could ever be a weapon in the world where these people lived and fought, but she crushed such doubts with a gentle shake of her head. She belonged here, and her purpose would reveal itself in the course of war, just as her love for Keiron would sustain her no matter what happened next.

"I know that we fight for the survival of the skies, and any connection to the past must be controlled. In the wrong hands, it's nothing short of the apocalypse. I can't tell you why this is true, but the Evocation was no accident. The connections between here and then cause a kind of inversion, and it's fatal to every House in the air. It will kill life as we know it, and the remains of our Houses will fall to the earth, flaming and at the mercy of whatever waits under the clouds. We can discuss reasons later, but for now, I will stand with you and fight, so that we might have another day in the sun to chart our future," Livvy declared, and it was the confirmation Windhook needed to understand that the war with Selinus was nothing short of an extinction event.

Cressa stood by Livvy, hand on her sword. When she spoke, it was in the resigned tone of a soldier leaving for battle. "Fight now, and win. We can save the world again if we have to."

"Let's hope once is enough," Livvy said, but no one countered her wish, and she knew her fight was only beginning.

CHAPTER TWENTY-SIX:

BATTLE FLAGS

" Impressive, isn't it?" Maev was smiling, one brow quirked as she surveyed the sky filled with battle angels and their various mounts. She stood easily on Electra's pier, wearing twin swords clasped to each hip, their hilts plain, but well-worn. Around her stood or hovered an array of forces that defied explanation. Arranged by house and skill, there were entire wings of Scholars, their various tools of arcana already in hand. Vasa noted wands, staves, sorcerous daggers and even a trio of grim angels from House Atlas, carrying short spears that pulsed with magical energy verging into the ultraviolet. Some flew about in nervous circles, others stood silently, waiting to board the dozens of windships that would transport the army to the outer reaches of the growing storm. Sails snapped in the constant winds, and angels swarmed over the decks of each craft, adjusting and readjusting each length of rope that kept the craft buoyancy neutral along the pier. Some ships were painted the color of flame, others in the muted tones of Houses long since fallen. They'd spared no expense to see to it that every battle angel arrived at the front with rested wings and full stomachs. Armies do not move on will alone, and House Windhook knew this.

Among the combatants were Watershapers, including

Vesta and Banu, and four of Matriarch Torga's sour-faced daughters within their ranks, every girl wearing an expression of barely contained disgust at the need for their collusion. House Lixa did not play well with others, but they could certainly fight, and for that, Windhook and the others were grateful. Torga's daughters could open a hole in any defense, given enough time. Since no one truly understood the storm's threat, having Watershapers who could twist the sky made everyone breathe a bit easier. Owning the elements meant stopping the storm, and *that* opened a path to the sisters of house Selinus and their sorcerous trap.

In the midst of the growing chaos, Vasa regarded Maev with open respect. It took a steel spine to wage war for a living, let alone consider nearly a thousand angels in full armor as anything less than a spectacle. In the centuries since the Evocation, the arrayed forces around Electra represented the largest army ever assembled, and she was certain that many of them didn't fully grasp the danger of House Selinus and the storm they'd created.

They would understand soon enough.

In the previous hours, three more reports of missing angels trickled in, lending even more credence to the idea that Selinus had to be removed from the skies, no matter what the cost.

And they were waiting on Windhook for orders.

Saiinov raised his voice in a raw bellow of command. "Soldiers, board. You've the order of battle once we debark—do *not* approach the storm until the Watershapers have punched through the outer walls. Watch for unseen threats, and never turn away from your squad. More than one hundred angels are already missing and presumed dead. Do *not* be the next to die." He looked them over, wondering how many would be alive at the end of the day. "Do your job, and fight within your chosen field of expertise. You are the finest warriors in the sky. Now, reclaim what is ours and close this unholy gate to ruin!"

As one, a thousand angels roared into the winds, their voices ringing off the whorled surface of Electra. Flashing wings and weapons filled the air with light and noise as squads, wings, and individuals found their ships and boarded, faces grim or exultant with the promise of incipient battle. In a series of smooth motions, windships began to roll away from the pier at a sedate pace. Within seconds, they gained speed, their sails straining with the bellows of wind as they entered open air.

Livvy stood in awe of the spectacle. Angels strung bows or placed spears across their backs, the heads gleaming wickedly in the morning sun. Some sharpened swords or coiled boarding ropes, and others merely stood still, letting the air move around them as they prepared their minds for battle. Every color of armor was at hand, dozens that Livvy had never seen before. The same was true of the angels. There were Easterners, like Cressa—each of their squads seemed to favor the short, vicious spears that were so effective at hunting smaller creatures in the clouds. She saw olive-skinned angels with shaved heads, their eyes golden brown and keen. On a triad of wide ships with green sails, angels with skin the color of midnight busily assembled crossbows that fired two arrows at once, the heads rounded and heavy. Their task was to handle anything armored, and they were fully prepared to bring down any threat that proved immune to the lighter weapons many angels preferred.

It was the mounted cavalry that took Livvy by surprise. On a flat decked ship of medium length, no less than twenty Airdancers rested in full saddle, their wide, colorful flanks flashing nervous messages to and fro.

"Airdancers? I thought Windhook was the only house that used them as mounts?" Livvy asked Utipa, who stood next to her watching the army take wing.

"There are few who can gain the trust of such animals. You're looking at the Lancers of House Cygnus. They fly at suicidal speeds and have uncanny accuracy with those long spears. They'll be the vanguard for any large scale action we might face, but either way, I'm glad they're on our side. See the stirrups, just there?" She pointed to thin strips that ran around the broad, undulating animals who looked like nudibranchs from a forgotten ocean. "The animals have a hidden jet of air that can be triggered by stress. The riders will accelerate into combat and clear a path wider than their spear can reach. I've seen them in action, once." Utipa made a show of shivering. "It was over before it began. They'll see first blood if I'm any judge of their mood from this distance."

As the ship passed by, Livvy took note of the animal's general movement and mood. Though they had no discernable face, their body language seemed eager, and the light cells flashing down their sides beat out a cheery pattern in bright, colorful waves.

"How do they stand there?" Livvy couldn't see any legs. They beasts seemed to hover.

"Gas neutral. They're floating unless they want to crush something in a charge. Like I said, effective allies." Utipa admired the creatures and their riders before turning to Livvy. "Enough of them. Have you considered staying on board, no matter what happens?"

"Why?" The blurted answer came out before Livvy could think. She sounded angry, even to herself.

Utipa motioned that they should make their way aboard the *Alu*, the personal windship of Outpost Electra. It was a behemoth, with a deck so wide that it felt like stepping onto land for Livvy, who found the pier to be both narrow and unsteady. The decks were organized and free of clutter, much like the outpost. Habira, the twins, and Vasa all walked aboard together, followed by Cressa and Saiinov, who were deep in a conversation that demanded they both examine a long knife with great interest.

The business of war was demanding, and there was little chatter among the crew and soldiers who were already on board. Looking up into the sun, Livvy watched as the great sails were lowered, filling with wind as the rigging began to sing. With a sickening lurch, they were away, leaving the long pier behind in less time than it took Livvy to notice Theobald waving to them from the control house above the base of Electra, where the dock connected.

Livvy felt herself wave, though she knew he couldn't see—but his smile widened as he shouted something meant for her. *That'll teach me to assume*, she thought, returning to the orderly frenzy of the deck. A shadow passed in front of her eyes as Theobald continued his wave.

Danila smiled down at her from the railing, casually balanced on her toes like a dancer. "Thought I might join you for the spectacle."

"Danila! What—why are you leaving Electra?" Livvy felt herself say before putting a hand over her mouth.

"Dad will be fine without me, and I have some insights to war. I'm not just a shopkeeper, you know," she told Livvy, then leaped down to land silently on the bobbing deck.

"Sorry, didn't think it through. What are you going to do?" Livvy's blush began to fade immediately when she realized her friend wasn't angry but grinning coyly.

"I'm rather handy with a bow if I do say so. I'll stay on deck and guard the *Alu*, but, in a pinch, I can throw some defensive spells around. We train for contingencies on Electra."

Livvy hugged her, glad to have the addition of Danila's cheerful competence. "Thank you."

"Don't thank her yet. We haven't even gotten underway," said Utipa, holding the railing with hands that itched for war. She was a realist, if not an enthusiast.

"How long will we sail?" Livvy asked, looking out into the blue.

"You haven't answered my question. Why not stay onboard?" The Factor's dark eyes widened as she gave Livvy a searching look. Her black hair was pulled into a severe knot, wrapped in a cord of shimmering scaled metal. It was a weapon, leaving no doubt as to her intentions for whatever House Selinus would bring to the field. The ensemble gave her a bright, capable look tinged with menace, and Livvy could see her as an attorney or judge in another life. Here, she was a warrior in a floating army filled with them.

"I didn't because I choose not to waste my breath, but I'll answer now." Livvy raised her voice slightly when she saw Saiinov and Vasa listening, turning his voice from that of a young friend into that of a fighter whose mind is made up. "I will leave this boat to fight whatever and whoever comes up out of the clouds. No one will stop me, nor will you get in my way. If you do, I can assure you the results won't be pretty. I may not be experienced with this thing," she looked at her sword, "but I know how to cut an apple in two. I have a heart of Windhook and my will. I have a thousand years of kinetic magic in me from a spell that would kill anyone else, and I aim to be in the thick of the fighting because I won't allow you to sacrifice yourselves for me twice. Is that clear?"

Vasa's laugh was low and filled with admiration. "I told you, love. She's no observer."

Saiinov offered Livvy his hand with great dignity, winking at Utipa's discomfiture at the depths of her passion for fighting. "I thought you might say as much. If you'll come with me, then? There's one more thing you'll need to join the fight."

"Where are we going?" It was a huge ship, with angels vanishing down a series of stairwells into unseen decks.

"The fo'csle." They wove through the crowd to the bow, descending a ramp into a wide, sunlit space that filled the entirety of the ship's first quarter. When her eyes adjusted, Livvy realized it was part gym, part armory.

"I have a sword," she protested, but Habira waved her off, impatiently pulling her to a wall, where weapons and sets of translucent armor rested on dummies made from boiled hide. "Oh." Her small reply was covered by the laughter of their group, who were clearly excited to try on their armor. Six sets of metal and hide armor waited, each a slightly different color and cut. The breastplates consisted of interlocking plates so thin that Livvy could see through them, like the delicate edge of a shell. Whatever had been done to the leather, it was sorcerous, leaving a pliable framework onto which scaled mail had been painstakingly sewn, one piece at a time. There was a set for everyone who would be in direct combat, save Prista. She was in the command tower of the *Alu*, where her analysis and skills might do the most good without exposing her to open magical warfare.

"Have you forgotten your visit to Rauta?" Vasa asked. The music of a hidden laugh ran through her question, and Saiinov smiled at the gentle reminder of Livvy's travels. She'd seen a great deal in a short time. She was about to see even more.

Livvy studied the armor in silence, save an occasional noise of approval—until she approached the set that could only be meant for her. Mute with awe, Livvy reached out to touch the armor, running a finger over the slick surface with a purely instinctive reverence. Slightly to one side, the suit was unique in every way, from the graceful curves to the artistry of the chest. Somewhere between a pearl and the strands of a nebula, the colors whirled and danced within the ethereal plates, molded perfectly to her size and frame, and each plate was designed to cover her body from head to foot. She began to count the pieces of the chest, her lips moving in silent wonder at the graceful pastiche forming the shape of a heart. When her finger brushed the heart shape, it moved like the scales of a Windbeast, perfect in its fit and purpose.

"May I?" she asked, but her hand already lifted the suit awkwardly upward, jerking the feather-light material with a soft rustle. "Sorry. Thought it would be heavy. Heavier, I mean. It's almost," she hefted the suit easily in one hand, taking its measure. "It's like air. But so tough!" Livvy rapped a knuckle against one of three overlapping shoulder plates that would protect her entire upper arm and back.

Habira motioned that she should hand the armor over. "Time to prepare. All of us, and fast. We'll be in combat before we're ready."

Obediently, Livvy waited for instruction, but Habira only lifted her arms and began to undress her in front of everyone mechanically. Flushing crimson, Livvy relived the first day of school, and birthdays where no one came to her party. Her throat tightened, and sweat broke out on her lip until Vasa put a calming hand on her shoulder.

"We'll all dress together, Livvy. Forget whatever is clouding your mind right now, and focus on this moment." Vasa's words were like a drug, soothing everyone around her as they began to hurriedly slip on their armor in movements learned over decades, centuries.

Habira began to slide the armor onto Livvy, leaving only her light shirt underneath. She kept an informative dialogue going, partially to calm Livvy, but also for her benefit. She was dressing a Heartborn for battle, and it might be the last time she ever held a part of Keiron in her grasp.

Sensing that, Livvy took Habira's hand when she put an arm into place, sliding hidden tabs together with a silent lock. "I don't plan on dying today. I'm not even sure what to do, but dying isn't on my list."

Habira stopped, leaving the family in motion as they tuned their suits to battle readiness. "I know. It's whatever waits for us. Down there."

"The storm?" Livvy asked.

"No, that's something I can understand. It's whoever is using the storm as a weapon. The missing angels are—we spend our lives training for war. We don't get taken by silent killers, so to lose a hundred fighters makes me think we're going to have a bad day if we aren't careful. The twins can punch down to the surface, and we'll have some access to whatever the source of magic might be, but it's a two-way path. Just as we expose the enemy, we are exposed to them. That transition will be the most dangerous moment of the fight."

With a final click, Livvy's armor was in place. She ran her hands over the chest where Rauta had worked the image of a heart into embossed segments, each one further protecting the vulnerable center of her body. She felt like a statue or a knight. Maybe both, though her first movements in the suit felt like she wore nothing at all.

"Good?" Habira asked. Behind her stood the family, their faces ripe with approval.

"I feel like I was made for this." Livvy started to dip her chin but stopped. That was a motion for someone who didn't exist. She looked at Vasa and Saiinov, considering her words with great care. "I can fight." She inhaled, slowly. "I can feel him, you know."

Vasa looked down, but Saiinov met her gaze as his eyes grew hot with the threat of tears. "I know you can, Livvy. We see it in your face. Between all of us and Keiron, and you, we're going to win. Trust us, and trust each other. Stay close and if ever you have the chance, strike first without hesitation. Remember, sorcery is almost always a single point. One spell. One source. You'll know it when you see it."

Saiinov handed Habira a small object wrapped in brilliant white hide. "There was a bit of extra material from Livvy's armor. Rauta sent this to you as a sort of gift."

With great care, she unwrapped a long, savage spear point, translucent and unearthly in its beauty. "It's exquisite." Nearly a foot long, it danced in the low light of the ship's hold, more art than weapon. Without a sound, she selected a short spear from a nearby rack, testing the heft with a practiced hand. Without fanfare, she removed the bone blade and seated her gift. In three swift turns, the hide and metal clasp held the new spear point in place, its edge glimmering with the untapped promise of violence.

"Now I'm ready, too. Don't forget, Liv. Whatever looks dangerous, cut." Habira nodded severely for emphasis.

"I will"—Livvy's promise was cut off by a deep,

shuddering groan as the ship began to list seriously, down and away in a stomach-clenching pitch. "What is it?"

A chorus of shouts rose to high-pitched fear as chaos erupted on the deck above. Unseen objects smashed into the planking above and to their sides as heavy, rolling sounds told of a ship in peril. It was a gravid moment before the screams died away to shouts of anger and the thumping of booted feet.

"Up and out," Saiinov said, turning to the hatch as it lifted to reveal muted sun and flashing lightning. "It seems the storm has come to us." He was calm, even quiet, urging everyone up the stairs, freed from the danger of going down in a ship without the chance to fly free. Emerging onto the *Alu*, the war party from Windhook was buffeted by swirling wind and the debris of countless ships coming apart under magical torment.

Vasa lifted her hands, weaving a complex spell of defensive magic even as the twins did the same in perfect syncopation. The captain's cabin was gone, sheared off in some unseen act of raw violence that left shards of wood and hide fluttering in the erratic lashing of a storm that blackened the air around them.

The howl of wind made speech impossible, leaving Saiinov with no choice but to use basic signals to urge everyone toward the shelter of a massive stump where the main mast had been only seconds before. "To the lee side!" Saiinov screamed, his words torn away into the raging clouds that enveloped the remains of the fleet. All around, ships were going down or exploding into showers of debris, their crews fighting a desperate battle to extend their wings and ride the wind to safety.

"Sarkany!" Habira shouted, pointing to the closest boiling storm cloud. It looked oddly substantial, a billowing gray wall that surged upward to enclose a nearby windship.

Before Livvy could ask, the Sarkany revealed itself. Long, red arms reached out of the cloud and seized a pair of battle angels trying to stroke downward through the mist. The creature that emerged was like no Windbeast Livvy had ever heard described. Longer than a ship, it was blood red, covered in glistening scales, and firing steaming vapor out of two tubes that extended grotesquely above its cruel mouth. The steam was cloying, thick, and toxic. Any creature flying into the miasma was slowed or rendered unconscious, letting the Sarkany feed at its leisure, which it was doing with gusto as the two angels were jammed into the coffin-like mouth.

As the ship began to list even further, the wind began to die, letting Saiinov speak once again. "We need to"—

Silence fell. A yawning hole of pure blue opened up beneath the foundering wreck of the *Alu* as dozens of Sarkany ringed the eye of the storm, spewing vapor and slaughtering angels with wanton fury.

"We're alone," Vasa said into the quiet. Her voice sounded like a violation after the roar of the wind, but it was true.

"Not completely," came the quiet voice behind them. Danila and Garrick stood with Maev, their armor already in appalling condition. Maev was cut over one eye, flicking the blood away with annoyance as it blurred her vision.

"Prista?" Vasa asked, stricken. Saiinov's intake of breath was audible to everyone on deck, or what was left of the deck.

Garrick shook his head. "Gone."

Vasa paled further, reaching out to Saiinov. They held hands in defiance of the hideous reality. Banu sobbed into Vesta's shoulder before wiping her eyes in a gesture that made her look like a child again. Their sister was dead, the fleet gone, and the battle hadn't started. All around them came the faint shouts as angels began to organize against the Sarkany and their murderous rampage. In flashes and shadows, they saw Spearwoods and Corvids riddle one with thrown weapons, then rush the beast as one and begin stabbing frantically. Then, the scene was replaced as the outer ring of wind moved the battle forward to reveal three angels firing arrows in a blur, ripping into the howling face of yet another Sarkany. The survivors were fighting back, but the eyewall was too dangerous to pierce. That left one choice.

"Down?" Cressa asked, looking into the swirling column of clear air that terminated in a dry, foreign landscape.

Saiinov's face was hot with rage. His eyes gleamed with a lurid hate that made Livvy take a step back. When he spoke, it was in the rasp of a parent with nowhere else to go. "To the end. To the finish."

"Can you fly?" Vasa asked everyone and no one. She shook her head to clear the glassiness in her eyes, but they were hooded with a loss that would settle in her bones, never to leave.

Muttered assent greeted her question, but no one knew what to do.

"I can." Livvy stepped to the shattered railing, pointing with her sword. "What's that?"

A thin golden light shot upward, dispersing into the outer ring of clouds. It started on the ground, of that much she was certain. The others moved forward to look at the anomaly as the beam fractured, reformed, and broke again, always terminating in the savagery of the ongoing storm. In the silence, no one spoke, assessing the sight through a lens of shock and loss.

"A spell," Vasa croaked. She squinted to adjust her sight

to its farthest capability, then added, "It's *the* spell. The one creating the storm. The one we're meant to end if it doesn't end us first."

"Just one? All of this from a single spell?" Livvy asked, incredulous.

"All of this death, and uproar. All of it. One being. One caster. One spell, which means I can end it," Vasa growled, stepping out into clear air as her wings spread with a spray of dust and debris. Saiinov followed, as did the twins and Garrick. Danila hesitated but joined him. Soon, it was only Livvy.

She peered into the atmospheric depths and *knew.* Down there waited her past, a place of heat and dust. A land of scorpions and power that called to her across time and distance, demanding that she descend in this column of quiet air and face her purpose.

She jumped, folding her wings to dive downward through the light of days, drawing her sword like a talisman meant to save the world. With her fall, she bent time to drive downward into the past, piercing years and centuries in a flickering blur. Behind her came Windhook and the sole remains of the Corvids and Crescent Council. Together, they fell, gaining speed until the earth began to give up details like hills, then dunes, then individual rocks.

A black shape detached from the barren ground, rising to meet them. Huge wings the color of midnight spread, folded, and spread again as the being launched itself upward at an impossible rate of speed. Gleaming blades reflected the line of light that punched downward through the storm, resolving into paired swords in the hands of a black winged angel with skin the color of death.

I have been waiting. The sounds exploded in Livvy's

head, rocking her in the air as she faltered, only to regain her direction with a herculean effort of will and trust. She was of Windhook, and there was no air in the sky that could best her ability to fly. Her pride and confidence kept her aloft long enough for her wings to catch up. Rage began to boil in Livvy, a feeling she knew nothing about.

"I am here," Livvy spat, knowing that the speaker would hear. Over her shoulder, two bolts of bright blue light sizzled past to strike at their attacker. Both missed, but a lance of ice cast by the twins shattered onto the dark angel's shoulder, spinning it out in a wild tangle of limbs.

The response was swift. Livvy's stomach dropped as the attacker rose again, even faster, hurling magic that shaded into the ultraviolet. Cressa screamed overhead, then Saiinov hurtled past to slam into the enemy at a suicidal speed. In an impossible move, he swept the enemy swords away and raked her with his weapon, leaving a spray of black feathers in the air even as he fought his inertia to turn around and attack again.

Saiinov was not unwounded. Blood sprayed from wounds in his leg and chest, his armor ripped in places from the impact of his airborne assault. With flagging strength, he fought to gain altitude and attack from below, but the goddess had other plans. In a blur she shot upward on a column of sorcerous power, slamming into Maev and Utipa who both cut downward with their swords. The clash sent all three combatants flying apart as Utipa's armor shattered, falling from her body like a discarded shell. Maev spun in place, launching a short spear up at the goddess with an inhuman throw. With an unearthly scream, the goddess beat higher as Maev's spear dangled from her left calf muscle, having pierced both armor and flesh to punch all the way through. As an afterthought, the goddess sent a wave of magical torment at the Corvid commander, who faltered in the air as she tried in vain to throw up a defensive wall against the shimmering attack.

Maev's wings began to smolder as she spun, and she howled in fury, lacing the air with expletives even as she threw a pair of daggers at the retreating form of the goddess, who was closing on Livvy and Banu with sickening speed. Utipa cast two spells in quick succession, neither landing on the goddess but serving their purpose. The respite was long enough that Vasa sent a vicious wall of flame to scorch the air where the goddess prepared to engage Livvy in a fight with swords. The battle unfolded in seconds, not minutes, and by the time Livvy could raise her sword to parry the dual weapons of the goddess, every member of the surviving war party was bleeding and wounded.

In a continual blaze, the magical column pulsed forth from the land below. Saiinov barked a command at the twins. "To the ground! Crush the spell at all costs!" As he shouted, he flew upward to strike at the goddess from below, suffering a horrific kick to the face. Doggedly, he grabbed the spear that pierced her leg, twisting savagely as she deflected a terrible downstroke from Livvy's sword.

Filled with rage, Livvy's first real taste of combat was a slashing cut from the goddess' silver blade. The force of it spun her around, throwing her arms outward like a doll as she fought to regain her balance. Wings snapping, Livvy's sight cleared in time to see a fist just before it struck her on the cheek.

"Mine!" The goddess roared as she struck Livvy again. "Mi"—

Saiinov and Utipa, their weapons deflected by her brilliant swordplay, slammed into the black-winged demon from opposing sides, but the goddess couldn't escape simple physics as their bodies delivered punishing blows. Vesta and Banu shot scalding lances of vaporous magic as the entire fighting group began to follow the goddess downward. She was losing altitude from the effects of battle, but still deflected the spells Vasa launched at her with repeated curses. Every spell that missed pounded the ground below with thunderous strikes, sending sprays of scalding mud and water outward in gelatinous jets.

Undaunted, Saiinov dove at the goddess again, stabbing forward in a lightning strike of his sword only to be rebuffed casually as she sent up a wall of ancient magic. Stars exploded around him as the strike was turned, wrenching his sword arm with a hideous crack. He began to fall, regained himself, and then started settling inexorably to the ground that rushed up to greet them. "Vasa! The source! Take the twins and crush that spell! End the storm; we have to get help!" Saiinov's shout was nearly lost to the growing roar in his ears. He faltered again, his sword in the offhand and wavering. Grit began to cloud his eyes as they neared the surface of a desert that was as alien to him as he was to it.

In a streak too fast to follow, Garrick made his pass, attacking from above in the glare of the midday sun. His cry of triumph was cut short as the goddess slashed him with both blades, parting his armor cleanly. The force of her blows froze him in space, leaving an opening for her follow through. With a meaty thump, she drove her knee into his temple, leaving him a fluttering wreck as he fought to control his landing. From above, the goddess showered him with ringing taunts as he plummeted, wings flailing like an infant.

Vasa folded her wings in a dive as the horror beneath her came into focus. They were hurtling toward a primitive pyramid, towering upward with a circular hole built into the middle of the hulking structure. Hollowed out in the middle, the shadowed central column was hemmed by mud bricks, scaling upward to leave a small, open space at the bottom. She could see through the spell's beam to the cloistered hollow far below, and the sight made her weep with pain.

It was an angel, mouth agape in a rictus of agony as the magical beam poured forth from her chest. She was collapsing inward, her tortured body wingless and pinned to the ground with spears in each foot. Vasa saw this from an altitude of nearly a thousand feet, and her eyes narrowed to focus on the inhuman scene of abuse that kept the storm alive and hungry. At the end of a circular tunnel, Brigha looked up into the sky, beseeching anyone who could see to end her suffering.

"It's an angel! The gateway is an angel!" She bellowed to her daughters, who were joined by Utipa in their headlong fall toward the broad, dusty plain. The decision was clear. Sick with grief, Vasa launched a killing spell at the open mouth of the angel as she drew close enough to see the jeweled tears in her haunted eyes.

As the carmine beam shot downward, the Brigha mouthed her thanks, closing her eyes in ecstasy as the spell struck home and knocked her sideways into the wall of her circular brick tomb. In an explosion of ash and bone, she was gone.

So was the spell. A deep rumble tore the sky as the last golden rays began dispersing into the outer cloud ring far above, but it would be some time before the tunnel could fully close. The fight raged on as Saiinov and the goddess fell together, Maev harrying her with thrusts from a broken spear shaft covered in black blood. They were losing because the goddess was still fighting, and the longer she lived, the worse their collective wounds would begin to slow them down. Even with the storm collapsing above, they had to kill a goddess of unknown power, and quickly lest she escape.

It could not be done. Habira soared into sight only to be crushed with an invisible spell of devastating power. As she slid past in a semi-conscious spin, a casual stroke of the goddess' sword slashed her wing, cutting feathers with a spiteful flick of her wrist. Now in freefall, Habira tried in vain to soften her landing, flapping her shredded wings before vanishing into a rising cloud of steam from the vaporized river.

Nearby, the twins continued to unleash their stunning power as Watershapers, their spells condensing all the water on the plain into destructive energy that reduced the pyramid to steaming mud.

The soaring structure collapsed in a drunken tumble as the giant bricks exploded from latent moisture deep in their stony cores, lashed to weakness by the sorcerous incursion of water. Rain appeared in skies that were clear and bright, sheeting sideways with the assistance of howling winds brought on from the sheer force of Banu and Vesta's training. They were masters of wind and water, and they unleashed every ounce of their will to pummel the citadel of pain that caused the deaths of untold angels high above. Their power held in the column of light and air that connected into the future, but it was fading. In the distant past of the plain, magic would not remain effective for long, and they could feel it slipping away.

"Above!" Screamed Utipa, who dodged away as the smoldering corpse of a Sarkany thudded into the growing plain of slushy mud. "We're winning!"

Another Sarkany fell, its body nearly sheared in two by

magical attacks. The animal slammed into the slouching column of a support wall, degrading the pyramid even farther. Its ribs sizzled with white light, lingering evidence of a spell well struck during the heat of battle.

Beneath the falling angels lay only scorched destruction. Wave after wave of magic punished the earth, setting fires and boiling away the small river. Mud exploded outward in a ring more than a mile across as the ruthless sorcery pounded the tower of brick and wood, finally collapsing with a roar of spattering earth and splintered timbers.

As a family, Windhook, Maev, and Utipa fell. Danila landed last, her wings torn backward by a languid wave of the goddess' hand. The unholy angel wasn't done exacting revenge for a reason none could understand.

No one except Livvy.

Bleeding and dizzy, she looked up, struggled to her feet, and swayed in the stinking humidity of the battleground. When her eyes locked with the goddess, Livvy knew fear. Around her, she saw flashes of wings, mud-spattered, singed and bloody. She would finish this fight on her own or not at all, and the creature before her radiated cold hatred of a kind she'd only seen once before. With a hand that trembled in anticipation, the goddess raised her scepter above Livvy, holding it over her like a benediction of hate.

Livvy closed her eyes, and let the rage burn inward.

CHAPTER TWENTY-SEVEN:

QUEEN TAKES PAWN

Livvy, forced into a kneel by the pain, looked up at the perfect rage of the goddess and once again felt the kind of fear she'd experienced every day while she waited for a heart. It was a chill that went into her marrow, a potential for death that stalked her like a ghost for her first seventeen years. She hated the memory, and fought to understand why, deep inside, a spark of something new began to glow.

The goddess drew back the scepter, now covered in blood, and brought it down on Livvy's cheek with a thunderous crash. Livvy's eyes filled with streaking comets of red agony as she tried to right herself, looking up through tears and a righteous fury that gave way to something far more damaging.

It was a pity.

It was not unseen by the goddess, whose eyes flickered like the hidden reaches of a distant storm. She drew her hand back again, but this time, it was the one holding the knife. When she spoke, her voice was a low, triumphant hiss. "I'm going to be a queen. More than a goddess, more than a toy, like you are. I know how to open the skies to my rule. I'll keep another stupid child in a new tower until the sun burns out, and the path between worlds will be open forever. It was done once. It can be done again."

Her laugh was fevered and desperate, every sound a hunger pang for something she'd wanted since the beginning of time. Above all else, the goddess wanted to be loved, rather than feared. Her withered heart meant she could not discern the two. Deep in the recesses of a mind gone mad for power, the goddess knew it, and it left her sick with unrequited need.

Livvy paid no attention to the blade, choosing to respond with something far more damaging. She chose the truth.

"Queens belong to everyone except themselves. That's what is—no, that is only *one* of the differences between us. I lived my entire life in fear, and then, for a short while, in the grip of a love so pure that it burned me, maybe even ruined me for the rest of my days. With each second, I could feel him, feel his heart, and I knew what sacrifice was all about. Being a queen or a ruler of any kind is a sacrifice that I never thought possible or could even imagine. That is, until Keiron. Now I understand why I have this heart. It wasn't to make me into a weapon because weapons are only used for one thing, to bring pain, and death, or fear. I don't want any of those things, but I'm not ashamed to admit that I see their purpose, too."

Livvy gave a rueful laugh, and it was the sound of a young woman under a great weight. "I'm not Livvy anymore, and you're not the incarnation of death. You were a god, of sorts, though I don't think you understand what that means. To be a queen is much like being a god. You belong to the people and the realm. You are trapped by the very ties that bind you to the people who seek your guidance, or a steady hand during times of storm and wind. I don't know if I can be that, but I know that I am capable of bending my knee to assume a responsibility that goes well beyond the satisfaction of my childish lust for power."

"You know *nothing* of godhood!" The goddess spat with a venom that split the air. Each word was a curse so vile it made most of those listening recoil with horror.

Most, but not Livvy. "Why me?"

"What?" The goddess held her hand, wavering in uncertainty. She was unused to being questioned, but that didn't mean she wasn't curious.

"Why have you chased me through a world and time? Is it because I got away? Surely you can't mean that of all the people you've come for. I'm the only one who slipped the noose. You're death incarnate. You're Thanatos or *Terezza* or Miss Henatis, or whatever idiotic name you've chosen this time around." Livvy's voice was low, calm. It infuriated Thanatos that she would be exposed, but the true rage came from Livvy's very existence. She had *belonged* to the goddess of death, teetering on the void for years only to be saved by a selfless boy with wings who knew, in his soul, that the blood of a queen pulsed in Livvy's veins. Somehow, they all knew, except Livvy, and that innocence made Thanatos quiver with hatred of a kind she had never known before.

She was going to savor taking this one. The heart, twice used and strong, would be kept in a box next to her throne, wherever that might be. Thanatos flipped the scepter around in a blur, exposing a silver plated tip on the base. It glistened with something evil, a concentration of the pain she would bring to Livvy's bright light.

Livvy tilted her head as a look of pity flooded her eyes, along with a slow smile of loss and melancholy. On her freckled face, red with effort, they didn't sit well. Livvy was meant for many things, but pity wasn't one of them. She'd lived with that look for most of her life, and wouldn't cause anyone else to suffer under such twisted mercy.

From her kneeling position, Livvy raised a hand, extending it out to Thanatos, who stared at it like a coiled snake. "I'm offering you a chance at peace, goddess. You can't win every time, and certainly not now. You wormed your way into the harbor that Keiron built for me, under a disguise, but you are exposed now. I know. We all know.We *are* going to bring harmony to the skies. With the help of my family, the lands Brigha connected us to will know peace as well, for I will not abandon these people to your devices. This I swear, so I ask you only once. Will you have peace?"

Thanatos' answer was a ringing laugh, echoing across the ruined plain of mud and debris. "I think not, child. I choose blood."

Livvy's face went blank, but a tear slid down her freckled cheek to streak the dusty skin. It was the essence of her, a young woman who would choose to avoid war at all costs, and death under all circumstances save one. When she spoke, it was in a tone that the angels would remember for all their lives, because it was the first order Livvy ever issued.

"Even the gods are wrong. You chose beauty over wisdom, and lust over logic. When the choice was between power and mercy, you failed. You've had an ocean of tears around you, purely from the darkness of your own flawed heart. You were weak, and now? You are ended." Livvy bowed her head as the goddess brought her hand down halfway, only to stop with a strangled, wet cry. From behind the goddess came Habira's laugh, tired yet triumphant as Habira's strike drove her spear directly through Thanatos' diseased heart. The scepter dropped neatly into Livvy's palm, sprayed black from the blood pouring off Habira's spearhead, its ethereal beauty now hidden in the oily residue of purest evil. She dropped it in disgust, stomping it into the mud with a savage kick. Livvy wanted nothing so heinous to touch her, let alone the symbol of a being who lived by taking joy through pain.

"Sorry, sis. I thought she'd never stop talking, so I had to shut her up myself." Habira rose from the earthen berm as Thanatos collapsed, her mouth moving in a soundless scream as the millennia of sin came home to rest in her bones, a tidal wave of agony that ended only when her body turned black, then gray, and finally to ashes. A dry, hot wind took the remnants of the goddess away, eventually to be carried by some nameless rivers all the way to the hungry ocean. In the end, Thanatos would be no different than her victims, whose ghosts waited for her in the tides, eager to question the harbinger of their pain. For Thanatos, eternity would be a long time, indeed. The dead had much to ask of her, and she had much to answer for.

"Habira, I never thought I'd say this, but I want to go back to Windhook. I want to go home." She sagged into her sister, who began waving to Vasa and Saiinov, dropping from the sky with exhaustion. Their armor was torn, scorched, and split, and both had faces grimy from the aftermath of the savage battle. Saiinov had a gash over one eye, and his right shoulder slouched dangerously low from a wicked separation. Vasa leaned against him, her face grave with lines of exhaustion and sadness. There had been enough death for a lifetime, and they would begin by leaving the fly-ridden plain now covered with muck, bones, and rivulets of ashen water.

High above, Vesta, and Banu rode Airdancers in a looping patrol, but they, too, were wounded. Most of

Vesta's hair was gone along with her helmet, and Banu's mount let out a piteous cry, its side opened to the air in a vicious wound from some well-placed blade or spell. No one was unscathed, and the remaining warriors would need a long time to recover from the battle for a place that would soon be lost to them, once Livvy closed the corridor. By an unseen signal, the remaining angels began to slip away into the eye of the storm, now a slowly turning whirlpool of gentle blue light.

Last to leave, Maev raised her sword in tribute, the light flashing on a blade that was chipped and bent from ruthless combat. With a piercing cry of victory, she passed up and through the diminishing circle of opportunity linking the two worlds. Livvy raised her hand in thanks to them as every survivor dipped their wings in tribute to their newest leader, a young woman who was becoming something far different from the hesitant girl who craved only a deep breath. Her powers were now beyond that of a Heartborn, proven in the forge of battle and tested by the bonds of an ethereal love so powerful it could draw from the light of the moon. She was Moonborn, and Heartborn, and Livvy. She was many things and all things to the people of the sky, who would have been slaves to an eternal monster had it not been for the shy girl from a time when wings were myths, and so was magic.

Livvy felt herself smile as the familiar feeling began to warm her chest, a sensation of purest love.

It is time.

"It is," she said to the wind and to Keiron.

Habira didn't have to ask what she meant; the set of Livvy's jaw was enough to reveal a truth that the skies would learn soon enough.

Standing to the side in a puddle of ashen sludge, Danila

sagged into Garrick, their faces streaked with dirt and ash. "I've seen all the bad," she said, taking his hand. There was hope on her face, an honest, brutal truth of the possibility that the moment might pass them by, never to be seen again. She knew that, now, and made her decision. She chose him, as he had wanted all along despite not admitting it to his soul. "Now, show me the good." His answering smile was the grimace of a survivor, but it was there. Together, Garrick and Danila turned their faces into the sun as the last of the storm dissipated high above. The final wisps vanished, torn apart by the eternal winds. They would follow the storm's echo to return home, but not yet.

They walked a few steps, steadying each other until the family could meet, to link arms and stand in the dying embers of the battle and prepare to fly home through the narrow gap in time that lingered directly above. No one spoke, as there was nothing to say. After a time, Livvy turned her head to look back. A single figure approached, skulking across the ruined land.

Arad.

He raised his hands in supplication, a filthy, bedraggled creature covered in mud and ash. When he spoke, it was in a muffled tone, as if he feared reawakening the chaos. "Is it over?"

"For now," Saiinov said. He squinted up into the sun with a grimace. "We will fight again someday, but not here."

Vasa nodded. Habira said nothing.

"Are your people alive?" Livvy asked.

"My people?" Arad seemed surprised. He was master of nothing. He had been nothing, under the boot of Death.

"Yes, yours. They're yours now, Arad. They're scared. They'll live in fear unless someone speaks to them of the future. That tower, or whatever it was? You must turn it into something useful. Plow it under, spread the bricks, and bury the dead. Give it a name of hope, instead of death, and never, ever forget. Do you understand? It's your place now. You know the truth, and on your shoulders must go the burden." Livvy pointed to a distant palm grove, partially flattened during the fight. Silent survivors emerged from the debris, their faces perfect circles of fear. They lived but would need guidance. She hoped Arad could be strong enough to save who he could. To build again, but for the people, not for a vengeful god.

"I'll try, but something happened during the fight. I don't know—it's as if no one can hear me, or perhaps, they no longer understand now that the—now that she is gone." He twisted his lips in a rueful grin as the enormity of Thanatos' death began to settle in his mind.

Livvy gave him a searching look. "Arad, what's the name of the nearest village? One not touched by the goddess?"

He thought for a moment before crooking a finger to the east. "Just there, a small town that avoided her notice, for some reason. It's mostly refugees who escaped her lash. I don't know if it will survive, now, what with all the chaos, but"—

"Arad." Livvy's voice was like iron. It seemed she already knew some things about being direct. "The name. Of this place. Now."

He dipped his head out of habit, used to obeying the sharp tongue of the goddess. "Of course. We call it Babel."

CHAPTER TWENTY-EIGHT:

INHERITANCE

ab-el was a cursed place now. Stinking of mud and death, even days after the battle no one came to pick through the ruin.

Except for one person.

In the failing light just before dusk, Arad picked his way along the drying field, following his footprints. With a careful hand, he explored the dirt with a lover's touch. For several long, silent moments he worked, moving from spot to spot until a low hiss of pleasure escaped his lips. His teeth gleamed in the growing night, a smile of cunning satisfaction.

Digging, he freed the object, admiring the gleam in the final rays of light. Ever the fox, Arad looked around, sly and smug.

I have found it.

In his hand, he wrapped Thanatos' scepter in greedy fingers. The weapon felt heavy, jeweled, and sticky with blood.

The only sound on the plain was his laughter. Let them hear. He feared nothing, and never would. "It fits. Oh, but I always knew it would fit. I think it's time I had wings, instead of crawling through the dust like a serpent." Arad's words were exultant with the possibility of untold vengeance.

With the swagger of a tyrant, he began walking back to the town. *His* town, he corrected himself, as another grunt of animalistic pleasure erupted from his throat. Soon, he would have the people singing his praises, but first, there were things to be done. Standing on a muddy outcropping, he surveyed the ruined land, thinking of a cousin who told him his fortunes always lay in the west. There must be better things where the sun sets, a place free from the stench, the flies, the circling birds, ever watchful for prey ripening in the punishing heat.

Can he make the people take him west, to the untold riches he deserves? There were rumors of a sea filled with gold and gems, so pure that one could drink from it on the hottest day of the year. The body of water was an inland ocean surrounded by mountains and myth, perfect for someone of his ambitions.

He'd need soldiers, of course, but not for his personal defense. Ruling a land—and more-- required thought, but the road was long. He could consider such things on the way, protected by his people, and if they aren't willing to serve him, well—there are means to overcome such problems. He looked at the scepter, glowing softly in the dark, and thought of the things the goddess did with it. Hefting the weapon, he imagined himself with wings the color of nightmares, and a temper to match. Immediately, a prickling fire began to spread across his shoulders as the first black feathers emerged, lending the chill scent of death to the air around him. Arad smiled in amazement even as the pain began to lacerate his senses, but some things were worth hurting for. Wings were one such reason. *I will be a god.*

Thanatos had been powerful, but in Arad's mind, she was too kind, even weak. He would not make her mistakes.

He turned to the village at a measured pace as the wind lifted his hair, then swung the scepter like a sword. The air whined with potential violence. He smiled.

For the first time in his life, Arad was ready to go to work.

EPILOGUE:

"She's here?" Garrick barked. After a grimace, "Sorry. My nerves are tight."

"I'm not surprised, son. This isn't any ordinary day for you. In truth, for any of us. Yes. She's here, you may put that worry to rest," Saiinov confirmed, dropping an arm of equals across his son's shoulders. Just months earlier, such a gesture would have been unthinkable, perhaps even leading to violence. But now, it was caring, companionable. It was welcome.

I have told her where to go, in case she does not remember her last visit. It has, after all, been some time. For you. For me, it was as a blink. If I had eyes, that is. Windhook's casual joke made Saiinov's brows lift in surprise. It seemed that the day would be filled with the unusual, if not the unexpected. After a mental note of thanks to the house elemental, Saiinov guided his son toward the aerie, where the Revealer stood, squinting from the aftereffects of her long flight.

"I'm in time?" Her smile was warm, nurturing. An air of confidence clung to her like a second skin, her wings folding neatly back to reveal a small bag hanging on one hip, the four pointed star of her House embossed in lurid red. An angel of middle years, her hair was only now beginning to gray, pulled back in a complex braid she wore like a crown. Eyes of hazel danced in cheekbones that were high and sharp, her generous lips dabbed with shining ointment. Clearly, this was an angel who spent a many hours aloft as she plied her trade from house to house. Every part of her flying armor was worn supple, creases in the light blue hide like the wrinkles of a Windbeast reaching later years, proud signs of experience earned and cherished.

"You are, as every other time you were here, friend. It's good to have you back, Catron. I trust the skies were free of trouble?" Saiinov asked, his tone light, welcoming. They were old friends, though Garrick had never seen her before, leading to his quizzical expression.

"We have met before, young Garrick, but you might not recall the event." Catron's voice was rich with laughter as she reached up to pat his cheek. "I delivered you, as I will deliver your"—she hesitated, lifting her face upward like an Airdancer sensing currents. When her eyes opened again, they sparkled with mischief. "Would you like to know, or shall we wait until the babe is here?"

"I—you can tell? Just by?" Garrick sputtered, unsure if she was truthful or teasing.

"Of course I can, lad. It's my business to know who's coming to the party. As for *how* I know, that's rather simple. I listen. They're quite chatty, you know, especially when they know that a love greater than the sky awaits them." Tears begin to glimmer in her eyes as she recalled the hundreds of births she'd attended, using only her hands and a few tools, handed down from a time that descended into the haze of the past. "I never tire of this, you know. I was made for it."

"By all means, then. Let's go meet our new friend." Saiinov gestured grandly, falling behind his son and the Revealer, who began issuing soothing instructions to the nervous young father. Saiinov grinned at the memory of

Catron doing the same for him, watching as Garrick's shoulders began to loosen with each word of her sage advice. This was her arena now, a place where she was born to be.

When they arrived at the hall's end, there was no door, only a wide opening in which a silken curtain rustled from the eternal currents of air that gave Windhook its vibrant feeling. Vasa looked up from the bedside, her face schooled into a neutral welcome. As the mother of many, she knew that the first time was hardest, and atmosphere mattered.

"Catron, you're beaming. I take it the babe has said hello?" She rose to kiss the Revealer's cheeks before stepping back to look at her old friend. Together, they'd spent many nights in the same room, hoping, laughing, crying, but always waiting, until it was done and the time had arrived. As mothers know, there is no schedule for the babe outside its wishes, and Garrick's progeny was no different.

"Aren't you perfectly radiant?" Catron leaned to stroke Danila's glistening forehead, pausing long enough to wipe tears from her eyes as well. She did so with a confidence that was unrushed and practiced, the result of decades in the presence of first-time parents. The turbid emotions were running hot in the young mother, a state of change that was understood to be the sign of an impending birth. Angels didn't merely arrive; they tended to make a statement with their birth, a racial trait that seemed logical given the beginning of a life spent flying through dangerous skies.

"Take my bag, place it just there. It used to be more difficult, delivering the babes, but the caul keeps our kind in order. You'll see, shortly. You have the things I required?" Catron craned her neck, nodding as her eyes scanned the water, wine, and swaddling, all in place to her right-hand side. "Good, good. Just so, as every other time I've been here. Oh, but it's a pleasure being in a house where cooler heads prevail. Last week I had a father nearly faint when I asked him if he'd like to cut the caul. He's a Skywatcher, so it wasn't as if the boy hadn't seen his share of blood, not leading patrols in the wild south. In point of fact, he still had score marks on his armor from something rather nasty, so his swoon seemed a bit excessive to me. Naturally, I assured him that he was quite brave once he'd come to and had some rather potent wine. I suspect the arrival of his son was the only time he'd ever been nervous in his adult life if one can call a warrior with less than thirty years an adult."

Catron chattered away while her hands danced, placing brilliant white fabric within easy reach. Each segment was cut in long strips and shimmering with moisture. A sharp tang wafted throughout the room, heady but not unpleasant. There was medicine present, and the smells of sun and blossoms, light but noticeable. All of these drifted in the room, specters of an event so rare that most angels only saw it every few decades, if at all.

With a decisive shrug of her shoulders and long exhalation, the Revealer let herself be felt by the attendees as she began to inhabit her true purpose. It became *her* room, and soon, it would belong to the babe. Until that moment, she entered a place where every gesture was sacred, every outcome critical—a landscape rife with emotion of such intensity that the air began to hum with unspoken promise and awe. Looking over the crowded room, her features shifted subtly from amiable to commanding, a trick of such nuance that Saiinov tilted his head in respect at the gesture. Along the wall stood Theobald, rubbing his enormous hands with worry, then

Prista, pale, smiling and still healing after being pulled from the floating wreckage of the *Alu*. She would never be the same as her former self, but she was alive, and fighting to learn how to speak again. Nearby, the twins stood in quiet reverence at the enormity of the event, sharing whispers and smiles in their secret language.

Opposite but closer were Vasa and Saiinov, along with Habira. To their left, the beaming face of Cressa, now fleshed out in the planes of adulthood. Time and battle may have taken her youth, but the angel left behind was remarkable in every way. Her dark almond eyes radiated a suffusion of joy that was hard won and not easily dispensed. She'd come a long way from the girl with smudged wings, living her days in fear of the past.

A hulking, nervous shadow clung to the wall, saying nothing. Theobald had flown via windship, arriving earlier in the morning amid the general excitement of his first grandchild. His sightless eyes darted about, following the cacophony of noises with the lifelong practice of someone trained to listen. Occasionally, he would moisten his lips with wine, but was otherwise still, nervous but smiling as the symphony of birth unfolded around him.

Livvy crouched against the wall, her face awash with the conflict of emotions from every aspect of her life, be it far or near. Looking around, Livvy knew that no one in the room was the same person.

Nor would they be after the birth.

There was a silent anticipation even within Windhook, who could often be heard emitting a low hum of satisfaction as the family went about the business of living. Now, there was nothing. A holding of the breath, but on a scale of such size that if fit no imagination save that of Heike's beasts, who were of like size and temperament.

"Unfold the chair, if you please," Catron commanded. Springing to action, Livvy and Garrick made quick work of the slender bone frame, locking its sections into place with mechanical clicks. The structure was part throne, part recliner, and covered incrementally in hide so thin that light shone through with little resistance. It was an old thing, but a fine thing; a masterwork of engineering and thought made real to keep the mother in a semi-standing position. The angle would bring the babe to light safely, and quickly.

"Danila." It was a statement, a warning of sorts. Catron's voice was low, steady. She held a small silver knife in her left hand, the other was bare but dripped with the powerful wine she'd requested. "It's time to move to the chair now."

"Can you hear?" Danila asked, easing ponderously into the frame with the help of Garrick, Livvy, and cooing words from nearly everyone in the room. Only her father remained silent, his lips moving in a prayer of unknown origin but unquestioned sincerity.

Catron nodded by way of answer before kneeling, the knife flashing in the light falling through Windhook's broad windows. The breeze was cool but tolerable, a boon, given the heavy perspiration now running freely down Danila's face and neck. Garrick leaned to kiss her, their skins a contrast of shadows and light, beautiful to behold. He murmured something to her, yielding a smile before the babe began to arrive.

"I can hear." Catron frowned, cocking her head to and fro in disbelief at some unknown conversation. "Ahh, that is, your *daughter* wishes us to hurry up. She informs me that she's rather impatient to meet her family, after being kept away from you all for so long." She laughed, a ringing sound that filled the chamber and startled Danila into movement. "No, dear stay still. She'll be along directly. She also *insists* that her grandparents teach her to fly as soon as her wings are dry. Seems she doesn't like being kept away from the skies."

"I think she takes after you, love," Vasa said to Saiinov, who kissed his wife with a muffled laugh. "She's true to our house, and not even arrived. I think you'll have your hands full, son of mine."

Garrick blanched but managed a watery smile. "I'll need a full fighting wing of Skyatchers to keep her safe," he said, then reconsidered. "Two wings."

The laughter stopped as Danila cried out, pressing against the frame with a strength that surprised everyone in the room save Catron and Vasa. "She's here." The words were ground out between teeth clenched so tightly the noise was little more than a growl. Motherhood did not come without its dues.

A silver caul slid into view, transparent, tinged with hints of blue and yellow, and encasing an angry young angel who had no interest in remaining caged. With a swift, decisive cut, Catron opened the caul in the four sacred directions after taking a long, close look inside at the babe, who faced her from within.

"Yes, much easier with the caul," she murmured, beginning her cuts. After a contemplative pause, the knife blurred in her hand as the years of expertise made all movement smooth, founded in muscle memory, and certain. Deftly catching the babe with her free hand, she lowered her to the waiting swaddle.

"Should she look so—whatever that is?" Garrick asked, stricken.

"Gray? She's perfect, don't you worry. She'll start pinking up immediately, once we rub her feet a bit—gently, now. No, keep her face down, I've my reasons, and this is no concern of yours, I assure you. Let the first hands be Garrick's, not just mine, and then we'll take her to breast once she's drawn her first fill of Windhook air. You're doing wonderfully, Danila. She's a grand, plump little thing and her wings are formed by the hands of the gods. Long, sweeping, oh, trust me when I say, she'll be fast in the air and quicker with her wits." The wings were plastered against the babe's back, but already, individual feathers began to separate under the brisk cleaning of the Revealer.

In the midst of her ministrations, Catron cocked her head again, giving a minor twitch as the psychic bond between her and the child was broken. Jeweled tears sparkled on her cheeks, just as with every birth she'd been present for since taking the vow and caring for the newborns who would fly into the teeth of danger for centuries to come. The angels would go on, and Catron would have a hand in it. "Ahh, she's gone from my mind. Time for her to begin learning, as it were." Revealers could speak to infants, but only until they were free of the silver caul. Then, the young angel would begin the arduous task of growing well enough to regain their use of language, a feat that left many youths frustrated and prone to fits.

Then again, it *was* a toddler, and they tended to do that regardless of who or what told them to be calm.

There was wonder on Garrick's face, and, in truth, everyone in the room. It had been a swift birth, free of complications and trouble. Danila was helped back to the bed, collapsing into the mass of covers with a grateful sigh. She fairly pulsed with the radiance of birth, her cocoa skin flushed in undertones of pink and red. Birthing was hard work, and she was new to it all.

"It's time to hold her, Danila. Your daughter," Catron

said, her voice holding a note of neutrality that hadn't been present before. Instantly, the family pressed around like children clamoring for starshine, a press of bright faces transfixed by the magnificent arrival of their new ally, friend, and blood.

Livvy blanched, and in a flash of terrible recognition, she knew what had given Catron her earlier moment of pause. Then Vasa saw, and Saiinov. One by one, the jubilant faces began to collapse inward on the weight of the truth, a fall of such intensity that Theobald gasped and went to his knees. The big man's body made an audible *crack* as he put a meaty hand on the floor to steady himself from complete collapse. Now, the tears streaking Danila's serene beauty took on a quality of fear or bitterness, but, in all likelihood, there was no word for the maelstrom in her mind and body as she looked down into the wide, perfect, colorless blue eyes of her daughter.

The babe looked like Garrick, although she was a deep golden brown like the hour before dusk. Her nose was straight, tiny, and perfect, just like each plump hand that grasped instinctively into her mother's sweat-curled black hair.

Danila looked at Livvy, an ocean of mistrust in that gaze, but then that faded into open bitterness and confusion. She kissed her daughter, lingering, inhaling. Creating a memory to serve her later for what would inevitably come.

"She's like you, isn't she? And you're—the one before? Keiron?" Danila's words were thick, accusatory. Shaming.

Livvy regarded the open, curious stare of the tiny angel, her wings beginning to flex in the first motions of their kind, an experimental motion that looked alien and familiar at once.

Yes, she is. And yes, you are. The words sifted through

her awareness from that other place, where Keiron may have been, or perhaps it was only her soul confirming the reality of what she was seeing. The babe was Heartborn, of that there was no doubt. Her eyes were open, aware—brilliant with curiosity and underpinned with wisdom, a look that should be on the face of no creature still held in the arms of its mother. Keiron had been born just as this child, eyes open and knowing.

And Keiron's heart now beat in Livvy's chest, a steady song of life, and memory, and love. Since she had no need of a heart, that meant this child was destined for something else. Something unknown, but ultimately, it would be a sacrifice of such importance that to deny it was to refuse the movement of the stars. A useless gesture, then, and yet wholly natural given the innocence of the tiny face looking back at here.

Danila was utterly still in the midst of tears and denial, only bending to kiss her daughter in a heartbreaking slowness, stroking the crown of her tiny head with fingers that were still sweat-slicked and shaking. She leaned in, even closer, until her mouth was at her daughter's ear, to deliver a message meant only for the newborn soul who lay in her arms, waiting to be told that her life was not her own.

Livvy, close enough to hear, nearly broke. Danila's voice was so faint as to be a rumor, the sounds funneled to her daughter in a tender song known to mothers and children since the first days of life.

"I thought I'd seen all the bad, but I was wrong," Danila whispered, pausing to kiss the baby's cheek once again. "Sometimes, it's even worse."

Reviews

If you enjoyed *Moonborn* please consider leaving a rating and review on the site where you bought it. All genuine comments and feedback are welcome.

Reviews and feedback are extremely important to Terry Maggert, as well as other potential readers, and would be very much appreciated. Thank you.

Acknowledgements

The more I write the larger my circle of friends becomes, and so, here we are again. To Desirre Andrews goes my undying thanks for her advice about the science of midwifery and just how babies arrive. As to how babies are made, I saw that film in seventh grade Health class, and it really left an impression.

To Staci Hart, I wish you clear skies and plentiful bicycles in your new adventure. Wear thick socks. Wooden shoes are clunky. That's a thing, right?

Speaking of the sky—Rocket Girl Rachelle, there are Seven Sisters swooshing silently skyward. Thanks for the heads up, and fly well.

For my friends who offer feedback, suggestions, and encouragement on social media-- I'm thankful, I'm reading your comments, and I use your encouragement as fuel.

To my bride, Special Agent Doctor Professor Missy-- thanks for all of it.

As ever, any errors are my own, and I'll try to do better next time.
Terry
Nashville, Tennessee, May 2017

About the Author

Left-handed. Father of the World's Tallest Nine Year Old *. Husband to a half-Norwegian. Herder of cats and dogs. Lover of pie. I write books. I've had an unhealthy fascination with dragons since the age of-- well, for a while. Native Floridian. Current Tennessean. Location subject to change based on insurrection, upheaval, or availability of coffee. Ten books and counting, with no end in sight. You've been warned.

Contact Terry Maggert

Author's Blog: terrymaggert.com

Additional Social Media:
Twitter: https://twitter.com/TerryMaggert
Facebook:
https://www.facebook.com/terrymaggertbooks
Goodreads:
http://www.goodreads.com/user/show/20617266-terry-maggert
Pinterest: http://www.pinterest.com/terry68/terry-maggerts-author-swag/
Amazon Author Page: http://www.amazon.com/Terry-Maggert/e/B00EKN8RHG/

Signed Paperbacks: Contact author directly via Facebook, or at terrymaggertbooks@gmail.com

More Books by Terry Maggert:

Halfway Witchy: Come for the waffles. Stay for the magic.
Halfway Dead
Halfway Bitten
Halfway Hunted

The Fearless: Three lovers. Two demons. One Problem
The Forest Bull
The Mask of the Swan
The Waking Serpent
A Bride of Salt and Stars

Short Fiction
Cool to the Touch
Call of Shadows

Banshee
Cities Fall. Dragons Rise. War Begins

Halfway Dead
Halfway Witchy Book 1

Carlie McEwan loves many things.

She loves being a witch. She loves her town of Halfway, NY—a tourist destination nestled on the shores of an Adirondack lake. Carlie loves her enormous familiar, Gus, who is twenty-five pounds of judgmental Maine Coon cat, and she positively worships her Grandmother, a witch of incredible power and wisdom. Carlie spends her days cooking at the finest—and only—real diner in town, and her life is a balance between magic and the mundane, just as she likes it.

When a blonde stranger sits at the diner counter and calls her by name, that balance is gone. Major Pickford asks Carlie to lead him into the deepest shadows of the forest to find a mythical circle of chestnut trees, thought lost forever to mankind. There are ghosts in the forest, and one of them cries out to Carlie across the years. Come find me.

Danger, like the shadowed pools of the forest, can run deep. The danger is real, but Carlie's magic is born of a pure spirit. With the help of Gus, and Gran, and a rugged cop who really does want to save the world, she'll fight to bring a ghost home, and deliver justice to a murderer who hides in the cool, mysterious green of a forest gone mad with magic.

Halfway Bitten
Halfway Witchy Book 2

The circus came to Halfway, and they brought the weird.

When clowns, vampires, and corpses start piling up in town, Carlie has to break away from her boyfriend, Wulfric, to bring her witchy skills to the table- or grill, as the case may be.
When the body of a young woman washes up in the lake, it unleashes a spiral of mystery that will bring Carlie, Gran, and Wulfric into a storm of magical warfare. Spells will fly. Curses will rain. Amidst it all, Carlie will make waffles, protect her town, and find out if a man from the distant past can join her in happy ever after.

With love and honor at stake, Carlie has no peer.

Halfway Hunted
Halfway Witchy Book 3

Some Prey Bites Back.

Welcome to Halfway; where the waffles are golden, the moon is silver, and magic is just around every corner.

A century old curse is broken, releasing Exit Wainwright, an innocent man trapped alone in time.
Lost and in danger, he enlists Carlie, Gran, and their magic to find the warlock who sentenced him to a hundred years of darkness. The hunter becomes the hunted when Carlie's spells awaken a cold-blooded killer intent on adding another pelt to their gruesome collection: hers.

But the killer has never been to Halfway before, where there are three unbreakable rules:
1. Don't complain about the diner's waffles.
2. Don't break the laws of magic.
3. Never threaten a witch on her home turf.

Can Carlie solve an ancient crime, defeat a ruthless killer and save the love of her life from a vampire's curse without burning the waffles?

Come hunt with Carlie, and answer the call of the wild.

The Forest Bull
The Fearless Book 1

Three lovers who stalk and kill the immortals that drift
through South Florida (tourists are a moveable feast,
after all) are living a simple life of leisure- until one of
them is nearly killed by woman who is a new kind of
lethal.

When Ring Hardigan isn't making sandwiches for, and
with, his two partners, Waleska and Risa (they're cool like
that), he's got a busy schedule doing the dirty work of
sending immortals to the ever after. Wally and Risa
provide linguistics, logistics, and finding the right place
for him and his knife- together, they're a well-oiled
machine, and they've settled into a rhythm that bodes ill
for the Undying. Warlocks, vampires, succubae and the
odd ghoul have all fallen to their teamwork. Life is tough,
but they soldier on killing the undead, liberating their
worldly goods for charity, and generally achieving very
little.

Until Ring wakes up after nearly dying at the hands of a
woman who may or may not be the daughter of Satan.
Ring's a tough character, for a boat bum (killing
immortals sort of rubs off on you that way), but twelve
days of comatose healing are enough to bring out the ugly
side of his temper. When a letter arrives asking for their
help finding a large collection of stolen heirloom jewelry,
they form an uneasy friendship with the last Baron of a
family hiding in a primal European forest.

Cazimir, the Baron, has two skills: Jeweler and preserver of the last herd of forest bulls. It's an odd occupation, but then, Ring, Risa and Wally aren't your everyday career folks, and Cazimir's lodge might be sitting on something that looks a lot like hell, which, according to a 2400 year old succubus hooker named Delphine, is currently on the market to the strongest immortal. The Baron's impassioned plea to find the jewelry comes with some conditions- he doesn't want the collection back as much as he does the thief, Elizabeth, who happens to be his daughter- and the woman who nearly sent Ring to his grave.

In a tapestry of lies, it's up to Ring, Wally and Risa to find out what is evil, who is human, and exactly who really wants to reign over hell.

The Mask of the Swan
The Fearless Book 2

Killing immortals is easy. Becoming one is hard.

When three lovers (Ring, Waleska, and Risa) take a vacation after losing a fight with an elegant monster named Elizabeth, their time for healing is cut short by a new threat, and this time, innocent blood will spill. Reaching for the crown of Hell, Elizabeth gathers Archangels around her to fuel her power-mad ascent— but she has powerful enemies who will fight her every step of the way, including Delphine, the 2400 year old succubus hooker who knows that inside her beautiful body rests a very human soul. Joined by an honorable priest who finds himself in the middle of a war he never knew existed, a demigod and his partner, and the stage is set for another round in the battle to determine how much of Ring, Waleska, and Risa is still human, how tough their immortal side can be—and how far they are willing to go to protect the people they love from a creature who would burn their world to ashes.

The Waking Serpent
The Fearless Book 3

Evil is never still.

Something wicked is crossing the sea, a creature so old that none even remember its name-- but it has not forgotten the taste of blood. With a succubus ally, a brave priest, and new friends who seem a little less human than most, The Fearless will meet the greatest challenge of their lives. An ancient adversary is stopping by to avenge a wrong from the depths of time in a fight to the death that will bring a goddess to Florida for the best reason of all: Revenge.

A Bride of Salt and Stars
The Fearless Book 4

From a secret tomb beneath the ashes of a Mexican volcano, something has broken free. Something luminous. Beautiful. And deadly. From the deepest part of our human legends, she is known simply as The Bride, and she's visiting Florida for dinner, but her arrival has not gone unseen. The Fearless will make certain her reception is memorable.

In a place where creatures like The Bride hunt each night, The Fearless will go to any lengths defending humanity. But only after dark. That's when the hunting is best.

In this battle, new warriors emerge against this timeless evil as Ring, Wally and Risa rejoin their stalwart friends to turn demons into dust --and justice into reality. They're joined by Aurelia, the Romanian stripper who fights better than she dances. Aurelia brings a legendary weapon to bear against The Bride—but first, she'll have to guide Ring through a maze of warlocks, a clever deity, and the ongoing reclamation of the succubus Delphine's soul. Along the way, The Fearless will feed the dog, collect the rent, and act like every day in the sun might be their last.

Banshee

Cities Fall. Dragons Rise. War Begins.

The war for earth began in Hell. First came the earthquakes. Then came the floods. Finally, from the darkened mines, caves and pits, the creatures of our nightmares boiled forth to sweep across the planet in a wave of death.

On the run and unprepared, mankind is not alone. We have dragons.
Emerging from their slumber, giant dragons select riders to go to war. Their forces strike back at the legions of demons that attack on the night of every new moon. The Killing Moon, as it becomes known, is the proving ground for warriors of skill and heart. Among the riders is Saavin, a brave young woman from the shattered remains of Texas. Her dragon, Banshee, is swift and fearless, but they will need help to fight a trio of monstrous creatures that Hell is using to take cities one by one.

With the help of French Heavener, a warrior of noble intent, Banshee and Saavin will launch a desperate defense of New Madrid, the last city standing. But first, they'll have to go into the very cave where demons bide their time until the sun fades and the moon is black.

The hope of mankind rests on dragon's wings and the bravery of Saavin and French.
They have the guts. They have the guns.
They have dragons.

Made in the USA
Lexington, KY
13 June 2017